Lizzie Bright and the Buckminster Boy

MORE NOVELS BY GARY D. SCHMIDT

Straw into Gold

The Wednesday Wars

Okay for Now

Trouble

What Came from the Stars

Orbiting Jupiter

Pay Attention, Carter Jones

GARY D. SCHMIDT

Lizzie Bright and the Buckminster Boy

HOUGHTON MIFFLIN HARCOURT

BOSTON   NEW YORK

For information about permission to reproduce selections from
this book, write to trade.permissions@hmhco.com or to Permissions,
Houghton Mifflin Harcourt Publishing Company,
3 Park Avenue, 19th Floor, New York, New York 10016.

hmhbooks.com

The text was set in 15-point Bembo.

The Library of Congress has cataloged the hardcover edition as follows:
Schmidt, Gary D.
Lizzie Bright and the Buckminster boy / by Gary D. Schmidt.
p. cm.
Summary: In 1911, Turner Buckminster hates his new home of Phippsburg,
Maine, but things improve when he meets Lizzie Bright Griffin, a girl from
a poor nearby island community founded by former slaves that the town
fathers—and Turner's—want to change into a tourist spot.
[1. Progress—Fiction. 2. Race relations—Fiction. 3. Moving,
Household—Fiction. 4. Clergy—Fiction. 5. Maine—History—
20th century—Fiction.]
I. Title.
PZ7.S3527Li2004
[Fic]—dc22

ISBN: 978-0-618-43929-4 hardcover
ISBN: 978-0-358-20639-2 paperback

Manufactured in the United States of America

2 2020
4500816903

CHAPTER

TURNER Buckminster had lived in Phippsburg, Maine, for fifteen minutes shy of six hours. He had dipped his hand in its waves and licked the salt from his fingers. He had smelled the sharp resin of the pines. He had heard the low rhythm of the bells on the buoys that balanced on the ridges of the sea. He had seen the fine clapboard parsonage beside the church where he was to live, and the small house set a ways beyond it that puzzled him some.

Turner Buckminster had lived in Phippsburg, Maine, for almost six whole hours.

He didn't know how much longer he could stand it.

Maybe somewhere out West there really were Territories that he could light out to, where being a minister's son wouldn't matter worth a . . . well, worth a darn. He hoped so, because here, being a minister's son mattered a whole lot, and pretending that it didn't matter to him was starting to peck at his soul.

He did have to admit that their arrival had something to it. Every member of Phippsburg's First Congregational—as well as lost reprobates from other denominations—had gathered to greet the new minister and his family. A quartet of slick trombones played a Sousa march as the steamer *Kennebec* came in sight of the wharf. A red, white, and blue welcome banner unfurled at the end of the dock: WELCOME PASTOR BUCKMINSTER! The church deacons stood properly at the foot of the gangway, their hands grasping the lapels of their dark suits, their hats lifting in unison as soon as Mrs. Buckminster appeared on deck. A cheer at the sight of the new pastor, the quartet sliding into "Come, Ye That Love the Lord," and the bronze bells of First Congregational suddenly tolling.

Then the three of them had stepped onto the shore of their new home, and the deacons grabbed their new pastor's arms, and the women of the Ladies Sewing Circle of First Congregational grabbed their new pastor's wife's arms, and Turner . . . Turner stood alone at the edge of the dock, faced by the sons and daughters of the deacons and the women of the Ladies Sewing Circle. Not a single one of them grabbed his arms. They looked at him as if he'd stepped in something they didn't want to be around.

He held up his hand. "Hey," he said.

But it appeared that what he had heard in Boston was true: folks in Maine spoke a whole different language, and didn't care for those who couldn't speak it themselves.

That was the first time Turner thought about lighting out for the Territories.

Though things did get better. The Ladies' Sewing Circle set out a picnic with enough cold chicken, cold pork, German potato salad, hard-boiled eggs, cucumbers, tomato slices, dill pickles, bacon strips, ham-and-butter sandwiches, apple-cranberry muffins, rhubarb muffins, gooseberry muffins, and strawberry and boysenberry preserves to feed the Five Thou-

sand. And after Deacon Hurd had prayed long enough to ag-
gravate the prophet Elijah, Turner sat down and began to think
that maybe Phippsburg wouldn't be such a bad place after all—
once he learned the language.

And things got even better when Deacon Hurd called the
sides for the afternoon baseball game. Turner's mother grinned
at him, and he grinned back.

With whistles and calls and impossible boasts, the men
and boys of First Congregational strolled across to Thayer's
haymeadow—mown just the day before—and marked out the
lines. They circled the pitcher's mound, and squared the batter's
box beside the plate. Then Deacon Hurd, now Umpire Hurd,
took off his jacket and held a bat out to Turner.

"You ever play this game before, young Buckminster?"

"Yes, sir," said Turner.

He wanted to say, "About a hundred thousand times." Or,
"About a hundred million times." Or, "Mister, I can shimmy a
ball down a line so pretty, there isn't a soul on God's green earth
that can even get near it." But he held back and just grinned
again.

"Then you're the first man up," said Deacon Hurd.

"Yes, sir," said Turner, and took the bat, the resin on it feeling like home.

It wasn't exactly the kind of field he might lay out on
Boston Common. It was more stubble than grass. Home plate
was tilted up and stamped on top with a cracked mollusk fos-
sil. And since the other bases were set wherever a slab of
granite showed its back, they weren't playing on anything you
could rightly call a diamond. But Turner saw that the pines sidled awful close to the left-field line, and he could spin a ball
to make it touch in fair, then scoot off into the trees. He
imagined that would be at least a triple. And even the trees in

dead center were near enough that the sea breeze could take the ball into their branches—if he could hit it high enough.

And he could.

Turner decided that the second time up, he'd finesse the triple. But now, just to establish himself, he would double past the second baseman, who was playing too neighborly to a second base that was way too close to third.

He stepped to the granite plate and took a couple of slow swings. He straightened his left leg and cocked his right—this usually confused the pitcher, though it didn't seem to confuse this one. He was another Hurd, Willis Hurd, and he smiled as he tossed the ball up and down. It was the kind of smile you give to a chicken whose head you're about to cut off.

That was the second time Turner wondered about lighting out for the Territories.

He stepped back and took two more slow swings, feeling the groove he left in the air. Then he stepped up again, set his left leg, fixed his eyes, and waited for the quick swing of the pitcher's arm, the flashing slant of the ball through the blue-and-white air.

It never came. Willis held the ball a long while, still smiling, then slowly leaned forward, swung his arm down low, and lofted the ball into a high arc. Turner had never seen anything like it. The ball went about as high as a young pine, then turned, slowly spun its seams once or twice, and sauntered on down until it bounced softly on the granite plate.

"Strike one!" hollered Deacon Hurd.

Turner looked at him. "Was that a pitch?"

"That was a strike."

"It landed on the plate."

"That's what a strike will do. I thought you said you'd played this game before."

"Let's see another strike," said Turner.

And he did. Another high, lofting ball. No human being had ever pitched like that before, Turner decided. It added an entirely new aerial dimension. And when the ball meandered down from about a mile above his head, he flailed at it as if it were a bumblebee.

"Strike two!" shouted Deacon Hurd. "You know you've only got one more, son."

"Maybe you'd better bend that front leg," called still-smiling Willis.

"Are you holding the bat high enough, boy?" suggested one of the Ladies' Sewing Circle from the sidelines. She turned to another of the circle. "I don't think he's holding the bat high enough. He's not holding that bat high enough at all. It's too heavy for him."

Turner stepped back from the plate and let the bat swing low a couple of times. He wouldn't go for the double—just a single. Someone clapped, and when he looked up, it seemed that every member of Phippsburg First Congregational was standing on the lines figuring that he didn't have any idea what he was doing.

Willis waited a moment, letting Turner settle in, and Turner wondered what Willis's smile would look like if the ball went crashing back into his face. Maybe that wasn't something a minister's son should want to see—but he did want to see it. He was almost startled that he wanted to see it so badly. He took another couple of swings; then he straightened his front leg and waited.

"You sure you don't want to bend that leg? You'd balance better," suggested Deacon Hurd.

Turner did not move. He waited with the bat held over his shoulder, absolutely still.

And Willis looped the pitch up to him.

It must have peaked somewhere in the stratosphere, because this time it came down screaming. Turner watched it come. He wanted it to come. The ball was big and fat, getting bigger and fatter, and he knew that when he swung at just the right second he would shoot it out into center. He would feel it pop against his wrists, would watch it leap as he trotted easily to first.

Rushing, rushing, rushing, waiting, waiting, waiting—swinging.

And the ball dropped onto the granite plate, bounced up against his knee, plopped back onto the plate, and rolled still against his ankle.

"Strike three!" yelled Deacon Hurd.

"Bend your front leg next time," offered Willis.

"You'll catch on, Turner. Next time, you'll catch on," called Reverend Buckminster, and turned, laughing, to one of the deacons, who had thumped him on the back.

Turner looked away from his father. He handed the bat to Deacon Hurd and sat down on the grass. No one else struck out the rest of the inning.

No one else struck out the rest of the game—except Turner. He never could time the descent of the ball. It always seemed to cheat on him. In Boston, baseball was honest. The pitcher threw as hard as he could, the ball came flat and fast, or maybe spinning into a curve, but still fast. Here it just seemed to hang in the currents of the air until it found the convenient moment to plop onto the granite plate. No matter how he timed the thing, he was always off, and the most he could manage was a weasel of a hit that looped back to the pitcher's glove.

"Good, Turner. You got it back to me," said Willis.

"That's the way," added Reverend Buckminster.

Turner thought he might as well die right then and there. It was probably too much to hope for the Apocalypse.

And so his first failure in Phippsburg. He suspected he'd hear about it for a long time.

That first night, while the congregation sat around the haymeadow eating the ice cream Mr. Newton and Mrs. Newton and all the little Newtons had brought up from their grocery store, he heard about it from the Ladies' Sewing Circle: "Turner, don't you think you need a lighter bat? That one is so heavy for a boy your size." While bits of light flitted around so thickly that Turner could not tell which were fireflies and which were sparks the sea breeze kicked up from the blue-gold logs, he heard about it from Reverend Buckminster: "Couldn't you have done better than that? It didn't look like you were swinging right." And while the fire burned low and the moon came up to silver the haymeadow, he heard about it from Deacon Hurd: "Son, maybe Willis can show you how to stand up at the plate sometime. You be sure to ask him." Turner nodded. He'd be sure to ask Willis about standing up at the plate sometime in the next millennium.

He didn't hear about it from his mother, but later that night, she did explain to him the purpose of the small house behind the parsonage.

"You don't mean that," said Turner.

"Yes," she said, "I do." She handed him the Sears, Roebuck catalogue.

It was, Turner thought, a fitting end for the day.

And the next day wasn't so promising. Bright and early, Mrs. Hurd stood on their front porch, a fresh blueberry pie for the new minister and his family in her hands and the baseball game on her lips:

"I'm sorry you had such a difficult time last night. Did you ask Willis to show you how to play?"

"He will," said Reverend Buckminster. "Turner should have a grand time with Willis. He's been looking forward to living here in Phippsburg."

"He's been looking forward to lighting out for the Territories," thought Turner.

But the grand time came before he could light out.

That afternoon, the dignitaries of Phippsburg arrived to conduct Reverend Buckminster around his new parish, and the sons of those dignitaries arrived to conduct Turner to "the best spot to swim in the whole state," according to Willis.

"Is it safe?" asked Mrs. Buckminster.

Turner was impressed that Willis could smile at his mother and sneer at him at one and the same moment.

"We'd never swim where it wasn't, ma'am," said Willis. Then he looked at Turner. "You can swim, can't you? You have done that before?"

Turner wished he had a baseball bat in his hand.

He walked behind the other boys, and tried not to hear the stifled laughs, tried not to see the flailing swings. They crossed Thayer's haymeadow and passed among the firs and cedars and yellow birches, then began to climb up. Turner was a bit confused; even someone who had lived in Boston knew you climbed down to the sea. But then the trees gave way, and they came to a granite outcropping that jutted out over the cold, green Atlantic. While the other boys draped their shirts over the blueberry bushes, Turner stepped to the edge and looked down at the blue-black rocks. He figured this was where people who'd had enough of Phippsburg came to end it all.

Willis came up beside him. "You jumping in with your Sunday shirt on?"

"It isn't a Sunday shirt, and I wasn't planning to."

"I suppose all Buck*ministers* wear Sunday shirts every day of the week. You do know how to jump, right?"

"I know how to jump."

"Wait for the wave to come in, so you don't splatter yourself all over those rocks. If you do, there won't be much of you left to wash out to sea." Then Willis moved to the edge, waited for his wave, and, with a last smile at Turner, leaped.

It was beautiful. He fell slowly, like a baseball, reaching the wave just as it covered the rocks, disappearing in white and green, and then rising out of the water as the wave drew past and threw itself against the cliff. The sun gilded the spray that fell around him.

Turner thought he might be sick.

One by one, the boys jumped off the granite outcropping and fell perfectly into waves that had just covered the rocks. And one by one they rose out of the sea into a golden spray.

Until there was only Turner.

He left his clothes on the blueberry bushes and moved to the edge where his pale toes clenched the rock. The sea swelled rhythmically beneath him, and he leaned forward whenever a wave folded in and broke to a yellow froth. He looked down at his legs and was surprised to see that they were shivering, since he couldn't feel them at all.

He flexed his knees. Below him, the boys, standing on the blue-black rocks waved at him to jump. "Now!" they yelled with each swell, and then groaned with disappointment when he didn't go. "Now!" More groaning.

Turner hated their guts.

Somewhere there was a baseball diamond yellow with dust and green with summer grass. And there was a kid stepping up to the plate, swinging his bat low, the pine tar sticky on his palms. He was moving his back foot behind him and trying not to eye the gap down the right-field line big enough to run an eight-wheel locomotive through.

But Turner was standing forty feet above the writhing sea, waiting for a swell big enough to keep him from splattering on the rocks and hoping he wouldn't throw up before he went under.

"You coming or not?"

"Hey, Buck*minister,* you coming?"

Turner leaned over. He edged the tiniest bit closer to the tip of the rock and wondered how far away the Territories were. He hoped that they never smelled of sea salt, that they never heard the urgings of the ocean, that they were so lonely that being a stranger in them hardly mattered.

And then he saw the sea surge that was coming in.

Already the boys were scrambling up to a higher rock. "This is it, Buck*minister.* This is the biggest one you'll ever get."

Turner had no doubt it was the biggest one he would ever get. The surge moved like a wallowing mountain range, roiling to a whiteness at its peaks. He saw the water begin to pull back from the rocks below him, saw the seaweed sucked out in long green tresses, saw the ocean yanked away from the dark, sharp mussel beds.

"You see it, Buck*minister?* You see it? That's the one!"

Of course he saw it. God and all creation saw it.

He flexed his knees again, unclenched and clenched his toes. It would take a second and a half, maybe two seconds, for him to hit the wave. Not hard to judge. Keep the knees bent so he wouldn't hit the bottom. Blow out the nose just when he hit so he wouldn't come up spurting. Be ready if it spun him over . . . *when* it spun him over. No screaming. Oh Lord, please no screaming.

By now, the mountain surge had drawn all the water along the entire coast of Maine up into itself, and it was no longer wallowing. The top ridge began to fall over and disintegrate into churning confusion. Turner felt himself leaning, leaning more and more, his legs about to spring. Then the wave crossed where he knew he must jump and exploded into chaos, water avalanching in every direction, roaring at the sky, tormenting the rocks, and bursting into a spray that blotted out the sun.

And when that spray fell back in sheets to the following waves, it left Turner still standing on the top of the cliff, knees still flexed, toes still clenched.

He was breathing about as hard as any human being can breathe.

Then the laughing hollers began to come up from the rocks below the outcropping. He tried to slow his breathing, to stop the shivering in his legs. He found his clothes, put on his pants, and stretched the suspenders over his shoulders. He didn't wait to put on his shirt but willed himself to climb up the ledges and start for town even though his legs were still shivering.

Around him soft bright moss curled up the yellow birches, lichens roughened the rocks, and crushed needles let go their piney scent. But Turner hardly noticed. If only he were on Tremont Street, the gold on the State House glowing in the sun, the horsey smell of the carriages and the brogue calls of the cabbies filling the air, the bells of Park Street Church singing the hours, the grass of the Common—oh, the sweet grass of the Common.

He tried not to cry.

He came out of the woods and onto Parker Head Road a little below Phippsburg. Ahead of him, the sky pirouetted on First Congregational's sunlit steeple. Beneath it, the bell tower angled down to the clapboard front and granite steps, hewn a hundred years ago by the first congregation. Aside from the granite and the green window shutters, the whole building was shining white with a new coat of paint for the new minister.

In fact, all the buildings up and down Parker Head Road were white, and though most looked as if they had seen more winter storms than any house should have to, they all stood with corners as straight and trim and proper as if they wore invisible corsets. All of them had green shutters and all of them had green doors—except for one, whose shutters were as yellow as sunlight and whose door was as red as strawberries.

Turner skipped a rock down Parker Head, trying to keep it between the lines of grass. It threw up yellow dust for three skips and then skidded off. He wondered if Willis could hit a pitch thrown honestly, and tossed another rock, more fiercely, that skipped five times. He wondered if Willis could hit a pitch that had spin and speed, and skipped another stone, which skidded off after the first skip, jumped over the grass, and smacked sharply against the picket fence that bound the narrowest, sharpest, most peaked house on the street. The elm that draped over its roof shadowed its high windows

It was not the house with the yellow shutters and the red door.

"Oh no" whispered Turner when he heard the smack.

"Doggone," he muttered when he saw the green door of the house open.

"Darn," he said aloud when a woman came out with a hand up to shield her eyes so she might see him all the better. It was a large hand, attached to a large woman. "You the new minister's boy?"

Turner nodded.

"A boy that belongs to a minister should know how to answer a lady."

"Yes, ma'am. Turner Buckminster."

"Well, Turner Buckminster, what are you doing standing in the middle of the road half naked like that, throwing stones at my house in the middle of the day?"

Turner wondered wildly if there was a better time to throw stones at her house, but all he said was, "I'm on my way home. From swimming."

"We don't run around half naked in Phippsburg. Maybe that's the kind of thing they do down to Boston, but not here. Not in a God-fearing town. And especially not the minister's son. Throwing stones at my house—my very house! You're supposed to set some kind of example. Don't you know that?"

"I'm just on my way home."

She shook her broom at him. "Then put your shirt on so you don't walk down the main street of Phippsburg like that, in front of God and everyone. And find something to do fitting for a minister's son, instead of being a trial and a tribulation to an old woman. Standing in the middle of the road, throwing stones."

"Yes, ma'am." Turner wondered if this was a third failure. It seemed almost too much to bear—three in two days.

"Your father is sure to hear of this. See if he doesn't. You tell him that Mrs. Cobb will be down to call on him."

Turner thought he might start bawling right there in the middle of the road, in the middle of Phippsburg, in the middle of Maine.

And then across the road, the strawberry door on the sunlight-shuttered house opened, and a tiny, frail bird of a woman stepped out. Turner figured she had reached her peak of height sometime around the Civil War and from that time on had been folding and shrinking until someday she would probably just disappear. The white of her dress had faded to yellow and matched her skin almost precisely. One hand held a pale blue shawl tight around her chest, and the other held a book, which she used to beckon him.

Turner glanced back at Mrs. Cobb and her large hand—he could imagine that even a tidal wave wouldn't shiver her—and crossed over to the yellow-shuttered house, buttoning on his shirt and strapping on his suspenders again.

"Turner Buckminster," she said, her voice the dry rustling of fallen leaves. "Turner Buckminster III. Well, you never mind that Mrs. Cobb." He heard the green door slam across the street, heard the gate of the picket fence open and shut, felt a disapproving presence move behind him like a wave frothing up the street to the parsonage.

"Yes, ma'am."

"She's more thunder than lightning. I'm more . . . a cloud. A wispy one. Mrs. Elia Hurd, mother of the present deacon."

She held her hand out, and Turner went up the steps to take it. It felt as dry as her voice, like one of those pastries with layers that flake off, thin as paper.

"Turner!"

His father, coming up Parker Head in the custody of the town dignitaries. Since he was smiling, Turner figured he had—who knows how—missed the thunderous Mrs. Cobb, and that God had given him at least a brief reprieve—which he deserved after the last two days, not to mention the Sears, Roebuck catalogue.

"Come along with me," Reverend Buckminster called, his arm out and gesturing.

Mrs. Elia Hurd looked at Turner, her head a little to one side, her old eyes as pale as her shawl. Her lips parted, closed, parted again, and then she said what he had never expected anyone else in the wide world to say: "So, Turner Buckminster III," she asked, "when you look through the number at the end of your name, does it seem like you're looking through prison bars?"

Turner fell back one step.

She came closer and laid her hand against his cheek. He did not move. "Sometimes," said Turner softly, "I just want to light out . . ."

"Oh yes," said Mrs. Hurd, her hand still on his cheek, "I do, too. Just light out for the Territories." And suddenly, Turner thought he could smell sweet grass.

"This instant!" called Reverend Buckminster.

The sea surge that had drawn up the coastal waters of Maine poured past the cliffs and tore along the ragged coast. It covered the high rocks—dry for more than three months of high tides—all the way from Small Point up past Harpswell. When it had finished its fussing, it seethed back down the New Meadows River, sluicing between the mainland and the islands. It spent its last surge on one rock-shouldered heap just a spit or two off the coast, frothing over the mudflats, setting the clam holes flapping, and carrying a small, startled crab out from its weedy hiding place. It tumbled upside down up the island shore and onto a toe stretched toward the water.

Lizzie Griffin, who belonged to the toe, grinned at the crab's frantic turnings as it tried to sort out claws and legs. Its shell was so pale that she could see the mess of the inner workings. Another almost-spent wave came up behind and tumbled it off—claws and legs all to be sorted out again. Lizzie plucked her toe and the rest of her foot out of the covering mud and slowly backed up the shore, letting a wave catch her and cover her ankles, then moving away some until she was on the thin line of gravelly sand that marked the reach of the water.

She looked out at the thrusting tide, clenched her toes into the loose sand, and smelled the salty, piney air. At thirteen, she was, as her grandfather liked to remind her, one year older than the century, and so a good deal wiser. Too wise to stay on Malaga Island, he said, but she planned to stay there forever. Where else, after all, did the tide set a pale crab on your toe?

She turned and scrambled up the outcroppings, picking up the hatchet that was to have been splitting kindling all this time. But she could hardly help it if there was something so much better to do, like watching the tide come in. She balanced the hatchet on her finger as she walked, carefully keeping herself under it while her feet guided her through the scrub and tripping roots. When she came to the pines that stood as close to the ocean as they could and still reach sweet water, she tipped the hatchet into the air, caught it by the handle, and swung it back over her shoulder. She set her eye on the heart of a youngster pine and flashed the hatchet through the scented air; it tumbled over and over itself in jerks, like a crab caught in a ripple, until it slapped high up into the trunk. Lizzie looked around to see if anyone might be nearby, half wanting to show off, half wanting to be sure that no one had seen Preacher Griffin's granddaughter throwing a hatchet around. No one had, and Lizzie slicked up the tree, her feet finding the branches easily.

She jerked out the hatchet and let it fall to the soft pine needles beneath her. Then, since she was already partway up, and since the set of the branches made it so easy, and since the pine was young enough that she could get it swaying pretty good if she got close to the top, she kept climbing until she felt the tree moving with her from side to side. She let her weight into it, back and forth, and the whole heap of Malaga Island rushed beneath her—ocean, sand, rock, scrub, mudflat, pale little crab, all rushing back and forth as the soft boughs laid their gentle, dry hands against her laughing face.

The day might come, she thought, when she would take her grandfather's dory and row to the mouth of the New Meadows. She'd take it out past West Point, past Hermit, past Bald Head, and drift until she was alone with the whales in the open water. Then she'd come back in close and follow the coast, maybe row all the way to Portland, maybe even to Boston.

And then she'd row home. She would always come back to Malaga Island, just as sure as the tide always came back.

And that was when Lizzie looked across the water to the mainland and saw the group of men gathered high on the granite ledge above the tide. If Lizzie had been down on the beach, they would have towered above her, but up in the pine, she was just about eye level with them. They wore dark frock coats, top hats they held against the sea breeze, and shiny shoes that probably hadn't walked on honest granite ever before. Standing there, they all looked alike: too much weight in the front—for that matter, too much weight in the behind—and dressed for a deacon's funeral. All except one. A boy wearing a shirt so white it hurt to look at it. Why would a boy wear a shirt so white this side of paradise?

One of the frock coats pointed, and then another, and Lizzie knew where they were looking. At the turn of the island, where the slack water let the tide in soft and easy, where the clams buried themselves so thick you could gather a meal with just one rake, Lizzie's house watched New Meadows with weathered eyes. Its boards were warped beyond hope, and its roof slumped in the middle like a fallen pudding—

and there wasn't a house in Phippsburg where she'd rather live.

The afternoon bell of First Congregational tolled, and one of the men turned his eyes toward Phippsburg. When he looked back, he saw Lizzie. He said something to the others, who turned with him and stared, some smiling. Then he pulled back the side of his frock coat and laid his hand on the pistol it had hidden.

The gorged sound of their laughter stained the sea breeze that came in over the tide.

2

"WOULD you look at that monkey go? Look at her go. She climbing down or falling?" Deacon Hurd watched the last leap to the ground. "Sheriff Elwell, I believe she thought you might shoot her."

"Wouldn't have been any trouble, Mr. Hurd. One less colored in the world."

Standing beside the frock-coated men, Turner shivered with the sea breeze that had come up to him and circled his feet. The gulls that rode it screeched overhead.

"More to the point," said the tallest of the group—the one with the most expensive frock coat, the most expensive top hat, and the most expensive shiny shoes—"one less colored on Malaga Island." Laughter from the group, louder than the gulls. "Though the issue is much larger than one colored." His eye searched the pine shadows across the water for the girl, as if he sensed her watching him. His hands moved to the lapels of his coat. "The issue is how to relieve Malaga Island of the girl, her family, her neighbors, what she would call her house, what they would call their town."

"All it should take is a good sound storm." Sheriff Elwell pointed down to the turn of the island. "Good high tide running up there, lift that shanty right on out to sea, Mr. Stonecrop."

"God has not seen fit to be so helpful." Mr. Stonecrop stared down across the water. "Reverend Buckminster, behold the cross we bear in Phippsburg: a ragtag collection of hovels and shacks, filled with thieves and lazy sots, eking out a life by eating clams from the ocean mud, heedless of offers of help from either state or church, a blight on the town's aspirations, a hopeless barrier to its future."

Mr. Stonecrop said this mouthful without taking a breath. It was, Turner thought, quite a trick.

"If the shanties were gone, think what a resort site this very cliff might be." Mr. Stonecrop spread his arms out wide. "Imagine the white porticoes of the place, the gracious stairway, the glass doors open to bring in the sea breeze, the red carpet of the lobby, the tinkling of the glass chandelier. I tell you, Reverend, a resort here would be the salvation of Phippsburg."

"Still," said Deacon Hurd, grasping Reverend Buckminster's elbow, "if the governor takes them off the island, he'll add every blessed one onto Phippsburg's pauper rolls. Before we know it, the town will be paying for them to live somewhere else, and paying a proper penny year in, year out. Phippsburg couldn't afford it—and not a single soul will stand for it."

Mr. Stonecrop began to shine his rings against his lapels. "The days of shipbuilding are coming to an end here, Reverend. Traditions change, and we must change with them. If Phippsburg is to survive long enough for your boy to grow up here, it needs new capital, new investment."

"Tourists," said Reverend Buckminster.

"Exactly so. Tourists from Boston, New York, Philadelphia."

"And tourists will not come if there are shanties by their hotel doors."

"You see the situation precisely. The question that remains is, How to do it?" Mr. Stonecrop leaned toward Turner. "Perhaps you would enjoy exploring the coastline, young Buckminster. Take a half hour. You may find some tidal pools to wade in."

"It's high tide," said Turner. "There are no tidal pools at high tide."

"Another quick study, just like his father," said Mr. Stonecrop. "Deacon, he's figured out the tides already. And you said he wasn't very bright."

Shame filled Turner, and his heart beat against his chest so loudly that he imagined it could be heard above the waves.

"Go on along," said Reverend Buckminster, his voice tight. "Things may be different along this coast."

Things would not be different along this coast, Turner thought. Tidal pools came at low tide in Boston, in Phippsburg, in Timbuktu. It didn't take someone very bright to figure that out.

He climbed down the ledges, his heart still beating loudly. The afternoon had become as hot as meanness, and since the shirt he was wearing had enough starch in it to mummify two, maybe three, pharaohs, he began to feel he could hardly breathe. The only thing that saved him from absolute suffocation was the sea breeze somersaulting and fooling, first ahead, then behind, running and panting like a dog ready to play. And he followed it, pulling at his collar, trying not to wish what a minister's son should not wish.

Beneath the granite ledges, Turner found two gnarled pines that begged to be shinnied up, a cave that would just about die to be explored, and mudflats where herons longed to be chased. But he was wearing his white shirt. He felt the starch

21

stiffening against his sides, felt his sweat accumulating in places he could not reach.

So it wasn't exactly fair that when he and his white shirt climbed back up the ledges—after thirty-seven minutes—Mrs. Cobb had appeared among the frock coats. He wasn't surprised that God hadn't given him much of a reprieve. His father's face was red, and Turner knew that supper would be very quiet that night, and that sometime later he would hear about his sins, repent sincerely, and learn what he should do to make amends.

He groaned, quietly.

Reverend Buckminster glared once at his son as they followed the frock coats and a satisfied Mrs. Cobb back into town. Turner wondered if he should grab the Sears, Roebuck catalogue and hide in the outhouse when they got back to the parsonage, even though the day's heat might give it a ripeness he wouldn't care for.

No one spoke to him.

On Parker Head Road, Mrs. Cobb took her outrage into her house, but Turner looked across the road, and there, sure enough, was Mrs. Elia Hurd, watching by her yellow shutters. He waved, then felt his father's hand on his arm.

"You don't want to be getting to know her," said Deacon Hurd. "She's daft as a loon. Will say anything to anyone—not that it will make much sense." Turner heard Sheriff Elwell laughing behind him.

⚓

Turner was right about the ripeness of the outhouse, so he came out for supper, which was as quiet as he had expected. Later on, he heard about his sins, and he repented sincerely, but he thought the amending was harder than it had any right to be.

Even Mrs. Buckminster was surprised. "Does that seem fair?" she asked.

"Yes," said Reverend Buckminster.

"For the rest of the summer?"

"Yes," said Reverend Buckminster, and that was all.

So the next afternoon when it was hot and close, Turner climbed the steps to Mrs. Cobb's house with the sea breeze at his heels, urging him to play. The green door jerked open before he even knocked—as if Mrs. Cobb had been watching for him. "So you're here," she said.

"I'm here to to read to you . . . every day . . . for the rest of the summer . . . if you like," Turner said. He wondered if he was supposed to say something about being sinful and hoping for forgiveness and grace. But he wasn't sure he could muster any real hope in this heat.

Mrs. Cobb eyed him. "So you want to read to me."

Turner nodded. He hoped a nod wasn't the same as an out-loud lie, since he might need one in the near future and didn't want to waste it when things weren't too awful.

"Did you know my grandfather built that picket fence?"

"No, ma'am."

"Well, he did. And it's stood all this time and not a single scratch to it. Not until you started stoning it." She took a step back. "You may as well come in."

With a sigh, Turner decided he might as well. The sea breeze rolled in before him and stirred the fern by the front door. But then it fell panting in the hall, gasping for breath.

Mrs. Cobb strode on in front of him, passing a stairway that rose up too steeply, and then a library hoarding shelves of dark volumes—the arts of necromancy, Turner figured. Though probably they weren't nearly so interesting.

She followed the worn tread in the throw rugs, and Turner went after her into a house as hot as it could possibly be without the whole place flaring up. He looked back, hop-

23

ing the sea breeze might revive, but it lay in the hallway, stricken and still.

They went into a parlor where no one but Mrs. Cobb had stepped since the century had turned over. The windows had been shut against sea breezes long ago, and they let in only a little sunlight. An organ with yellow ivory keys and threadbare pedals leaned back in the shadows beside a black leather chair whose horsehair stuffing cantered out from every crack. Another chair, straight-backed, cushionless, waited beside a dark round table with a dark book on it. Turner picked up the book—*Lives of the English Poets*—and the red dust of its leather cover came off in his hand.

Mrs. Cobb sat down on the leather chair and the horsehair galloped out. "I thought you'd enjoy reading something entertaining," she said.

"Yes, ma'am." He sat down on the straight-backed chair.

Silence. It was too hot for words.

"Would you like me to read now?" Turner asked, almost as if he meant it.

"I'm going to die in this room," said Mrs. Cobb.

Turner stared at her.

"I said, I'm going to die in this room."

"Today?"

"Not today," she snapped.

"No, ma'am," agreed Turner. He was relieved.

"I'll be sitting here reading and I'll set the book aside on that table and lay my head back right here." She laid her head back. "And then I'll fall asleep. Just like that. Fall asleep." She closed her eyes.

"Yes, ma'am."

"The only thing I'll regret is that nobody will hear my last words. People are always remembered for their last words. They're almost like a message from beyond the grave."

Turner nodded. He wondered if his father had known that Mrs. Cobb was absolutely and completely crazy when he'd sent him to read to her. He guessed that he probably hadn't.

Suddenly, her eyes opened and she lifted her head. "Have you thought about what your last words might be? You're never too young to know what your last words might be. Death could come along at any moment and thrust his dart right through you." She jerked her arm out at him, and Turner shot back against the organ.

"I suppose," he whispered, "something like, 'The Lord is my shepherd.'"

"Too expected," she said, shaking her head. "Nobody would care to remember that, and you'd have wasted your one opportunity. You don't get two chances to say your last words, you know."

Turner suddenly felt sick with sadness, as sick as when he had been standing on the rock ledges waiting for the sea to come crashing in on him. Mrs. Cobb was so alone, sitting in a dark room as hot as Beelzebub and waiting for Death's dart to come so that she could say the one thing people would re-member her for—knowing all the while that there would be no one there to hear it.

"Well," she said, "your father said you were coming to read."

"Yes, ma'am."

"Best get on, then. Start with John Milton. Then we'll get to Alexander Pope."

"Mrs. Cobb, if I could just have a glass of—"

"You're young. You don't need it. Get on with Mr. Milton."

Turner got on with Mr. Milton. He was reading Mr. Milton when he heard the clock chime three with a weary, half-hearted chime. He was reading Mr. Pope when the clock chimed the half hour. He was reading Mr. Addison when the clock chimed four and Mrs. Cobb fell asleep. At least, Turner hoped she was asleep. Her head was back and her eyes were closed and she hadn't said anything since he'd started on Mr. Addison.

He hoped she hadn't missed her one opportunity.

He set the book down, quietly. He stepped out into the hall, quietly. Wondering if there was any water left in his body that hadn't been drawn into the starch of his shirt, he walked down the hall—quietly—past a dining room, and finally to the kitchen. He didn't bother looking for a glass; he just held his face by the spout and pumped. At the second pumping, a rush of warm water rusty with iron flushed out, but at the third it was cold and clear. He drank in gulps, then let it come down over his face.

Turner wasn't sure he should leave Mrs. Cobb asleep and alone, but he was sure he needed some air that hadn't been wrung out inside the house. Slowly, quietly, he went back down the hall. Slowly, quietly, he looked in on Mrs. Cobb to see if she was breathing. He couldn't quite tell, but he decided that the odds were pretty good that she hadn't left the world this very afternoon. He went on to the front hall and stepped over the sea breeze. If he could just open the door and gulp some air, he'd be able to sit with her through Mr. Addison, and his amends would be over for the day.

So he opened the door—and stared beyond the picket gate at Willis Hurd and his friends, who all broke into sudden and uproarious laughter—all except Willis, who was smiling his chicken-killing smile.

"Nice shirt, Buck*minister*," sneered Willis. "You calling on your girl?"

A sea surge of laughter from the road.

"I'm not calling on my girl."

"Oh," said Willis, turning to the others. "He says he's not calling on his girl."

Turner reached behind him for the door.

"She wouldn't have him anyway, scared as he is to jump into a wave. Hey, Buck*minister*, you jump about as good as you swing a bat."

Turner let go of the doorknob and went down the porch steps.

"You got him mad now, Willis!"

"Sure. He's coming to fight for his girl." Willis held the gate open. "You know how to fight, Buck*minister*? You know how to throw a punch as good as you swing a bat?"

Turner threw one. Even before it landed, he realized that Willis had never believed he would. It crashed into his cheek and slid over onto his nose, and Turner knew that Willis's face would probably be all blood in a second or two. He also knew that Willis, who was a head bigger than he, would tuck into him faster than a ball screaming down toward first.

All this turned out to be true, and it wasn't much more than a minute before Willis landed an unsporting and sickening punch (which even he regretted) that had Turner on the ground, writhing and throwing up all the cold water he had swallowed.

Willis backed up and wiped a hand under his bleeding nose. He stood still, watching Turner crumpled, holding himself, his face coated with the dust of the road, his white shirt smeared with blood.

"You want us to call your girl?"

"Let's get on," said Willis. "He'll be all right. Let's get on."

But Turner didn't want them to leave with him sprawled in the road. He wouldn't let them leave with him sprawled in the road.

He pushed himself up from his knees, winced, and reached out for the picket gate, not caring much whether he got blood on Mrs. Cobb's grandfather's work. He missed it the first time, organized his eyes so that they were seeing straighter, and grabbed at it again. Slowly he came up, trying to sort out his legs underneath him, wishing the world weren't spinning as fast as it was. But he was standing. His knees wobbled and he was bent over, but he was standing. Turner didn't look to see if Willis was watching him, but he figured he was, so he walked slowly, as unbent as he could under the circumstances, up the steps and onto the porch. He tracked down the doorknob, turned it, and went inside, making sure to take a quick but necessarily shallow gulp of air just before he closed the door behind him.

He would not cry. He was trapped in the dark pit of the world, but he would not cry. God and all the heavenly host were witness that he had every reason to, but he would not cry.

There was a satisfaction, though. He flexed his hand and looked down at his bloody knuckles. Willis's blood. He remembered the feeling of his knuckles striking Willis's cheek, and he didn't care a doggone bit that he had enjoyed hitting Willis, minister's son or not. Not one doggone bit.

Still bent, Turner shuffled back to the kitchen, checking once more to see if Mrs. Cobb was asleep—or dead. She was, one or the other. Taking off his shirt, he pulled at the pump again and put his head under it, spitting out the bile in his mouth. The water was as cold and wonderful as before, and after a quick check, he realized that none of the blood that had spurted all over the place was his own—another satisfaction. But his or not, it had spurted all over him, and the shirt—and the pants as well—might be beyond hope. Still, they were worth a try, so he held the shirt under the streaming water to wash off as much as he could of Willis's blood; then he took off his pants and held them under the stream, too. He set them on the back of a chair to dry, which, he figured, would hardly take any time in a place as hot as this. If he did get them dry, he could wear them home and no one would be the wiser. Except maybe his mother. He might have to account to her for any bloodstains that were left, but that was the kind of thing he had saved his out-loud lie for.

Now, Turner had heard his father say more than once that there are times when things spin away, when they go from bad to worse, then worse again. We should thank God for those times, he said, since they are God's reminders that we poor and lowly creatures need His help.

Turner had never liked this line of thinking. He figured that if things got bad through no fault of your own, then God should stand up and do something about it. It seemed only right.

He was thinking that now when he wheeled about at a sudden breath behind him and saw Mrs. Cobb staring. She had one hand up to her open mouth, and her eyes were as shocked as if the Seven Horsemen of the Apocalypse had come riding down into her kitchen.

"What in the name of all that's holy are you doing?"

Turner sighed.

"You are standing in my house, my very house, naked."

Turner sighed again.

"Turner Buckminster, you are standing in my house naked."

"I'm wearing my underwear," he said weakly.

Mrs. Cobb spurted back into the hallway, fast enough that the Seven Horsemen themselves would have had trouble with the pace. He heard her clomping up the steep stairs.

There was nothing to do but take up his wet clothes and

put them back on. He dripped down the hall, across the stoop, through Mrs. Cobb's front yard, past the picket gate, and most of the way home. He figured he might get there before the news reached his father. He had a while to wait and wonder why God hadn't handled things a little bit better.

But he had enjoyed smacking Willis. He smiled and flexed his hand again.

❧

The problem of God's not handling things well troubled Lizzie, too. She had been watching a pale crab in a low pool for about an hour—maybe the same crab that had tumbled onto her toe the day before. And after all that watching, she figured the crab deserved a name, and so she gave it one: Zerubabel. When she called, it waved its tiny pink pincers at her frantically. "You like your name, don't you, Zerubabel?" She twirled a finger and let Zerubabel catch her. She pulled it up, right out of the water, and then shook it back in with a tiny splash. "A toughie." She smiled.

Lizzie peered up at the ledges across the way. Not a frock coat in sight. Not a white shirt in sight. The grainy rocks, the swaying pines, the cascade of stubborn blue mussels, the water splashing up green and streaming back white—they were all the same, as if the frock coats had never been there. They would always be the same.

And it was right then that God didn't handle things too well.

A sudden feathered swooping startled her back. A splash, a labored beating of wings, and Zerubabel was in a gull's beak, its pale, pink shell already crushed, its tiny pincers loosely dangling.

And Lizzie was crying.

Golly Moses, she thought, it was only a tiny crab, after all. There were crabs under every patch of floating seaweed. There were crabs in every pool up the shore. And gulls had to eat, too.

But she had named it Zerubabel, and it had held its little pincers so prettily.

So she cried. And she was still crying when she heard the splash of oars and saw a dory just digging its nose into the gravelly beach around the turn and Sheriff Elwell jumping out and getting his pants wet to the knees so that the other frock coats could step out onto the shore of Malaga Island.

Lizzie stopped crying and ran. It might be that a dolphin could swim faster than Lizzie through the water and a fish hawk dive faster through the air, but nothing alive could run across Malaga Island faster than Lizzie Griffin. So before the five frock coats had clambered out of the dory, Lizzie's grandfather knew of their coming. And before they had climbed up the shore, the sea breeze blowing back their frock coats like beating wings, most of the folks who lived on Malaga Island knew of their coming, too, and were standing on their doorsteps.

"Preacher Griffin," called out Sheriff Elwell. "Preacher Griffin!"

Lizzie came out of her house hanging onto her grandfather's arm. He held a ladle in his hands and blinked against the bright sunlight. Lizzie loved him like this: stooped a little, as though something were dragging on him by the shoulders, his eyes the tiniest bit closed, his mouth pulled up on one side, his tread sort of slow. She knew he was strong. He could heft a dory right up onto its blocks, dig out a rock that a glacier had dropped into his garden patch, and cart enough firewood in his own two hands to warm their house and the Tripp house through a whole winter day—and the Tripp house had more sunlight between its boards than board.

But you could never tell this by looking at him. Unless The

Change happened. When he took his Bible in hand and stood up in front of God and all Malaga Island to preach, he'd be straight up, his eyes opened wide and glinting like mica. His voice would drop down three, four, five notes, and he'd hold the Good Book level, and you'd think he had the angels at his command. Golly Moses, he looked as if he could stamp his foot on the ground and the rocks would split open beneath him and fire and thunder come out.

Lizzie prayed that The Change would come on now. She saw that not a single one of the frock coats understood what might happen if her grandfather decided to stamp his foot on the ground.

But The Change did not come on. Not yet.

"You all well, Preacher?" asked Sheriff Elwell.

Lizzie's grandfather nodded. "Thanks for asking," he said.

"Your fence here needs fixing."

"It usually does, Sheriff."

The sheriff nodded. "I haven't heard tell of anything missing in town since last spring. Not a single chicken, all this time. I suppose you've been preaching right."

"I hope I have."

"That one yours?" He pointed to Lizzie. "You been climbing trees?"

Lizzie scooted behind her grandfather. "She's my granddaughter. Thaddeus's girl."

"She don't say much."

"Sometimes folks who have things to say don't say them."

Sheriff Elwell looked at him sharply.

Just then, twenty, thirty gulls rose from somewhere on the island coast and turned to face the sea breeze, screeching like broken promises. The gulls beat up into the air, speckling the shore with their shadows. Sheriff Elwell watched them, and when he turned back, he saw that Reverend Griffin had not moved. "Preacher, I'll get right to the point of it, us coming out here and all. These shanties"—he waved his hand across the island—"these shanties have all got to come down."

The gulls glided back around, all together, all yawing their wings to the drafts that brought them low to the water. Then they straightened and flew over the ledges on the far shore, out of sight.

"They in somebody's way?"

"They've got to come down and you've got to move on."

"By this fall," added one of the frock coats. Deacon Hurd.

"I see," said Reverend Griffin, nodding. Lizzie watched him for The Change, but she didn't see any signs of it. "And by this fall. I see." He thought some and tilted his head at Sheriff Elwell. "Someone worried about his chickens? Someone missing his traps?"

"It's our tax money," said Deacon Hurd. "If a single one of you comes onto the pauper rolls, where do you think the money to keep you will come from? It will come from the people of Phippsburg."

"We're awful glad to hear that the people of Phippsburg will care for us in our time of trouble. But Sheriff, when was the last time Phippsburg sent their taxes our way?"

"The schoolhouse," pointed out another frock coat. "And the teacher's salary to go with it."

"I guess," said Lizzie's grandfather slowly, "I guess I thought that every town in the state of Maine took care to find a teacher for its own."

"Exactly the issue," said the tallest of the frock coats, twirling the rings on his fingers. "Are you our own?"

"Times move on, Preacher," said Sheriff Elwell. "And sometimes when times move on, folks have to move on with them. You'll find some other place to squat. Lord knows it won't take long to build another shack like this one."

Lizzie put her arms around her grandfather, and he stroked her hands. "Lord knows it wouldn't," he said. "But we've got our own place here already."

"No, you don't have your own place here," said Sheriff Elwell. "There's not one of you that's got a registered deed to the land on this island. I've been to the town clerk about it. Not a single one of you owns any land on the island."

Lizzie felt The Change begin.

"My granddaddy built that house there, my daddy built the fence around it," said Reverend Griffin. "They worked like dogs tending your granddaddies' and daddies' places in Phippsburg so they could pay right for every nail. There's no one here lives on a piece of land like that, father and mother after father and mother, that doesn't own it."

The tall frock coat put his hands in the side pockets of his vest. "Your grandfather saw fit to build this house on land that did not belong to him—that does not belong to you now. The sheriff is trying to explain the consequences of that."

Reverend Griffin looked at Sheriff Elwell, who shrugged. "The law's the law. You got no deed that says you own this place."

"Then who does own this place?"

"The state of Maine," said Sheriff Elwell.

"And does the state of Maine have a mind to settle right here?"

Sheriff Elwell shrugged again. "The state of Maine does what the state of Maine wants to do."

A long pause. Lizzie waited for the gulls to return over the high ledge, but they didn't. Maybe they'd gone across to the Kennebec and were swooping down on more Zerubabels. She felt the movement of the day and knew that the tide would be running in soon, covering the Zerubabels. Covering the clams, too, and she hadn't dug hers yet. Now she probably wouldn't.

"Sheriff," her grandfather said slowly, "you've taken the trouble to come out here to tell us this."

"You'll let the others know, Preacher? They'll need to be out come fall."

"Before I do that, I wonder if all you might take a walk with me." Silence. "A little ways in."

He did not wait for an answer but turned, Lizzie with him and still waiting for The Change to drop his voice. He set out on a path that threaded through knots of pines, looking into them and nodding now and again. The path was clear enough that even the frock coats were able to keep up pretty well, though Lizzie doubted that they heard the sounds of those who had come off their doorsteps and now walked silently beside them, hidden by the trees. They all followed the path as it fell down between the sharp halves of a cracked boulder, came into pine woods again, and finally rounded into a sudden clearing.

Lizzie's grandfather waited for the frock coats to come up. "This here," he said, "this here's our deed."

In the clearing, sixty graves lay quiet and still, restful. Wood crosses with printed names too faded to read stood at their heads. Some had piles of pink-grained stones gathered from around the island placed carefully at the foot of each cross. Some had sprigs of violets, some fresh evergreen boughs. The pines quivered around them, and the moss softening the stones in the piles was so green that Lizzie wondered whether even the frock coats want to kneel down and smell it. It was all as neat and welcoming as if Nature herself had swept and tidied up her best room, figuring on guests coming to call.

Reverend Griffin stopped by a grave with a whitewashed

cross. "This here's Thaddeus," he said. "Next to his mother. And that there, that's her daddy." He held his hands out. "Their bones—our bones—they're all part of this island. We can't leave."

The tallest frock coat sniffed. "This will have to be cleared away."

Reverend Griffin turned for the first time to one of the other frock coats. "Sir, your collar says you're a preacher."

Reverend Buckminster nodded. "I'm the new minister at First Congregational."

"Then you know," said Reverend Griffin, "that when God gives you a place to live, you don't leave it even if all the armies of the Philistines come down among you. You don't leave it till God calls you someplace else."

Lizzie waited, and golly Moses, she saw that the new minister understood.

But . . .

"No," said Reverend Buckminster, looking at the other frock coats. "No. I'm sorry for your trouble, but First Congregational will help out as much as it can to see you folks settled somewhere. The Ladies' Sewing Circle has already begun to knit mittens, and scarves as well, I believe. Perhaps just mittens. We plan on a collection next Sunday."

"You be out by fall," said Sheriff Elwell.

Just then the flock of gulls appeared again overhead, calling and calling, as if searching for lost souls. The frock coats turned back toward their dory, and the sheriff walked behind them with Reverend Griffin and Lizzie. "You'll know what to tell them," said Sheriff Elwell, "the rest of the folks on the island. You'll have better words than I would."

"I'll tell them that times move on."

The sheriff nodded.

"That maybe God's calling on us to move on."

Another nod. "You'll find a place. You people always do."

"Just one more thing, Sheriff." The sheriff stopped and waited. "What'll happen when times move on again and it's your turn?"

For a moment, the sheriff seemed to understand. His eyes looked down. Then the moment passed, and full and sudden he laughed louder than the calling gulls. "Times will never move on that much," he said.

When they reached the shore, the frock coats boarded and the sheriff pushed the dory out until the water reached his knees, clambered in—carefully, so as not to splash the frock coats—and began rowing back up the New Meadows. "You'll know what to tell them," he called back. "By fall."

Lizzie held close against her grandfather as the people of Malaga Island came out from the pine woods, gathering around their preacher on the shore to hear what had been said. Before they turned, Lizzie felt her grandfather ebb as though his soul were passing out of him, the way the last waves of a falling tide pass into still air and are gone.

She took a deep breath, and she wasn't just breathing in the air. She breathed in the waves, the sea grass, the pines, the pale lichens on the granite, the sweet shimmering of the pebbles dragged back and forth in the surf, the fish hawk diving to the waves, the dolphin jumping out of them.

She would not ebb.

Then she turned with her grandfather to tell the gathering people of Malaga that times had moved on, and they would have to leave their homes.

CHAPTER

"By all that's holy, Turner, you couldn't wait before you decided to embarrass me in front of a new congregation?"

"I didn't mean to embarrass you."

"First you harass Mrs. Cobb, walking past her house without a shirt and throwing stones at her fence. And now you brawl in the street with Deacon Hurd's son. With the deacon's son! But perhaps you're right. I cannot possibly imagine how that would embarrass me, the new minister. 'Look,' people will say—are already saying—'he can't handle his own son. How can he possibly handle a church?' And that's not all they'll be saying. They'll be saying—"

A single high metal ring on the phone broke off what people would say about the new minister. Glaring, Reverend Buckminster went to answer it, and Turner wondered if he was free to go upstairs. His damp clothes were pretty much clamped against his skin, and as they dried, the starch was tightening. Soon, he figured, he wouldn't be able to breathe.

He supposed he'd better wait for his father. Heaven only knew what new sin committed by the minister's son was being announced over the phone. It was probably Mrs. Cobb doing the announcing.

Turner looked up and down the shelves of his father's study—the first room in the house that had been readied. Sunlight glinted on the gilt spines of the books. It smelled impressive, all that leather. Still, he wondered if there was a single book on those shelves that any human being really liked to read. "*The Heresies of the Modern World and the Infallibility of Orthodoxy*," he said into the still air. "*An Alphabetical Compendium of All Sects. A View of All Religions. Occasional Sermons of the Reverend Emmons.*" He decided he could probably come up with better titles: *Huckleberry Finn and the Merry Apostles*, maybe. *The Piratical Adventures of Peter on the Sea of Galilee. Occasional Sermons on How God Intended Baseball Be Played.*

He felt his father come back into the room. The door shut. Tightly.

"You were naked in Mrs. Cobb's kitchen," Turner's father said, slowly and quietly.

"Not naked."

His father waited.

"I was in my underwear."

"You were in your underwear in Mrs. Cobb's kitchen. Let us praise God that decency reigns."

The rest of the conversation went about as badly as it could go, particularly at the end, when Turner had to promise he would ask Mrs. Cobb's pardon the next day, and would, to improve his own soul and to bring light to her dark loneliness, resolve not only to read to her for the summer but to play the organ for her at least three times a week as well, taking care all the while to remain fully dressed. And while it was to be recognized that he was still a young boy, yet he would resolve to conquer his debased self so that he would not be an embarrassment to his father but would instead shine brightly as an example of Christian charity to all—much like Willis Hurd.

Turner left his father's study, climbed the stairs to his room, and put on another perfectly white and starched shirt. He was desperate to find a place where he could breathe.

Whatever that place was, it wasn't his room, which was long and narrow and slanted downhill. Someone had put up the wallpaper during the Civil War, Turner figured—for a girl, he was sure—and it had clung to the walls for longer than it should have. By the one window, all of its yellow blooms had faded to a general gray, and Turner had started to peel it away. He took a long strip off now, wondering if it would be a sin to open his window and lean out. It probably was in Phippsburg, Maine, and someone would call the new minister and tell him that his son was hanging out the upper story and being a bad example for younger children, who would unwittingly follow his lead and fall to untimely deaths without any of their last words being said, never mind heard. His father would be embarrassed again. Turner thought about getting to work on conquering his debased self, but decided that could wait till morning. He wasn't up to shining brightly, and he wasn't much inclined to do it anyway. He lay down on his bed, held his baseball glove up to his face, and breathed in its leathery scent.

He kept it over his face until his mother called him for supper.

Getting through supper was like being dangled on a spiderweb strand over hell. But he resolved to avoid the one misstep that might send his soul down to perdition. He was as polite as an angel all the way through the roast and potatoes. He ate the egg pudding without complaint. While carrying out the dishes, he was as helpful as St. Timothy.

One misstep!

He had avoided it all through supper.

Afterward, Turner climbed back to his narrow room. For a moment he held his glove to his face again; then he suddenly crossed the room, jerked open the window, and sat on the sill dangling one leg out, not caring if he was shining brightly or not.

He watched the day begin to settle into sleep. It yawned out a white fog the sea breeze carried in close to shore and then left hovering there. Aside from the low ringing of the buoy offshore, it was all so quiet that Turner thought he could hear the tide pulling away from the gravelly beachhead. The merry flight of the bats around the steeple of First Congregational stilled, the blurred stars began to come out, and the first owl call sounded, low and sonorous. Everything faded from gray to grayer to grayer still, so that soon there was hardly any color, and then the gray was so dark that Turner couldn't see through it. And suddenly there was the moon, joking around in the haze and tossing a dull light that shimmered the fog to the color of old pearls.

Turner thought that maybe there were times when Maine would do. Then he heard the phone ring and, after a minute, Reverend Buckminster hollering up the stairs. "Turner, you're not climbing out onto the roof, are you?"

Turner went to bed and lay awake most of the night. He figured if he couldn't light out for the Territories and had to stay in Phippsburg, he'd need to find a place to breathe—someplace where no one else would come around, someplace where no one was even likely to come around. And it wouldn't hurt for it to be by the water.

So in the morning, Turner set his face to the sea breeze and followed it down Parker Head Road, across the peninsula, and toward the water. He was perfectly dressed in another startlingly white shirt, and not a soul whom he passed on the street or who eyed him through a parlor window—and there were plenty of souls who eyed him—could find a single blessed fault. He walked as if he were in the company of the elect, so that even Mrs. Cobb would have had to stretch to find something to remark on.

Turner hated himself for playing the minister's son. He desperately wanted to pull out his collar, or to run, or just to holler. But he couldn't. I am not my own, he thought, but belong body and soul to every parishioner in Phippsburg who might have a word to say about me to my father. And there seemed to be plenty of words and plenty of parishioners to say them.

So he went on toward the sea. He passed the yellow-shuttered house, half wishing that Mrs. Hurd were on the porch. He passed the picket fence of Mrs. Cobb's, steering as clear of it as if it were the wall of Jericho about to fall. He kept his face to the sea breeze as the line of white houses at the end of Parker Head sputtered, revived in a solid row, and finally gave out and let the road twist by itself up into cedars.

Turner held himself to a slow walk, his hands politely out of his pockets. (Who knew if Mrs. Cobb might still be watching him from some murky spot where dark things lurked?) But as he climbed into the thicket of trees and the air grew cooler, and as the road thinned to a path, and as the cedars gave way to birches, then aspens, then pines, Turner felt as though he were taking off the black robes that enveloped his father. He unbuttoned his stiff collar as he passed through into scrub pines and laid it on a branch. And then he was out in the open.

He spread his arms wide against the ocean sounds: the rush of the waves, the manic giggles of the gulls, the sighing of the sea breeze against the granite. He put his back to all of Phippsburg—Lord, to the entire continent—till with a shrug he sloughed off its heavy stillness and looked for a way to climb down to the water. In the end, it was more of a tumble than a climb, and he left a little skin and a little blood in one or two places—though, thankfully, not on his shirt. There was a moment when he wondered if he would be able to climb back up and find his dang collar again, but finally he was down on the beach, breathing hard and deep, like something that was only just coming alive and drinking in the liquid air for the first delicious time.

He looked up and down the coast. If he saw even a single soul prowling the shore, he would light out. But there were only gulls. Across the water a line of trembling smoke rose high and then spread out. Otherwise, it was as if God had just remade the world for him, and he was Adam waking up, an entire globe to explore.

He figured there wasn't anything Adam would have wanted to do more than skip stones, so he began to fling rocks along the wave troughs, trying to skip one clear across the channel to the island lying offshore. But the water had rounded most of the rocks so that they were no good for skipping, and anyway, there was always a wave to grab them before they could reach the gravel. He searched and then saw an almost perfectly straight branch of driftwood, bleached and smooth as worn soap, right at the waterline. He hefted it in his hands and swung it once. Then he picked up a rounded stone, set his feet firm with the left forward, and tossed the stone high into the air. He swung at it as it came straight down. And missed.

He picked it up, set his eye to judge the vertical, and tossed it again. This time he connected—barely. The next time he missed, and the next, but finally the rap of the stone stung his palms and rattled his wrists. If he tilted the horizontal swing, he thought, maybe he'd have a better hit. He threw another stone up and connected again, this time with satisfying solidity.

And that was how Lizzie saw him as she came up the coast: his back to her, wearing a white shirt fit for glory, throwing rocks up into the air and swinging at them with a piece of driftwood.

If she had figured he had come for a place to breathe, she might have been more understanding—even if she had wondered about him some. If she had figured he was absolutely and completely crazy, she would have let him be. But as far as she knew, he was standing with his left leg forward on her shore, in a place where she had come to clam and to breathe. It was as if he were telling her to move on.

And she had had enough of that.

If her grandfather had been there, he might have told her that a peaceable spirit was the reward of charity. But it was awfully hard to be peaceable and charitable when a whole island was about to be swept out from beneath you, and so Lizzie felt she had a right to say what she said, even if it wasn't peaceable and was as far from charitable as she could get.

"Are you some kind of idiot?"

Turner wheeled around, and it did not help when the stone he had tossed up that very second—a particularly heavy one with sharp corners—came down off center on the bridge of his nose, starting a gush of blood that leaped eagerly and immediately to his shirt. Turner figured the pain would come along in just a second or two, but before that started, he realized he would have to explain another bloody shirt to his parents. And he would have to come up with a wonderful out-loud lie, since he could hardly tell them that he had thrown a rock at his nose.

Then the pain came on. He bent down so that the blood wouldn't fall on his pants, too.

Lizzie thought that maybe he really was an idiot, bending down that way, letting the blood spout out. "You're supposed to lie down," she called, "with your head back. So's the blood will stop." He did not answer her, so she spoke slowly. "Are you understanding what I'm saying?"

Turner was starting to sweat and feeling sort of weak. He was also beginning to seriously doubt that he would survive his first week in Maine. He knelt down on the beach, careful to keep the gushing blood away from his pants, and wondered if it was possible for all the blood in his body to drain out through his nose.

Lizzie set down the clam bucket and rake she'd carried from the dory and walked carefully up to him, a little wary because you never can tell what idiots might do. "Do you understand me?"

Turner nodded.

"Lie down and put your head back. Like this." He felt her hands on his shoulders and let her push him down. She put one hand behind his head and laid him back until he was flat. "Turn your head." The blood started to run down over his left cheek. "You better now?"

He was not better now. He would not be better now until he had put this entire state somewhere about a thousand miles away from him.

"You talk any? I mean, if you understand me and all."

"I talk," said Turner, "but not usually to people who hide out and scare someone so that a rock comes down on his face."

"Well," said Lizzie slowly, "as far as the rock coming down on your face, I'm not the fool who threw it up."

Turner was in no mood to allow that this was so.

"It looks like it's letting up some. Looks like it might be. A little, anyways."

Turner moved his hand to his face, hesitated, and then gently, gently touched his nose. "Is it pushed off to one side?"

"Not much. Not so that anyone would notice—unless they were up close. But not so much."

This was not the answer Turner had been hoping for. He touched his nose again and decided that he probably shouldn't try to push it back into place.

"What were you doing anyway, hitting at stones?"

"I was hitting at stones."

"You've got a reason to do that?"

"Yes, I've got a reason to do that."

Lizzie sat down on the ground to consider. "You don't have to snap so."

Turner sat up slowly, touched his nose again, felt a new spurt of blood, and laid his head back. Lizzie thought he looked like a dog trying to sniff out something but not quite getting hold of the scent. She decided she would not tell him this. "If you take that shirt off, we could try to wash out the blood," she said. "Salt water is fine for that. Salt water will do for everything."

"Maybe not," said Turner. He stood up, his head held carefully, and looked fully at her for the first time. He was surprised to find that he immediately liked her. In fact, he was almost shocked that he immediately liked her. He'd never even spoken to a Negro before. Never once. But he liked the smooth, easy way she stood, as if she were part of the contour of the shore. He liked the oak brown of her eyes and the grip of her long toes on the rocky ground, the tilt of her head like a sail catching the wind. She had lit out for the Territories and found them, he thought.

"I could teach you how to do that," she said.

"How to do what? Get hit in the face with a rock? I don't need to learn how to do that."

"No, you're plenty good enough at that as it is. I mean to swing a bat, if that's what you're doing. And my name, by the way, is Lizzie. Lizzie Griffin."

"Thanks, but I already know how to swing a bat. And my name, by the way, is Turner. Turner Ernest Buckminster."

"Doesn't look to me like you do. And I have a middling name, too."

"I do any place where they know how to pitch. And what is it?"

"Well, Turner Ernest Buckminster, your problem isn't the pitch, it's the swing. It's Lizzie Bright Griffin."

"Then let's see you swing, Lizzie Bright Griffin."

She picked up the driftwood branch that Turner had let fall. "Pitch one," she said.

So he did. The first was too high and fell short. The second was too long and lobbed over her head. But then Turner got used to the weight, and the third went somewhere in the middle, and Lizzie, Lizzie of the steady eye and firm hand, Lizzie Bright Griffin swung and hit the stone dead center. In fact, every time Turner pitched her a stone within shouting distance, she hit it dead center—no matter how high the arch, no matter how straight the descent.

"Good?" asked Lizzie finally.

"Better than good," said Turner.

"You don't look so bad when you smile, you know. Even if you are still sort of bloody and your nose is pushed off to one side."

"It isn't pushed off to one side. And you don't look so bad when you swing. You start with your hands low, don't you, and when the pitch comes down, you set them lower and draw in."

She nodded. "You're not an idiot after all. Not even halfway." She handed the branch to Turner. "Now you."

She was, in addition to being a better batter than he was, a better pitcher than he was. "Start lower and come higher," she said.

"If I start lower and come higher, I'll pop it up every time."

"Of course you'll pop it up every time. We'll straighten that out later."

Turner lowered the branch and looked at her skeptically.

"Here," she said, "I'll show you again." And she stepped next to him and put her hands over his, and together they swung the bat in an arc as graceful as a fish hawk's winging slide through the air. They did it again and again, until Turner suddenly shivered, stepped back, and looked at her.

"You never touch a girl before, Turner Ernest Buckminster? Or is it just that you never touched a girl with black skin before?"

"I've never even talked to someone with black skin before."

"Well," she said, "never mind. You're holding up your end just fine."

By noon, Turner could hit most every pitch she threw to him—and not just a glancing hit, either. He was starting to level out his swing, and he even tried sending one or two down a sideline. His hands were ringing with the hits, and blisters were starting to bubble up. It was only when a couple of them broke and started to bleed that he thought he'd better stop, since he was not sure how much blood he had left to lose.

"You can wash that in the water," Lizzie said.

"I know," said Turner. "Salt water will do for everything." He knelt down to where the sea lay flat and exhausted after tumbling in close.

"It'll sting some," Lizzie called as he held his hand down. "Maybe a little more than some."

It did sting. A little more than some. But Turner did not

mind all that much. He held his wet hand up and watched the salt sea drip from it.

"My granddaddy says it's the stinging that drives out the hurt."

"Your granddaddy?" Turner asked.

"Reverend Griffin."

And that was when Turner suddenly knew that he was late for dinner, that Reverend Buckminster would be figuring that he'd fallen into some rocky chasm or drowned in the sea, or worse yet, that he'd come up with some other way to embarrass the new minister. And he figured that when he showed up alive after all, his father would stand on the porch and look at him in a way that said Turner would never be the kind of son he had hoped for—it would be as loud as if he had just announced it from the pulpit.

"Lizzie Bright Griffin, do you ever wish the world would just go ahead and swallow you whole?"

"Sometimes I do," she said, and then smiled. "But sometimes I figure I should just go ahead and swallow it." And she held her arms out wide, as if she would gather it all in. And for a moment, Turner had no doubt that she could.

He clambered back up the ledges, retrieved his collar—it took some time to find—and so sprinted home, hardly able to breathe by the time he reached the front porch.

He was right. His mother and father did think he had fallen into a chasm or drowned, and when he showed up alive—and bloody again—his father did look at him in a way that said Turner would never be the kind of son he had hoped for. The thought prowled quietly among the plates on the dining room table. When his father started to read from Proverbs, Turner was surprised at how many verses about rebellious children he had been able to collect on such short notice.

"Do you think you'll be able to last the afternoon without bleeding over your shirt, Turner?" his father asked. He held a spoonful of yesterday's egg pudding in front of him, and Turner was fascinated by the delicate balance of the thing, the way it jiggled and threatened to plop off onto the tablecloth but never quite did—almost as if it didn't dare to, because it was the Reverend Buckminster holding it.

Turner nodded.

"I wouldn't be surprised if there wasn't a game down to Thayer's haymeadow this afternoon. You could get to know some of the boys."

Another nod. Egg pudding still jiggling. The spoon slanting a bit, so that a bulge of the pudding was about to slide off, nutmeg skin and all.

"You'll need to keep your clothes clean, though," Reverend Buckminster observed.

"Yes, sir," said Turner. He could just imagine himself running down to the field, wearing his starched white shirt and pretending he wasn't, begging to play with Willis Hurd. An afternoon couldn't look much worse. Maybe reading to Mrs. Cobb—that might be worse. He wondered if Lizzie would still be down on the shore.

"On the way back, stop by Mrs. Cobb's house to apologize. Then you can read to her as well."

Turner looked up from the egg pudding. Things were getting much worse indeed. "Do I play the organ for her today, too?"

"And apologize," finished Reverend Buckminster. "Turner, God does not want us to . . ."

But Turner did not particularly care just then what God did not want us to do. He watched as his father became The Minister. His face took on a kind of faraway look, as if he were seeing something no one else could see, as if he were eager to talk to anyone lower than the seraphim for a time. His voice got higher and slower, as if he expected it to be rising into the church rafters.

The egg pudding fell to the tablecloth, and Turner's father did not notice. It lay there, slowly spreading out, a yellow blob against the white.

And suddenly, Turner had a thought that had never occurred to him before: he wondered if his father really believed a single thing he was saying.

And suddenly, Turner had a second thought that had never occurred to him before: he wondered if *he* believed a single thing his father was saying.

The intoning went on, its bulk bloating and bloating so that Turner thought the very ceiling might be pushed up. It went on, pressing on his eardrums. It went on, threatening the very roof. It went on, until the last thing Turner thought could ever happen—the very last thing—happened.

"Buckminster, stop it!"

It took Turner a moment to figure out who had just spoken. He saw that his mother had stood, that she had one hand against her face, another clenched into the checks of her apron. Since there was no one in the room but the three of them, it had to have been her. But that couldn't be.

Turner looked at his father, who was coming to just about the same conclusion.

"Turner," his mother said quietly, "go upstairs and change into something you can hit a baseball in. And I'll stop by Mrs. Cobb's this afternoon."

Turner stood.

"Go on now," she said tightly.

He wondered what might happen as soon as he left the dining room, and he was more than a little tempted to dawdle. But his father's face—which no longer looked as if it were facing only the seraphim—was convincing enough. And the prospect of wearing something that had not been made for church was too good for him to wait any longer, so he sprinted upstairs.

When he came back down, he was in a shirt and trousers he had found lying at the foot of his bed, a shirt and trousers that would never have marked him as a minister's son. After just a single stealthy moment of listening at the closed dining room doors—there was absolute silence—he leaped out into the free air, and headed straight for the haymeadow, the memory of the driftwood in his hands.

But a storm was boiling up in more places than in his dining room. Dinner had taken long enough for thickened thunderheads to swell off the coast. Turner felt the heavy air they dropped, heard their rumbling like the distant chariots of the Assyrians. He ran to the shore to see them come in.

Before he reached the haymeadow, the first big raindrops were plopping down and exploding in the yellow dust. They fell sudden and cold on his back. The wind bucked up, shifted once, and then again, and set the buoys out in the Kennebec bowing toward him. When Turner looked over the river, he saw an iron sheet of rain coming toward him, lit up from behind through a rip in the dark purple of the clouds.

He thought suddenly of Lizzie on the shore and flung out his arms and opened his mouth as the sheet came upon him. If Mrs. Cobb had seen him just then, she would have thought he was grinning like a loon and would have scampered off to tell the new minister that his son hadn't the sense God had given him, that he was standing out in the middle of the storm with his arms spread out and his mouth open. And she would have been right—about him grinning like a loon.

4

THE rain passed Turner, swept across Thayer's haymeadow, charged up Parker Head, and swirled around First Congregational, ripping off some of the still-green maple leaves and sending them in whirling cones against Mrs. Cobb's grandfather's fence and up onto Mrs. Hurd's porch. By the time Turner had started to feel the chill of it, the rain had already run down through the cedars, over the shore, and across the New Meadows, and had begun to scatter on Malaga Island, where Lizzie was just running into her house before it soaked her.

It rained all night, and Turner up in Phippsburg and Lizzie down on Malaga Island lay in their beds in the deep dark, their arms up behind their heads, listening to the play of the drops on their roofs. The drops played long after Turner and Lizzie had fallen asleep, and they played while Turner's mother and father lay still and unmoving in the dark, and they played while Lizzie's granddaddy sat quietly at his door, an unlit pipe in his mouth. They played across the coast all through the night, until the soft new day shrugged itself awake, tried on amethyst and lavender for a while, and finally decided on a pale yellow.

The day was brighter by the time Turner finished his breakfast, and a whole lot brighter when he ran out of the house, his bat over his shoulder, his glove slung onto it, and the other tossing a baseball up and around, behind his back and over his head. He left in a shirt that he had hung carefully up to dry the night before, that was not white, and that Mrs. Cobb probably would not approve of. It surprised him that he felt a little bad that his father would not approve, either—but not so bad that he would change it. Still, he hurried by Mrs. Cobb's, trusting that maybe the Lord would get things right today and she wouldn't be out by her grandfather's fence.

She wasn't out. But Mrs. Hurd was, sweeping the leaves off her porch. When she saw Turner, she waved at him with a merry hand. She was still dressed all in white, her hair tied tightly into a bun. Turner wondered if she had ever looked any other way. Maybe God had created her just like this, plunking her down old and white and with her hair tied back, without any preliminaries at all.

He waved back at her. "Morning, Mrs. Hurd."

"Morning, Turner III. Did you enjoy the rain last night?"

"Yes, ma'am."

"Me, too. Did you go out in it?"

"Yes, ma'am, I did."

Mrs. Hurd leaned over her porch rail. "Me, too." She smiled like a conspirator. "You know why you got whipped, don't you?"

"Ma'am?"

"You know why you got whipped?"

"Whipped?"

"You were supposed to hit that boy in the eye."

Turner went to the bottom of her steps. "I thought I got whipped because I shouldn't have been fighting."

Mrs. Hurd sighed a mighty sigh. "Don't be such a Christian. You got whipped because you got only the first part right—when you're fighting someone bigger than you are, you've got to break his nose first, and you did that just fine. But then there's the second part. You have to figure he's going to be mad, and so you have to hit him in the right eye to shut it. After that you're even."

Turner stood, stunned. Mrs. Hurd went back to her sweeping. "Don't you know about these things, Turner III?"

"I'm sort of surprised that you do, Mrs. Hurd."

She smiled, a smile as beautiful as the yellow day, and came down the steps, leaving her broom against a post. "What a lovely thing to say," she told him, and she reached up and kissed him lightly on his cheek. "But remember"—she balled her right hand into a fist—"first to the nose, like this, and then a left up to the eye, like that."

"First to the nose, then to the eye." Turner was smiling, too.

"Now go on your way. The day's too bright to spend it fighting with an old lady."

He leaned down and kissed her on the cheek.

"And it won't do to go courting an old lady, either."

"I'm not courting you," Turner said. "I just figure it would be smart to stay on your good side if I don't want to get my nose broken and my right eye shut."

"You learn quickly, Turner III. Go on now."

He went on now.

It had been dry too long for even an all-night rain to leave the dirt of Parker Head muddy, and Turner ran down the road and up into the woods. By the time he began to clamber down the ledges, he was wet through with the rain the branches had swiped at him, and he did not care, not wearing a shirt a minister's boy would have to be particular about. The day was bright and the sea blue and the salt air clear. It was all so perfect that Turner was hardly surprised when he reached the shore and found Lizzie was waiting for him, her dory pulled up by the chin onto the rocks and bucking a bit with the tide.

He tossed her the ball, and she caught it with one hand. "No more rocks!" he called.

"I don't know," Lizzie said. "You were getting on with rocks. You think you can hit something like this?"

"I think I can hit something like that." He tossed her his glove. She caught it and held it like a dream that had dropped right out of the bright blue sky into her outstretched hand. She tossed the ball back to him and then, slowly, as if it were a ceremony, she put the glove over her hand. She flexed it, held it up over her face and smelled it, then held it out again. She punched her right hand into it.

"Throw me the ball," she said. And he did. "Harder," she said, throwing it back. "Harder still," she called. At first she caught the ball down in the palm, but soon she had the trick of catching it up in the webbing, and she began to giggle with the pleasure of it, catching the ball and then whipping around and throwing it back to Turner. "You know," she said, "I never caught with one of these before." And Turner, watching the smooth flow of her arms and hands, the fine long fingers that twirled the ball just before they released it, the eyes that in the clear air shone with all the brightness of the day, thought that maybe he wouldn't need to light out for the Territories after all.

They never did use the bat. All Lizzie wanted to do was to catch the ball, for him to throw it harder, or higher, or off to her left, or off to her right, and she would snatch it out of the air, sometimes even leaning out over the water, and she would look as happy as the yellow-robed day, and she'd toss the ball back and flex the glove.

When they had thrown the ball back and forth about a million times, they sat down together on the stones, the glove between them, watching the ripples the tide was sending closer and closer in, watching it slurp up the seaweed beds and start to cover . . .

"The mudflats," Lizzie said. "I promised my granddaddy I'd dig up clams enough."

They threw the bat and ball and glove up above the tide line, and while Lizzie ran to the dory for her rake and bucket, Turner took off his shoes, rolled up his trousers, pulled up his sleeves, and began looking for a place to dig. He picked out a hole that the retreating ripples left bubbling, straddled it, and set to digging with his hands. By the time Lizzie was back, he had a pile of muddy sand but had lost track of where a clam might be.

"Here," she said, "take turns using this." She set her rake mightily in the mud, pulled back a layer, put the rake in again, pulled back another peel, and then once more, until the tines scraped against a shell and the clam lay like an ornery pearl, spitting at them. Lizzie lifted it. "Sometimes they don't mind their manners much," she said.

"I guess I wouldn't, either, if I was being dug up for chowder."

"I guess. Lately, it seems like there might be a whole lot of reasons for not minding your manners."

Turner nodded. He knew some reasons.

They dug clams until the water covered the flats—actually, as Lizzie pointed out, Turner mostly watched her dig clams until the water covered the flats. He held the bucket, leaning away from it to avoid the spitting, and lugged it full back to the dory. Lizzie knelt and packed it with seaweed, sending little crabs scuttling from underneath each handful she dragged up.

Turner was mindful of his toes.

"You want to come over?" asked Lizzie.

"To the island?"

She put her hand on her hip.

"I'll come over," said Turner. And together they waded out and climbed into the dory—it was floating freely now—and Lizzie, with easy hands, oared the boat around and with a few strokes set its bow and Turner toward Malaga.

He had seen the island from the far ledges, standing with his father and Sheriff Elwell and Deacon Hurd and everyone else important in the town. A stony beach, a stony ledge or two, some pines—a few toppled over with their heads in the water, a few tilted, most of them still straight. There had seemed nothing on the island that would set anyone but a gull to wishing that he could live there.

But coming on it now, from the water, with Lizzie stroking and angling her way to the point, Turner felt as if he was on the brink of a discovery. Ahead of him, the beach was covered with stones, their hard outsides rubbed off and smoothed so that they glowed as the waves gathered them up and down. The granite ledges were streaked by a thousand shades of gray and silver, separated by slices of pink quartz that glowed like happiness. And the pines! The pines threw their roots around the shore's boulders, grappling with the living rocks and wrestling them into position. And out of those rocks they thrust themselves into the air as if they might scratch the blue dome of heaven, and as they stretched back and forth trying to reach it, and as the sea stretched itself back and forth up the beach, Turner felt the world moving slowly and anciently beneath him, and he began to sway back and forth with the waves, with the trees, with the rolling globe itself.

"You're not going to throw up?" asked Lizzie.

"No, I'm not going to throw up."

"Good, because if you were going to throw up, I'd be sure to remind you that you'd best lean out over the side of the boat."

"You have a real way about you, you know that, Lizzie?"

"That's what my granddaddy says: a real way about me."

"What else does your granddaddy say about you?"

"That I'm the closest thing to glory he'll ever see on God's green earth. What does your daddy say about you?"

Turner didn't have to answer, since just then the dory scraped up on the beach a little above the point, and he jumped out the stern and began to push the boat in. (He thought just then that sometimes God could get things exactly right.) The rocks were cold and smooth and slippery under his feet and the water lapped up to his knees, but Turner hardly noticed. He watched Lizzie stow the oars neatly along the sides, saw her twist and reach for the hooked rock she would toss over for the anchor, felt the boat quiver a bit as she stood, balanced lightly, and finally jumped out the bow, her feet sending up a frothy splash. She turned and gripped the dory and pulled it higher, Turner pushing, and then she stood, hands on hips, and smiled.

"You coming?"

"I'm coming."

Maybe her granddaddy was right.

He pulled the pail of clams from the dory, and when she reached out a hand to him, he took it, and so stepped onto Malaga Island for the first time: the sounds of the water rushing through the rounded stones, the salt-pine scent of the air, the gaggling cry of a single gull flopping around with its head lowered, the sea breeze coming up suddenly against his back, the warm feel of Lizzie's hand as she led him farther up into it all. Lord, thought Turner. Lord.

Together they climbed up to the center of the island, where the trees were thick and high. She showed him the graves, and they stood quietly together and were careful where they set their feet. Then back up the shore and to the south end of the island, where shingled one- and two-room houses clamped themselves to the rocks like oysters, glad to be there and not needing anyone's say-so. In front of almost all of them was a dory or two, some overturned, some pulled up long ago for caulking or patching. Near them, half-moon lobster traps bleached under the heat of the sun, the salt dried to white streaks along their boards, their rope netting stiff and a bit ragged. High dune grass hid the paths up to the houses—in fact, almost hid the chopping block one man was using to split his cordwood.

"Hey, Mr. Eason," Lizzie hollered, and the man stopped for a moment and waved at them.

Turner shifted the pail of clams to his other hand, and they followed the curve of the beach past the schoolhouse—the trimmest building on the island—past more shingled one-room homes, where there was always someone at the window to wave to Lizzie and nod to Turner—the kind of nod you might give to someone who didn't belong but might, in time, come to belong—and then back around to the point where Lizzie's home and its tottering picket fence looked on up the New Meadows. And there was her grand-daddy, sitting by the front door, a Bible in his hand. He closed it as they came up.

"This the boy never talked to a Negro before?"

Lizzie nodded. Turner nodded, too. He thought Lizzie's grandfather must be older than Methuselah. He looked like a white-haired, fiery-eyed, God-haunted Old Testament prophet without the robes.

"How's he doing now?"

"Fair to middling."

"Fair to middling," her grandfather repeated. "Let's see, then. Boy, why don't you go ahead and say something?"

Turner had no notion of what to say to an Old Testament prophet. He had figured they were all dead.

"Maybe not quite middling," said Lizzie's granddaddy.

Turner opened his mouth and shut it again.

"Maybe not quite fair. How about something from the Bible? You know something from the Bible? I've just been reading in Philippians here."

"I do know something from the Bible."

"That's good to hear. Good to hear." He emphasized the "good" as if it really meant something. "Go on and say what that is."

Turner began. "'Abraham begat Isaac; and Isaac begat Jacob; and Jacob begat Judas and his brethren; and Judas begat Phares and Zara of Thamar; and Phares begat Esrom; and Esrom begat Aram; and Aram begat Aminadab; and Aminadab begat Naasson; and Naasson begat Salmon.'"

Lizzie's granddaddy put his hand to his cheek. Lizzie stared at Turner.

"I can keep on going," said Turner.

"No," said Lizzie's granddaddy slowly. "I expect you've gone on enough."

"Zara of Thamar?" said Lizzie.

"Maybe we should start with names." He put his hand to his chest. "Reverend Griffin."

"And he's Turner Ernest Buckminster," supplied Lizzie.

"Just Turner," he said.

"Turner. That's a fine name."

"So's yours."

"Well, thank you, Turner Ernest Buckminster. Now, if you're done with your begats, I'll go on ahead and shake your hand. But only if you're done with the begats."

"I'm done," said Turner, and took Reverend Griffin's hand. He wasn't surprised that it was strong, but he was surprised by how he felt every scar that ridged the man's palm, every cut drawn through by a quick and sharp pull on a fishline, every slit opened by an accidental knife.

"You can tell a man by his hand," said Reverend Griffin. He shook hands solemnly. "You hold your bat on the knob."

"Just on it," said Turner. Lizzie's granddaddy was a prophet after all.

"Good. Now, if you give me those clams, I'll see what I can do with them."

While Reverend Griffin carried the spitting clams into the house, Lizzie took Turner's hand that held his bat on the knob, and they walked back down to the shore. The water was so different here than in Boston Harbor. There was a cold wildness about it, and it didn't seem to care whether you looked at it. It would do what it was doing with or without you, as it had been doing for a long time before you and would be doing for a long time after you. They sat down and did not speak but watched the small waves chuck at the shore, frothing and foaming and disappearing into the sand and rocks, and then doing it all over again.

A loud screeching of gulls from behind the pines, louder and louder, and then it was no longer gulls that were screeching but a pack of five, or four, or six, or who knows how many children flapping their arms and running up and down and back and forth, screeching and cackling, and then careening down upon them, cawing and laughing and thrashing up the water until they flopped down like a flock of swarming birds all come to roost.

"You Tripps," scolded Lizzie, but she was not really scolding, and though she stood and put her hands on her hips and looked at them with a terrible eye, Turner knew right away that they had seen it all before, and not a single one—not a single one—felt any remorse.

Two of them grabbed Turner's hands. "Fly with us!" cried one. And they pulled him up and suddenly he was flapping his arms and running down the beach, and Lizzie was flapping hers and running alongside them, together in the midst of the swarm, and calling and calling and running and running, plashing through spent waves, cavorting up the granite ledges, wheeling around stands of pines. And when they were too spent to flap and screech anymore, they collapsed on the point, and Lizzie's granddaddy waved them to his door. Inside, there was bread and chowder in cracked white bowls, and they all— Tripps and Lizzie and Reverend Griffin and Turner—they all took the food and sat on the rocks, sun-warmed and briny, and Turner could not tell if it was the scent of the chowder or the sea that filled him, and he knew that he was late again for his own dinner and he did not care. Then there was quiet among the Tripps, and Turner and Lizzie looked at each other over their heads and smiled.

One of the Tripps who had held his hand came to stand on Turner's toes. "I'm Abbie," she said. "You the boy who throws rocks at his nose?"

Turner glared over at Lizzie, who was trying not to laugh. "Does Lizzie go around telling you stories?"

"Only all the time."

The Tripp who had held his other hand climbed onto his lap.

"That's Perlie," said Abbie. "She don't talk much yet." Turner began to tickle her stomach.

"And she ain't ticklish, either," said Abbie. "You could tickle that girl till half past tomorrow and she won't laugh none."

"She won't laugh, huh?" said Turner. He set down his bowl, shoved off Abbie and Perlie, picked up a round stone, and tossed it in the air. He let it fall just by his face, then began to howl and howl.

Perlie laughed, and Abbie laughed, and all the Tripps laughed. And they laughed louder and louder, and then they spread their arms and began to run in circles. They swarmed up the beach, and back down, and finally disappeared abruptly into the pines, Perlie the last in line, looking back at him and holding her nose.

It was, Turner figured, as good as a baseball game on Boston Common. Even better.

They carried all the bowls back inside the house. It was dark and warm and cozy. A shelf with pitchers was tacked to one wall, and underneath was another with a line of books, worn but serviceable. A small potbellied stove took up one corner, and next to it was a dry sink under a window that looked out to the sea. Lizzie's granddaddy took the bowls and stacked them in the sink—"Time enough for that later on"— and he pointed to a line of sepia photographs tacked to the doorway. "Those are our begats," he said, and he touched each one in turn: his grandfather, his own father, himself as a boy with his mama, Lizzie's mama, and another of her mama and daddy holding on to her as if she were a first-place prize they had just won.

"Where are they now?"

"You saw Mama before," said Lizzie. "Down to the grave-yard." They were all three quiet for a time, and they could hear the screeching of the Tripps, or maybe it was the gulls.

Turner and Lizzie spent most of the afternoon skipping rocks into the waves—he was better than Lizzie—and climb-ing up to sway in pines—she could go higher. And only reluc-tantly did they find themselves going back to the dory, getting in, and each taking an oar. They had trouble figuring how to work them together, and they circled and got slapped in the side by a wave that might have swamped them if it had been even a little bit bigger, but they straightened out and sat side by side, their shoulders working together as they crossed the New Meadows and landed the dory on the shore.

"You come around again, Turner Ernest Buckminster."

"I'll be around, Lizzie Bright Griffin."

She smiled at him as he shoved the dory off, and he waved as she oared her way easily to Malaga and when she landed, she waved once, twice, at him, then ran back up around the point. Turner blew his breath out slow and even. He did not know that Lizzie was doing the same.

Neither did Turner know that up in town, his father was blowing his breath out, too.

He got home in good time, and since he wasn't wearing his white shirt, the dirt showed no more than it should. He had run all the way and, truth to tell, skipped some as well, though he had stopped when he came to Parker Head to become the Minister's Son again, stared at from every parlor window. He had walked quietly and calmly, with only a skip now and then when he couldn't help himself. He figured he was smiling like a loon, but probably no one would fuss too much about that—probably.

The late afternoon was colder as he drew closer to home.

The clouds had mottled, and high winds had started to shred their undersides. He wondered how Lizzie and her grand-daddy got along on the island come winter, wondered if the New Meadows might ice over so that he could walk out there, wondered if Lizzie ever came into town. He figured she didn't, or at least not much. He thought for a moment of Willis Hurd, and he didn't need to worry any longer about keeping his skipping to a bare minimum.

He didn't need to worry about it at all when he got home.

He opened the front door and thought he had walked into a prayer meeting. The parlor was stuffed with his father, Dea-con Hurd, Sheriff Elwell, Mr. Stonecrop, and any other rich man who owned a house up to Phippsburg's Quality Ridge. The furniture seemed too small for them—the room seemed too small for them—and they scented the air with old cigars, starch, and sweat. Mr. Stonecrop stood like an actor posing on-stage, one hand set carefully in a pocket and the other gestur-ing toward the ceiling, or maybe to heaven.

". . . your duty to the town, Reverend. Your duty to the town, I say."

Even though Turner tried to close the door slowly and qui-etly, it shrieked out his presence like a guilty accomplice, and they all turned to look at him. Mr. Stonecrop took advantage of the moment.

"Good Lord, Buckminster, think of your own son here." He gestured toward Turner, then drew the eyes of his audience back. "This town is on the brink of economic collapse. Shipyards folding, one and then another. Families who have worked those yards for generations, who have used the hands that God saw fit to give them to build up a whole world, may see those hands empty. And what will this town be then? What opportunities will young Turner find then? I am a man of business, and I may not form the eloquent sentences of a preacher. But I say this: the day is coming when this town will perish, and young Buckminster will have nothing. Nothing at all."

Turner thought it was rather hard to be used as an example. He decided he should head up the stairs.

He did not make it.

"Come in here, young Buckminster," Mr. Stonecrop called. "Come on in here and talk to your father." He held out his arm to him as though he were looking for a stage prop to be delivered.

Turner went in, slowly, warily, feeling about as eager to go in as black molasses to flow on a wintry day.

"Gentlemen," Mr. Stonecrop said, "this is the boy we've all heard about. Son, is it true, your running around naked in Mrs. Cobb's house?" He draped his arm around Turner's shoulders and drew him in, into his strength and power and presence. Turner felt as if he were moving in close to a mountain. But when he looked up into Mr. Stonecrop's face, he shuddered. Mr. Stonecrop was laughing, and his mouth was pulled into a grin, but his eyes were as dead as marbles, almost as if there were nothing behind them. He was like someone out of a ghost story, and Turner tried to draw away.

Mr. Stonecrop held him.

"Son, tell me, is that true?"

Turner looked at his father. His face was pulled, too, but not into a grin.

"Mr. Stonecrop, it's not true, what you heard."

Deacon Hurd began to laugh. "The way I heard it, you were trying to wash blood off your shirt. You know, son, you'll learn that living in Maine is living more like a man than down in some easy city. But you have to be smart, too. You don't want to start throwing punches at someone a whole lot bigger than you—not if you don't want to get knocked around."

Turner felt his hands start to ball into fists; he put them in his pockets. He felt the slight laughter of the men in the room wash over him like a foaming wave lapping over a crab. He did not look at his father; he did not want to know if he, too, was laughing. But he did look at Deacon Hurd. "How's Willis's nose?"

"Willis's nose? Fine." His voice tight.

"Last time I saw it, it seemed pushed over to the side."

More laughter in the room, but not from Deacon Hurd.

"Willis's nose is fine."

"Gentlemen," said Mr. Stonecrop. "Back to the issue. Reverend Buckminster, we came here to ask you to help us rescue the town. You've seen the squalor on Malaga. There isn't a soul on that island who isn't a drunk or a thief. We tried educating them. We built a school and hired a teacher, all at the town's expense. But that didn't do a single bit of good."

"And besides," added Sheriff Elwell, "teaching those people is like teaching dogs to walk on their hind legs. All they know is living off others."

"I'm not sure but that it wouldn't be the Lord's work to put them somewhere they can be safe," said Mr. Stonecrop. "A place where they can be cared for."

"And since they haven't a one of them got a deed, there's no reason we can't." Sheriff Elwell smiled and held his lapels open so that Turner could see his pistol.

Turner tried again to draw away, but Mr. Stonecrop would have none of it. Turner felt the man's arm lean more heavily upon him, as if the cue to use him hadn't come yet.

"There will be those in town who insist that we should keep the school up, that we should spend even more money than we have from the town treasury on other schemes well-intentioned but foolish. You will hear talk of Christian charity and neighborliness and so on. We've tried it before, to no effect. But some people—say, the saintly Newtons—will come to you, Reverend, as a kind of rallying point—unless you make clear from the start that you stand with the interests of the town and against the dangers the island represents."

Turner felt Mr. Stonecrop's hand move down to his arm. He was being readied.

"I'm not at all sure where I stand yet, Mr. Stonecrop."

Turner felt the mountain shift, felt himself thrust forward. The cue had come.

"Turner, go on ahead and tell your good father where you left your bat and glove this morning."

"They're on the front porch," said Turner's father.

"My boy Willis brought them up," said the Deacon. "Seems he found them on the shore."

Turner felt the eyes of the room come upon him.

"I was on Malaga Island," he said.

Reverend Buckminster licked his lips. "What were you doing on Malaga Island?"

What could he say? That he had practiced with Lizzie, dug for clams, and eaten them later in a chowder so good that he might have given up Eden for it? That he had spread his arms and flown with the Tripps? That he had sat quietly by the water's edge and dreamed dreams? That he had found a place that was more home than home?

"Boating."

"In whose boat?"

"Reverend Griffin's dory."

Reverend Buckminster looked at Turner as though his son were Peter about to betray the Lord. Turner wondered what was so awful about going out in Reverend Griffin's dory. He wondered if there was some new rule for a minister's son that he hadn't come up against yet—if there could possibly be yet another rule that he hadn't come up against already.

"You went out in a Negro's dory. How do you know what might happen?"

"Nothing happened."

"It's not his fault, Reverend," said Mr. Stonecrop smoothly. "It's not his fault at all. That's how they are. They're sly and crafty, making out all the time that they're dumb. But they're thinking, thinking, plotting, plotting. Here's the minister's son, they think, and if we can just get him on our side, we'll get the minister. And if we get the minister, we get the church. And if we get the church—you see how it goes. That's how they used your son. And it wasn't the old Preacher Griffin that they sent out to you, boy, was it? No, sir. It wasn't the old preacher. Why don't you go on ahead and tell your father who you were with today."

"Lizzie."

"Speak up, son. I don't think your father heard you."

"Lizzie Griffin." And Turner felt dirty, as though he really had been caught doing something vile. And he knew that what Mr. Stonecrop was saying was an out-loud lie. A dirty, stinking, out-loud lie. But he couldn't figure how it was a lie.

"Lizzie Griffin. A Negress, Reverend, just Turner's age. The daughter of the only Jonah this town has ever seen. Good Lord, son, I hope you didn't enter her house. There are enough stories going around about you."

Silence from Turner. Reverend Buckminster blowing out his breath.

"So you did go in," said Mr. Stonecrop. "Well, a minister's son should know that stories tend to stay around and settle in,

70

so that after a time no one is asking whether or not they're true. They just become true. True about you, and true about all those associated with you."

"Gentlemen," said Reverend Buckminster slowly, "there clearly are real dangers I had not anticipated." He looked at Turner, and Turner saw in his eyes—distrust. "Perhaps the Lord is leading you in your efforts. And if so, then what else could the minister of First Congregational say but that he is with you in this?"

"That, Reverend, is what we came to ask," said Mr. Stonecrop. "And it will not be long before Phippsburg is free from this sordidness, and we can start to rebuild ourselves. Someday soon, the settlement on Malaga Island will be no more."

And that was the moment that Turner realized what was being plotted. And there wasn't a thing he could say without helping the plot all the more.

He thought suddenly of Mrs. Hurd. "First to the nose, then to the eye."

Mr. Stonecrop discarded his prop.

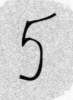

TURNER had been given a new commandment: Thou shalt not step one of thine feet upon Malaga Island, lest thou be smitten, and smitten mightily, saith the Reverend Buckminster. But if Turner happened to climb down the granite ledges to the muddy shore, and if Lizzie Bright happened to have come over in her dory to dig clams . . . well, Reverend Buckminster had said nothing about not talking with her, or throwing a baseball with her, or sitting by the green-blue sea with her.

And so he did. Almost every day.

And on the way back into town, he came up with something to tell his father. In fact, Reverend Buckminster was surprised at his son's new and urgent interest in bird watching. It was an interest, he remarked, that Turner shared with the young Charles Darwin.

Turner, who had never heard of Charles Darwin, cocked an eyebrow and nodded. He supposed that this was so. He was glad of it. And his father's smile made him feel as if he might be worth something after all—until he remembered he was out-loud lying.

Turner hoped Charles Darwin wasn't a minister. He hoped he lived in the Territories. He hoped he played baseball, because these high glory days of summer were baseball days if any days were baseball days, with blue skies, warm seas, and high clouds lazy above the ocean horizon. And every morning the sea breeze bustled up and called Turner until he followed it to the shore where Lizzie waited for him, her bucket half full of clams.

Blue days, as the tide washed away the twin footprints Lizzie and Turner left along the beach. Blue days, as they walked among the sharp-edged mussels, prying open their blue-black shells to tickle their orange tendons. Blue days, as they sprinted against the sea breeze and chased the gulls until Turner finally, finally, finally touched a tail feather. Blue days, as they dangled their legs over the granite ledges and felt the gigantic continent behind them.

And it was on one of their climbs, on one of those blue days that was gushing into a bright copper, that Turner reached up and put his hand on something wet and clammy and slimy and moving, recoiled with a yelp, and startled Lizzie beneath him. She tried but could not quite find her balance and fell down to the mudflats, striking her head on a granite outcropping just before she dropped to the bottom.

"Lizzie!" Turner cried, half falling himself until he was beside her, his hands under her head, startled by how quickly they were covered with her blood. "Lizzie!"

"Don't you get—" she said, then stopped. "Whatever you do," she started again, "don't get blood on that shirt." She put her hand up to her forehead, and it shook. "You better get me back to my granddaddy. I'm so dizzy."

She tried to stand up, Turner behind and holding on to her, but her feet didn't go where she wanted them to, and Turner had to steer her as she swayed and zigzagged to the dory. The blood leaked through her fingers and dripped to the sand.

"Almost there."

"I can hardly see," she said slowly, and Turner's stomach tightened.

When they reached the boat, Lizzie stood there stupidly, not quite sure what to do. "Climb in," said Turner, but he had to lift her front leg for her, and once she was in, she fell into a loose heap in the bow, and her eyes closed.

Turner figured that the more awake Lizzie was, the better she would be, so he hollered at her, and when she did not open her eyes, he splashed seawater into her face until she sputtered and opened them. "Keep them open, or I'll splash you again."

"If you splash me again, I won't help you get that blood off your shirt."

"Just keep your eyes open, Lizzie Bright." He shoved the dory out stern first into the New Meadows and noticed how choppy it had become, with even some whitecaps tumbling between him and Malaga. He settled himself, took the two oars and fixed them to the oarlocks, then dipped them in and was surprised at how the water took them, almost sweeping one oar under the boat and the other out of his hand. He imagined watching the oar drifting away out to the open bay and wondered how he would ever get across if that happened.

He kept turning around to look at Lizzie. "Are your eyes open?" he called. "Lizzie, open your eyes. Open your dang eyes."

"A minister's son . . . a minister's son shouldn't say . . . shouldn't say dang." Turner's stomach grew tighter and tighter with the slow sprawl of her words.

"Keep your eyes open," he said, and bent back to the oars, trying to get the stern steady and the bow pointed to the island. It was harder than he had realized. Much harder. The water was running out against him, and every whitecap that struck him broadside sent water into the bottom of the boat. The dory felt clumsy, and it would not keep its nose where it was supposed to go. Soon he was no longer trying to point it at the island's north end but at its south end, and with every stroke in toward the island, he felt the boat drifting down and away from it.

He began to row with a frantic energy, the oars chewing raggedly at the water. But the waves kept turning the bow from Malaga, and the oars kept slipping out of the locks, and by the time he had gotten them back in, the boat had skewed all around and was slipping up and down in the troughs.

"Head the dory . . . the dory into the waves," said Lizzie feebly.

Turner did not reply. He was watching the granite ledges slip past, the pines above them bending with the wind out to sea.

"Into the waves," said Lizzie again.

He turned around. "I know, Lizzie. I'll get it. Keep your eyes open. Both of them."

They were now well away from Malaga and heading stern first down the New Meadows. The waves chopped briskly as they rushed out to the bay and to the sea beyond, and Turner gave up any notion of trying to make it back to the island. Instead, he turned the bow against the running tide to maneuver the dory in close to the mainland, where he might find some mudflats to run up to. But now the ledges came right down to the New Meadows, and there were no open mudflats. The water was choppier in close, and twice he struck a stone ridge just beneath the surface, the second time so hard he was afraid it might bash in the boards. He moved the dory out farther again.

Lizzie, who had felt the bashing just beneath her, raised her head. "You missed the island."

"Yes."

"You missed the island. How could you miss the island?"

"The tide's too strong. It's taking us out with it."

Lizzie put her hand to her head, and Turner thought she might be sick. "I'm going to fall asleep," she murmured.

"You can't fall asleep, Lizzie. You've got to keep your eyes open."

"When you reach the point . . . when you reach Bald Head . . ."

"When I reach Bald Head," Turner repeated.

"The tide will slack some. You can ground. . . . The tide will slack some." Then Lizzie was quiet.

Turner looked ahead and saw the rock ledges streaking past and the shore bending away. He moved the dory in closer to the land and stopped rowing altogether except to keep the bow into the waves. His arms felt drained, and he wasn't sure he could make them do what he wanted them to do when the slack water came. But he waited and watched, hollering back to Lizzie now and again to be sure she stayed awake.

But she wasn't hollering back.

The copper of the sky had deepened into a dark red, and the dark red was now deepening into the purple of early night. When Turner looked over his shoulder to the east, more than a few stars had already yawned themselves awake and were stretching to begin their run. On the ledges above him there passed a farmhouse, then another, and still another, where yellow lamps were glowing out the windows. He felt the air cooling quickly.

Then the rhythm of the waves changed. In a moment they had lost their choppiness and had lengthened into long swells that came slow and syrupy. The boat smoothed out, and it was easy to keep the bow to the low stretches of water that swiped at the dory's nose.

Turner thought immediately that they must be at the point. When he looked at the shore, it was hard to tell whether it was bending away or whether it just got lost in the gathering darkness. But he turned into it anyway, rowing with all the might he could summon in his drained arms, pushing back with his legs and grunting with each pull, not even calling to Lizzie because he could not speak and pull at the same time. He felt the dory skim across the swells, cutting through their rhythm, and figured that finally, finally he was setting their course.

As the purple of the sky spread all the way across to the west, he rowed. As more and more stars roused themselves, he rowed. And as the wind picked itself up and wrestled with the tops of the swells, he rowed.

He rowed until he realized he had missed the point and they were well out into the bay.

And then he stopped.

Now the purple spread from horizon to horizon, and the stars that had clustered in the east were fading with the early light of the rising moon. The swells lengthened even more, so that the dory rocked up and down as gently as ever it might, and if it had not been for the farmhouse lights on the shoreline, Turner would hardly have been able to tell that the dory was moving at all.

He was not afraid, and was surprised to find that he wasn't. As long as he could keep the shoreline lights from dipping under the waves, he knew that he was in sight of shore. And he knew that the tide would have to stop flowing sometime and head back up the New Meadows. Already he could sense it weakening when he dipped the oars into the water. He could even make some headway into shore before his tired arms gave out and he was pulled back to where he had started. He was thirsty and more than a little bit hungry, but without the panic of hopelessness.

If only Lizzie were awake, this would be something out of a dream, something that, had he known he might do it, he would have longed for. But when he looked at Lizzie, there was a sickening tug down deep in his gut. It was getting harder and harder to get her to keep her eyes even half open, and though the bleeding from the wound had stopped, she seemed to be fading from him.

He shipped the oars and turned to face her. "Lizzie? Lizzie Bright?" He shook her by the knee. "Lizzie?"

"We almost there?"

"Almost."

"Turner?" she asked.

"Yes?"

"You ever row a boat before?"

Turner hesitated. He wondered if being on the swan boats in the Public Garden counted and figured that probably it didn't. "Not hardly."

"Ever in your whole life?"

"Not until today."

"I thought so."

"Keep your eyes open, Lizzie." Turner went back to the oars, turned the bow toward shore—it wasn't hard in the long swells—and tried to row in again. He kept his strokes slow and long, and though, when he finally turned his head, it seemed the shore lights were not much nearer, they were a little nearer, and he held to the pace until his muscles buckled, and he shipped the oars and watched the lights very slowly withdraw again.

And that was when he first heard the water ripping near him.

The moon had roused herself fully out of the sea and was tossing her silver bedclothes all around. Turner was sure that in that light he should have been able to make out any rocks. But he couldn't see anything breaking the surface. He listened, not moving, and heard the ripping again, but behind him this time, and closer to shore, and ahead of him—one after another. In the moonlight he saw a silver spray burst up into the air, a shower of diamond dust. Then another, and another almost beside the boat, so that he could feel the spray of it against his face, and the dory rocked to the rhythm of the new swells as a great Presence broke the surface of the sea and Turner knew, or felt, the vastness of whales.

Now he almost did panic. One could come right up beneath them and turn the dory over as easily as a pine chip, and he would be floating in the sea, holding on to the upturned dory, holding on to Lizzie, who he was sure could not hold on by herself. That is, he would be holding on to her if he could find her after they capsized.

But though the dory rocked back and forth with the swell of them, the whales never came so close that the boat might capsize. Turner heard them ripping the surface all around him, and felt the diamond spray sprinkle down on him in the moonlight like a benediction. He knew he was in the middle of something much larger than himself, and not just larger in size. It was like being in the middle of a swirling universe that could swamp him in a moment but had no desire to. He might put out his hand into the maelstrom and become a part of it.

But he didn't put his hand out yet, because as he watched, a whale five times as long as the dory surfaced, and rode quietly alongside him in the smooth swells. Turner could not breathe. The whale flipped its tail up a bit and began to roll from side to side, a great gargantuan roll like the roll of the globe, side to side, until it could slap the swells with the length of its flippers, gleaming silver-white in the moonlight. Turner held on to the sides of the dory and rolled side to side with it with this great vastness that had swum past the mountains and valleys of the sea. Together they rocked, and Turner wished that the rocking would never stop, that there would always be this moonlit moment.

But slowly the whale did stop rocking, and the seas calmed, and the rhythm of the swells took hold again. Quietly, more afraid than not, Turned slipped the oars into the water, and with gentle strokes, keeping the oars beneath the surface all the time, he eased the dory forward, hoping that the whale would wait on the surface.

It did. And so Turner reached the whale's eye, and they looked at each other. They looked at each other a long time— two souls rolling on the sea under the silvery moon, peering into each other's eyes. Turner wished with a desire greater than anything he had ever desired that he might understand what it was in the eye of the whale that shivered his soul.

He stretched his hand out across the side of the dory and reached over as far as he could without tipping the boat. But the whale kept a space of dark water between them, and they did not touch. Then slowly the whale sank, the water closing quietly along its black and white back.

And the whales were gone.

"Lizzie," whispered Turner.

There was no answer. He reached back and shook her leg, then her shoulder. Finally, he scooped up water and splashed it into her face—since saltwater will do for everything. "Lizzie, you've got to open your eyes."

"They're open," she said. "You splashed me."

"Lizzie, there were whales."

She didn't answer.

"Lizzie, whales."

"You touch one?"

"Tried."

She took a deep breath. "They only let you touch them if you understand what they're saying."

"What do they say?"

"You'll know when . . . when they let you touch them. Home yet?"

He set to rowing again. He did not know how long they had been with the whales. Maybe a century or two. But however long it was, he saw that the dory had not drifted out much from the shore lights, and that now, as he pulled steadily on the oars, the lights really were coming closer. Even though he was as hungry and thirsty as he had been before the whales, he was not at all as tired. The pull of the water against his arms and back thrilled him as he felt the dory moving through the lowering swells, sensed the bow cutting quickly and truly back up into the New Meadows with a new tide.

But the whales were gone.

Soon the lights were much larger, and sometimes they blinked out as though someone had walked past a window for a moment. He wasn't quite sure if he would hit Bald Head right on or if he could find the mouth of the New Meadows and row up to Malaga itself. But he decided he would take the first landfall he could find, beach the dory, and go for help.

His arms felt strong. There was no panic in him.

He had looked into the eye of a whale.

Finally, a light detached itself from the shore and began to bob up and down in the darkness. It tacked well off from them, and then, at the end of a long angle, it tacked again and came back in with the sea breeze; Turner began to row to cut across it.

He had rolled in a wave trough with a whale.

Then he heard a whistle, sounding shrilly over the smooth water.

"Here!" shouted Turner, and waved his arm.

"Why don't you go ahead and stand up and tip us over."

"Lizzie, you can close your eyes now."

The whistle came again, and Turner called out as loudly as he could: "Hello, the boat. The boat, hello. Hello, the boat." Suddenly, a sloop yawed toward them and the moon filled its half sail with bright light. It rode high above the waves, as if it preferred not to get wet. "Hello, the boat!" cried Turner again.

And then a cry from the sloop's deck: "Turner Buckminster! Turner Buckminster!" Deacon Hurd's voice.

"Here! Here!" called Turner. The sail dropped from the sloop's mast, and Turner rowed to its bow until he could make out Willis Hurd's face in the light of the lantern he was swaying over the water.

"Turner Buckminster!" called out Deacon Hurd again from somewhere back in the darkness.

"He's here," Willis hollered back over his shoulder. "Just off the bow. And it's true. He really does have a Negro with him."

"My God," Turner heard the deacon declare. "What is this world coming to?"

"I'll keep my eyes closed," said Lizzie.

Turner wasn't sure whether he wanted to sink then and there or maybe row back out into the dark and make their own way in.

"Slide on down to the stern," Deacon Hurd called. "Willis, throw him a stern line. We'll tow you in, boy."

"We need to get Lizzie on board first. She's hurt."

"Hurt or not, no Jonah's daughter is stepping foot on this boat. We'll tow you. Now, catch hold the rope, and while we're bringing you in, you'd best think of some story about what you two are doing out here. Good Lord, boy, don't you ever think?"

Turner caught the rope Willis threw out to him and knotted it in as good a knot as he could to a ring in the bow. It wasn't as good as he had hoped, though, and they hadn't gone very far before it unraveled and pulled out.

"The line's away," Willis called to his father.

"By all that's holy!" said Deacon Hurd.

Turner figured Deacon Hurd was getting more and more profane as the night wore on.

The Hurds tacked and came around again, and once more Willis hurled the line out to Turner. "Tie a hitch this time," he called. "You can tie a hitch, can't you?"

"I can tie a hitch," Turner hollered.

He tied another knot—another loose knot—around the ring and kept a length out long enough that he could hold on to it—which he did, for dear life.

"You don't know how to tie a hitch, do you?" said Lizzie.

"Close your eyes," Turner answered.

So he held on, and the dory jerked through the waves behind the Hurd sloop, the lantern in the bow now so that Turner couldn't see the Hurds at all. But the moonlight played on the sloop so that the boat seemed a lithe, living thing, and if Turner had been in some other moment and not being tugged along behind like a reluctant dog, he might have let himself marvel at the soundless beauty of sail.

He had looked into the eye of a whale.

The Hurd sloop towed them up the Kennebec, calling out to other lanterned ships as they went by. "Found him!"

"How far out?"

"Not so far."

"Is it true?"

"He had her, all right."

"Well, that does beat all."

Turner and Lizzie listened to the same exchange more times than they cared to.

They sailed past Popham, through the narrows off Cox's Head, past the lights of Parker Head, and then on up to Phippsburg, the water going more and more slack as they sailed. Any hope Turner had that they might slip in quietly was gone when he saw the score or more of lanterns down by the docks, and the crowd of people watching.

"Did you find him?"

"Sure enough," called Deacon Hurd.

"How many in the dory?" called the crowd.

Deacon Hurd let a dramatic pause cross the water and hover over his audience. Then, when they were all poised, he cried in a voice that sounded like God's, "Two."

"Oh," said the crowd. And then "Oh" again.

So they came up to the dock, with more than enough hands reaching out to take the bow and stern lines, and then more than enough hands pulling the towrope close in, and more than enough hands reaching down to tie it fast. They all stepped back as Turner guided Lizzie, woozy but with her eyes open, up the dock ladder, Mr. Newton reaching down to take her hand and bring her up. And then the crowd was pushing away from her granddaddy, and he was scooping Lizzie into his arms. She was putting her face in his chest and beginning to cry, and without saying more, they turned and walked off the dock together, the crowd carefully not touching them.

Turner was standing at the end of the dock, alone.

He thought of the whale, swimming so close to him but just out of his reach across the dark water, its skin glistening white and black in the silver moonlight, its great fins slapping the water, and its eye . . . its eye.

But now the eyes of most of the communicants of Phippsburg's First Congregational were on him. He felt guilt move toward him like a thickened fog—he could almost see it. The just and perfect Willis Hurd walked past him easily, but the fog embraced Turner like a vampire, and it whispered, "You are not one of us."

His father was coming through the crowd at the end of the dock. He came slowly and purposefully, as though the crowd were not there. Turner waited for him without moving. He could feel his father's footsteps on the dock.

"You're safe, then," said Reverend Buckminster.

"Yes."

"And the girl who was with you?"

"She was hurt. She's with her granddaddy now."

Reverend Buckminster nodded. "Your mother's upset. Come along home."

So they walked off the dock, Turner a little behind his father, but the vampire fog followed him up the shore, past First Congregational, and across Parker Head to the parsonage, where his mother was waiting at the top of the porch steps. She rushed him into the house and burst out with a cry the likes of which Turner had never heard before.

There followed all the frantic questions—his mother kept touching him while he answered. They told him of the sighting of the dory rounding Bald Head, the breathless news brought back to Phippsburg, the efforts of half the boats of the Phippsburg docks to find them before it was full dark, under the godly perseverance of the Hurds.

Then there was a silence, and Mrs. Buckminster stood. "That's enough. Turner will be hungry, and the Lord knows we could all do with something to eat, now that the excitement is over." She paused to look back at Turner, and looked back again just before she went into the kitchen.

"Turner," said Reverend Buckminster quietly.

Turner looked at him. He thought, He's going to come apart. He's holding himself together as best he can, but he's going to come apart.

"Turner, whatever were you doing with that Negro girl?"

"She was hurt. I was taking her back to the island."

"That's not what I mean. You know that's not what I mean. What were you doing with her in the first place?"

How could he tell his father what he was doing? How could he say they were chasing the sea breeze and putting the whole continent at their backs?

"Turner, no one on that island is fit company for a minister's son. Not a single one. Heaven only knows what goes on over there. But whatever it is, it's not for decent-minded folks to be around. Do you understand what I mean, Turner? Do you?"

"Lizzie's not like that. Whatever decent-minded folks are thinking, Lizzie's not like that."

"You're a child, Turner. You don't know how they can take you in, make you think what they want you to think. Tonight it could have cost you your life."

"Should I have left her bleeding on the shore?"

"You shouldn't have been on the shore. You should be up doing whatever the other boys of the town are doing. You should be playing baseball with them, or swimming, or whatever they're up to. But instead, you're down on the shore with a Negro girl and then swept out with the tide."

"I wonder," said Turner slowly, "if it's only the folks on Malaga Island who can make you think what they want you to think."

"So now you're impertinent, too."

Turner stood, and it suddenly seemed to him that his father was much smaller than he had been before. There simply wasn't as much of him as he remembered.

The only awkwardness the moment lacked was the omnipotent presence of Mr. Stonecrop, who soon remedied the absence. He knocked and opened the parsonage door at the same time, understanding that his importance in the town, his importance in the church, and the importance of his mission gave him the right to step in on the minister whom he paid every Sunday morning from his tithes and offerings.

"Buckminster!" he hollered. "Buckminster!" Mrs. Buckminster did not come out from the kitchen, but the iron skillet for the late dinner clanged sharply twice.

Immediately, Mr. Stonecrop's presence filled the parlor, and before either Reverend Buckminster or Turner had said a single word—before they had even thought a single thought—Mr. Stonecrop was announcing that all of the boats were back in, that the Negro girl had been taken to Dr. Pelham and there would be five or six stitches but that was all, that his bill would be sent on to the town, and that it was likely not to be inexpensive. "That's always the way of it," declared Mr. Stonecrop. "God sees fit to let something happen to a Malaga pauper, and Phippsburg pays the bill. It's a scandal."

"I will pay the bill," said Reverend Buckminster.

"Only appropriate," said Mr. Stonecrop. "All of First Congregational is wondering what on earth a minister's son is doing out in a dory with a Negro girl."

"She was hurt, and he was taking her back to the island. He didn't know the tide would carry him out."

Mr. Stonecrop raised a craggy eyebrow. "The congregation will wonder what he was doing on the shore with her in the first place," Mr. Stonecrop pointed out.

"Well," said Reverend Buckminster, "the congregation must think what it will think."

"The congregation, Minister, will tell you what it thinks, and what it wants you to think," said Mr. Stonecrop, and the words wound like barbed wire around the Buckminsters.

The door to the kitchen opened. "Pie, anyone?" Mrs. Buckminster asked, her voice quavery. They sat down to the blueberry pie, and Mr. Stonecrop thanked them for it by offering suggestions on household discipline: the ship to be more tightly run, the loose cannon to be tethered, the runaway colt to be penned in. "A minister's house in order, a church in order. A minister's house in disorder, a church in disorder." Mr. Stonecrop intoned his creed and smiled as if pleased with himself.

When Mr. Stonecrop finally left, promising to send Dr. Pelham's bill the next morning, the house breathed slowly and quietly.

"The whole pie is gone," said Mrs. Buckminster. "He ate half of it himself."

"'The congregation, Minister, will tell you what it thinks, and what it wants you to think,'" Reverend Buckminster repeated quietly. Turner's mother held him by the elbow. "'The congregation, Minister, will tell you what it *wants* you to think.'"

He looked at his son for a long time. He put a hand out to his shoulder. "Good Lord, Turner," he said finally, "you're getting so much bigger these days."

By the time Turner went to bed that night—having had his supper after his blueberry pie—the silver moon had set, and the racing stars had puffed out their fiery white chests. Turner looked at them through his window; he could almost see them puffing. In the dark, the cranked horn of a doryman sounded, and then another, higher pitched. Back and forth they talked to each other, braving the immense presence of the dark.

On that very same night, Turner had almost touched a whale.

C H A P T E R

6

TURNER was not surprised the next morning when Malaga Island was declared a forbidden place, once again.

He was not surprised when his father—and his mother—repeated the word *forbidden* four times during breakfast.

He was not surprised that his father watched him carefully during the "Community Notices" section of the Sunday-morning service at First Congregational, as he announced the formation of a group in Phippsburg to explore "new ventures" that might "improve the economic prospects of our town."

But he was surprised by his father's sermon topic—the fall of Jericho—which seemed to Turner strange to set among a new minister's first sermons.

Turner was sitting in a front pew as hard as Jacob's pillow, and he shifted now and again to let another part of him take his weight. The sanctuary had trapped the sticky heat of the past several days, which came close to stifling anyone wearing a starched white shirt with a starched white collar.

He felt the eyes of every member of First Congregational staring at the back of his starched neck. He felt Mrs. Cobb's outrage. He felt Mr. Stonecrop's disdain. He wished he could feel Mrs. Hurd's pale eyes, but she didn't come to church. Deacon Hurd's family was there, though, sitting across the aisle in the other front pew. From this angle, Turner could not tell whether Willis's nose was straight.

He hoped it wasn't.

The sermon slouched along as sermons will when every single soul in the building is wishing that the ushers would start passing around cool glasses of lemonade. Turner watched a small yellow hornet buzz listlessly around the pulpit as the priests of the Hebrew host organized their march. It meandered a bit, then settled down into one of the rosettes and went to sleep. Turner wondered what might happen if it woke up and decided to sting his father at some prominent moment— say, when the trumpets of Jericho sounded. He imagined the hornet turning on Deacon Hurd, and the general melee as he ran down the aisle, chased by the eager insect, hollering and swatting at the thin air.

He thought of swatting at thin air, of swatting at rocks on the shore, of Lizzie Bright Griffin, of tossing a ball back and forth, digging clams, sitting on the beach watching the tide heave in and out like the vast breathing of a whale.

Could it all have been a lie?

He had almost touched a whale.

By now his father had gotten onto the woes of Jericho, and he was finding his stride. Jericho, his father announced, was a place that needed to be rooted out so that God's good and perfect purposes might be fulfilled. So God had brought to its walls the Hebrew host to be His hands to carry out His righteous work. Reverend Buckminster paused and cleared his throat. He paused some more and cleared his throat again. He looked down at Mrs. Buckminster. He looked away.

"In this same way, good people of Phippsburg, God calls us to be His hands, and to do His will, to blot out spoil and contagion from among us, to bring His people to the place where He would have them be. Just as Jericho was wiped out and is gone to human history, and just as the Promised Land was taken up by the faithful, so also should we blot out what is not wholesome, what is not good, what is not pleasing, and take up our own promised future."

Turner felt his mother stiffen beside him. She reached out and took his hand.

"Amen," said the Reverend Buckminster.

"And amen," said Mr. Stonecrop behind them.

The organ turned to a melancholy last hymn, playing too slowly; after four verses, it sighed to silence a phrase or two behind the congregation. Reverend Buckminster descended from his pulpit and processed down the aisle. Mrs. Buckminster and Turner went behind him and stood with him at the back of the church to endure the handshakes and knowing looks. ("Did he really go out into the bay with a Negro?") Willis passed without looking at him, as, in fact, did most of the congregation, until he stopped holding out his hand. And when it was all over, he ran through the gossiping crowd and sprinted back to the parsonage, where the blue sea breeze laughed and swirled and invited him down to the water, down to the shore.

Oh Lord, if only Malaga Island hadn't all been a lie.

But no minister's son in Phippsburg, Maine, can follow a sea breeze to the shore on the Sabbath. Especially not to a forbidden shore. So Turner settled in for a quiet and still dinner, and a quieter and more still afternoon.

If he had been in Boston, where baseball was as it should be, he would be standing at home plate on the Common, the smell of grass and leather in his nose, his hands sticky with the pitch on the bat, waiting, waiting, waiting for the streak of white he would slash past the first baseman.

Instead, the quiet and still afternoon wore on like a too-slow hymn while Turner read some, stalked about the house some, looked out the window some, and wondered a great deal about why God had settled on Sunday afternoons to be dreary and miserable.

When his mother could stand the stalking no more, she sent Turner out—she used the word *forbidden* only once—and he strolled off, hands in his pockets—until he remembered that ministers' sons do not keep their hands in their pockets—down Parker Head, heading to Malaga but knowing he could not go there. He thought for a moment of trying to see if, by any chance, there was a ball game down in Thayer's haymeadow. He would risk breaking the Sabbath for one good hit. Even if it was only a hit to left field. But the thought of the greeting he would receive from Willis and his crew stopped him. And when the sea breeze sprang up again, it pulled him toward Malaga.

If it had not been for Mrs. Cobb standing by the gate of her grandfather's picket fence, as though waiting for him to try to sneak by, who knows how many *forbidden*s would have flitted away like yesterday's gypsy moths.

"So your mother got those bloodstains out."

"Yes, ma'am."

"It's too bad that she ends up with the work when you're the one out in the street brawling. And a minister's son at that."

Turner thought back on the day so far. He added one to the number of things in it that were almost more than God had any right to expect of him.

"Well, your father said you play the organ. You may as well come in and play for me."

"Mrs. Cobb, I wasn't coming to—"

"You weren't coming to what? To bring some peace to an old woman whose household you've thrown upside down? Is that what you weren't coming to do?"

Turner sighed. He ran his finger around his collar and followed her into the imprisonment of her house. He wondered why his father couldn't have chosen a decent career. A conductor, maybe. A conductor who rode trains with his family and lit out for the Territories.

Mrs. Cobb sat in her horsehair chair and pointed to her organ impatiently. Turner sat on the stool, and he heard her settle back, bones creaking and snapping. He started to pump, and the stale air of the organ dusted around him.

"You remember," said Mrs. Cobb, "that if I have to say my last words, you'll write them down."

"Yes, ma'am. I'll write them down just as you say them."

"There is paper there on the organ. And pen and ink beside it. And you won't need to pretty them up any, because they'll be pretty enough."

Turner nodded and decided he wouldn't play "Swing Low, Sweet Chariot," choosing instead "Shall We Gather at the River?" and realizing too late that Mrs. Cobb might figure that was an invitation. But when he heard her humming to it, he played the second verse, and then the third, and while his fingers took on the chorus, he turned to look at her. Her eyes were closed, and her mouth, too, with her humming, and she was smiling. She looked, Turner thought, as though there was a day once upon a time when she might have been happy.

Mrs. Cobb did not have to say her last words that afternoon. Turner played hymn after hymn, repeating a few verses when she hummed to the chorus, taking care to avoid the ones that suggested the pleasures of leaving this weary world. When he heard her tapping her foot, he sped up, and she always kept up the pace. And when he closed with a rousing "As Flows the Rapid River"—and it wasn't easy to be rousing with four sharps—she actually, really, honestly, truly clapped.

Turner supposed that if the Apocalypse had come, he could hardly have been more surprised.

When Turner left Mrs. Cobb, the sun was still high, his shadow was still small, and the mischief of a sea breeze was still hovering by the gate, waiting for him. And Mrs. Cobb was no longer there to stop him. He followed it down Parker Head, along the street as it dwindled toward the shore, down past the pines and through the scrub, all the while the salt in his nose and a hope singing in his ears that Malaga wasn't a lie, that there was some one person in all of Maine who wasn't playing him for a fool.

And when he came down to the beach, the tide was up and the gulls were circling, and the New Meadows flowed so high and strong that there was almost no beach to stand on. And across the water, Malaga's pines waved their boughs at him.

But no one stood on the shore.

And the island had never seemed so far away.

He waited to see if Lizzie might come around the point. He counted waves and told himself he would leave after twenty-five had tumbled in. After that, he skipped rocks and told himself he would leave after he skipped one seven times. (He did it with the eleventh stone.) After that, he counted fifty gulls—except they came almost all at once. And then, with nothing left to count, Turner climbed back up the ledges, with a pile of loneliness on his back as heavy as nightfall.

The sea breeze had scooted the heat of the day out in front of it, and Turner found himself shivering by the time he came back up to Parker Head. Mrs. Hurd was out on her porch now, and she waved to him. He wondered suddenly if this would be his life from now on: walking down Parker Head to see Mrs. Cobb, walking down to the shore to an empty Malaga Island, and walking back up to see Mrs. Hurd. The days stretched awfully long.

"I heard you playing the organ across the way," Mrs. Hurd called.

"Yes, ma'am. Over to Mrs. Cobb's."

"You're much better than that wretched Lillian Woodward. She hasn't played anything faster than a dirge since the Civil War."

"I didn't see you at church."

She smiled and winked at him. "I went every Sunday until my hair turned white, and in all that time I never heard a sermon worth that"—and she snapped her fingers in front of him, a dry, sort of soft snap. "So one day I up and decided I wouldn't go anymore. Imagine that, Turner III. After all, why should Sundays be so dreary?"

Turner wondered if his hair would have to be white before he didn't have to put up with dreary Sundays.

"Not that I think your father is dreary," Mrs. Hurd said quickly. "It's just that I've gotten into the habit of keeping the Sabbath here at home." She balled her hand into a fist and pounded—sort of—her chest. "Here is where God speaks. Here is where I listen."

A sudden gust of warm wind came up and swirled a moment around them both. But watching Mrs. Hurd's old white hand, watching that surprising fist, Turner shivered. He wondered what his father would say to Mrs. Hurd. He wondered if his father would believe—really believe—the things he might say to Mrs. Hurd.

"Do you think I'm wicked?" she asked.

"I don't think you could be wicked if you tried, Mrs. Hurd."

"Oh, it's not that difficult. You hardly have to practice at all."

"Mrs. Hurd, whenever I play over to Mrs. Cobb's, that's for you, too."

She smiled at him. "Turner, that is one of the nicest things you could ever give to me," she said. "You might play 'I Have Some Friends Before Me Gone.'"

"I'm trying not to give Mrs. Cobb hymns about dying."

"Good Lord, Turner III, she's almost as old as I am. Every second thought is about dying. And she doesn't have any friends before her gone anyway."

"But I'd rather she didn't think of dying while I'm playing."

Mrs. Hurd considered this. "No," she finally agreed, "you wouldn't want her to die while you're playing. That wouldn't be polite. But if she does die while you're working on 'I Have Some Friends Before Me Gone,' be sure you finish the chorus before you cover her up."

"Mrs. Hurd! That is wicked!"

"Well, I suppose you might stop to cover her up. But be sure to go back and finish the chorus."

Turner figured the likelihood was remote enough that he could promise to finish the chorus, and so he did.

"You see, Turner III, you're as wicked as I am. You hardly have to practice at all." He smiled, and felt then that some part of the dreary afternoon of the dreary Sunday had been saved.

He was almost whistling when he climbed the steps to his front porch. He was whistling for sure when he opened the door and went in. But he wasn't whistling when he saw his father, who took two quick strides toward him, opened his hand, and slapped it flat and hard against Turner's face.

Turner stood stunned. He felt his entire body grow taut and then begin to quiver with surprise and humiliation and ... anger.

"That's how it feels," said his father. "That's how it feels every time you humiliate me. Do you know what *forbidden* means, Turner? Do you understand the word *forbidden?* You were *forbidden* to go to Malaga Island. Absolutely forbidden. I could not have been more clear about that. Yet here comes Willis Hurd to ask me to tell you that when you come back from the island, you'd be welcome to join him and the others down on the docks. 'Oh no,' I say, 'Turner couldn't be down to the island.' But Willis tells me that he saw you heading down Parker Head. He tells me that Parker Head leads to Malaga, and he figured that's where you were heading."

Turner hoped wildly that Willis's nose was pushed so far to the right he couldn't even pick it.

"Is it true, Turner? Did you go to the island?"

"To the shore," answered Turner. "I couldn't get across to the island."

"You disobeyed me."

Turner thought this should be pretty clear. "Yes."

"May I ask why? Or is this something else that wasn't intended to embarrass the new minister?"

"Because I wanted to know if it was true."

"If what was true?"

"If Lizzie was lying to me. If all she wanted to do was to get me on her side so she wouldn't have to leave the island."

Reverend Buckminster sighed. "It doesn't matter if it's true. It matters what people think. It matters that my congregation can tell me what to think when my son goes out to visit a Negro girl on Malaga Island. It doesn't matter at all how she got you out there."

"It matters to me," Turner whispered.

"Speak up!"

"It matters to me."

The grim silence circled the room like an eager tiger. It

flicked its tail greedily at them, circling, circling, circling. Turner felt that it was about to pounce, claws fully out.

And then it did.

"*Forbidden* is *forbidden*. You will stay in the house for the next two weeks, Turner. If I cannot trust you not to go to the island, then I will have to keep you under my eye. You may not leave here except for church services. And this means that you may not go down to the docks today."

"They're not down on the docks."

"Speak up, Turner. Good Lord, don't mumble like a little whipped boy."

"They're not down on the damn docks."

Another circling silence. "I think I can trust Willis Hurd to be telling the truth over a boy who can't even keep his own mouth clean," said Reverend Buckminster, and took his presence out of the room.

That Sunday turned out to be the dreariest one on record. And it had to go some to pass a handful of others Turner could recall.

It seemed to Turner less and less likely that he would be lighting out for the Territories anytime soon. But as the days went by and he settled into his imprisonment, he was comforted by one thing: who knew how, but he was more and more sure that Lizzie had not lied to him, and that Malaga was as real as real.

And there was one other comfort, and it came from a surprising source. After three days of his absence, Mrs. Cobb appeared at the parsonage to ask if he had been sick. When she found out he wasn't, she asked if Turner might come to her house to play the organ for her. His mother agreed. Turner was not told how Reverend Buckminster came to agree to this, too, and he did not ask.

Turner dawdled on his way down to her house each afternoon. Not that there was much to see. But there was the sea breeze, and the trees were starting to yellow and blush. So he dawdled until he came to the picket fence, and every day Mrs. Cobb was standing at the door waiting for him, scowling and sour. And she stayed scowling and sour through the first hymn or two, and then she started to hum a little, and eventually, by "The Battle Hymn of the Republic," she was singing—"Glory, glory, hallelujah!"—and her voice trembled and then grew stronger—"Glory, glory, hallelujah! His truth is marching on."

And sometime after the glory, glory, hallelujahs were over, Turner glanced at her to assess her general state of health, and if she seemed hale and hearty enough, he meandered into "I Have Some Friends Before Me Gone," and played more loudly than it ought to be played so that Mrs. Hurd could hear it across the street.

And when he finished each afternoon, Mrs. Cobb leaned back in her chair and smiled, not a scowl anywhere on her face. "I've made it through another day," she said.

"No last words yet," Turner agreed.

"You're not such a bad sort after all, Turner Buckminster. I'd be pleased to have you be the one to hear them."

And Turner nodded, strangely glad with the honor—though not so eager to fulfill it—and headed on home. He would wave at Mrs. Hurd, who was sometimes rocking on the porch with her shawl around her shoulders, or sometimes sitting by a window watching for him. And he dawdled as the clouds turned their mackerel undersides to him and the cool of the late afternoon started to settle in over the town.

One afternoon, after another dreary Sunday, he walked home from Mrs. Cobb's with the sea breeze determined to shove him to Malaga Island. It scooted around him and pulled at his ears. It threw up the dust of the road into his face to turn him around, and when he leaned into it, it suddenly let go and pushed at him from behind, laughing. But with the iron word *forbidden* tolling like a heavy bell by his ears, Turner would not let himself be brought to Malaga. And so with a last abrupt kick, the sea breeze twisted around and left him. Turner watched it rushing pell-mell down Parker Head and toward the shore. "Go find Lizzie," he whispered.

And it heard him.

That night, after a quiet and still supper, Turner sat by his window watching the late dusk turn purple, and suddenly there was the sea breeze again, chuckling and rolling down Parker Head, whipping three times around First Congregational and then rollicking across the street, up the clapboards of the parsonage, and to him, rustling his hair and scooting down the back of his shirt so that he shivered and laughed.

"Is that you up there, laughing like a loon?"

Lizzie. Lizzie Bright.

He put his head out the window. "What are you doing here?" he called down.

"Well, I've missed you, too. I'm stealing chickens."

"We don't have any chickens."

"Your dog, then."

"We don't have a dog."

"I figured you didn't have a dog—or he was deaf as a post. What does a minister have to steal?"

"Books. Preaching books."

She paused. "I guess you can keep those. I'll try somewhere else."

"No. Wait a minute—right there." Turner figured that sneaking through a minister's house wasn't exactly something fit for a minister's son, but the scriptures never said, "Thou shalt not sneak," and that was good enough. He went down the front steps, hoping his father would be in the back study—he was—and his mother wouldn't be in the front parlor—she wasn't—and so on he went out the front door that would squeak no matter how much he comforted it. But then he was outside and the sea breeze found him again and chucked him lightly under the chin.

He followed the sea breeze around to the back of the house, and there, away from the light thrown out the study windows, stood Lizzie, one hand on her hip, her foot tapping impatiently.

"Why don't you have a dog?" she asked.

"We've never had a dog."

"That's no reason not to have a dog. If I had a big fine house like this, I'd have a dog. Even a mangy dog. And I'd run him all day, and then we'd come back here and throw balls back and forth till I couldn't throw one more ball."

"Then I'll get a dog," said Turner, "and we'll see how long it takes that arm of yours to give out."

"Longer than it would take yours."

"Probably so."

"You know it's so." She grinned and Turner grinned back. Lord, it was good to see her.

"How'd you know how to find me?"

"There's only this one church in Phippsburg, Turner. Doesn't take a whole lot to figure out where you'd be. You know why I came?"

"So I could row you back up the New Meadows."

She put her other hand on her other hip and stared at him. "Boy, you won't find me in a boat with you rowing anytime soon. I came to tell you I just don't believe it."

"You just don't believe what?"

"What Sheriff Elwell said."

"What did he say?"

"You always answer with a question, Turner."

"What did the sheriff say?"

"See?"

"Lizzie, what did—"

"That Willis Hurd dared you to come out to talk to a Negro. That he dared you to come out to the island. That you didn't care a penny's worth about me or my granddaddy. And that you can't hardly wait till we clear out—just like all the rest of the town."

"That's what the sheriff said?"

She glared at him.

"Lizzie, I swear to you, as sure as I'm standing right here— that's a lie. Every bit of it. Every single bit."

"My granddaddy said it was a lie, too." She leaned her head to one side and looked at him steadily. "So why haven't you been down to the island?"

"So only you get to ask questions now?"

"Yes." She waited.

"I haven't been down to the island because my father believes that you were using me to help you stay on Malaga Island."

"Well," she said slowly. "Well."

"I didn't believe it, either." The sea breeze lay at their feet panting, hoping they would play with it again.

"My granddaddy's been on that island since he was a baby," said Lizzie, as quiet as the dark. "He won't leave. He'd never leave my grandmama. And he'd never leave my mama."

"You won't have to leave. You can't have to leave."

"That's what Mr. Tripp says. He's got this shotgun he waves around like Ulysses S. Grant, saying how he'll fight to protect our homes and such. He's about ready to declare independency."

They stood together quietly, in the dark, in the growing cool of the night, and the sea breeze gave up on them and played in the dark leaves above, and the sound of the waves came in with the quiet. The stars popped in the night sky like distant firecrackers, and beyond them the great streak of the Milky Way came down out of heaven and draped a swathe into the ocean beyond. Turner could almost feel the globe sliding under his feet. Lizzie felt it, too and she reached out and took his hand for a moment—as if for balance—and then dropped it.

"My granddaddy said I shouldn't be out here long."

"Lizzie, you been clamming?"

"Some."

"Batting?"

"Some."

"Flying with the Tripps?"

"More than some. And you?"

"Mostly I stay in the house. I go to services. I read and play the organ for Mrs. Cobb in the afternoons."

"You play the organ? You do? Turner Buckminster, you play the organ?"

"Better than I bat."

"Oh," she said, smiling, "I thought for a minute you might be good."

"Come hear me."

"Sure. 'Please, Mrs. Cobb, may I come in and set a while and listen to Turner play your organ? Oh yes, thank you, I'll sit in your best chair. Of course, I'd love some tea. No, thank you, no cake just now. Thank you, yes, I am having a lovely time, Mrs. Cobb. He does play like all get out.'"

"Well, it might not be exactly like that."

"Lord, I guess it wouldn't."

"Come anyway."

Lizzie looked at him for a long time, tilting her head to one side as if trying to figure him out—which was what she was doing. "You're a strange person, you know that, Turner Buckminster? I wonder if you can see anything straight. What do you think your daddy would say if he saw us two standing out here right now? Or knew that I would be coming up to Mrs. Cobb's house just to hear you play?"

"He'd say hell and damnation. So you going to come?"

"I'll come. At high tide, when I can't be clamming anyway."

"Then I'll see you tomorrow at high tide, Lizzie Bright."

"Yes, you will," she said, and whistling softly, she turned toward the back of the yard. The sea breeze came down from the leaves and followed at her heels, jumping up now and again and frisking all around.

Turner snuck back inside, as quiet as could be, thinking of high tide.

By the next morning, gray clouds scuttled over the sea, muffling the sound of the waves and throttling hope of a sea breeze. But they were only the beginning. Around noon, all the clouds that had been gathering back of the White Mountains let loose and skittered across the lowlands with a slanting rain until they hit the sea, where they stopped to enjoy the view. The rain came down steadily, cold from the mountaintops, and had no intention of moving on. Turner watched the town soak.

Turner's mother suggested that he might not want to go down to Mrs. Cobb's that afternoon. She made the suggestion over a quiet and still noon dinner. Reverend Buckminster suggested that Mrs. Cobb might be expecting Turner, and it would be appropriate for a minister's son to keep his commitments, no matter what the weather. Turner said he would go later, maybe at high tide, when the weather might be clearing. Turner's mother raised an eyebrow and remarked that he had started to become a real Maine boy, thinking of the tide and the weather. Turner supposed that was so.

And that was about it for the rest of dinner.

High tide was indeed late in the afternoon, but it did not bring any clearing. Mrs. Cobb was waiting for him just inside her door, scowling and sour and wondering why he hadn't come yet.

"I thought I'd wait for the weather to clear."

"You may as well wait for Armageddon as that."

And then Turner heard a knock at the back door. A tiny, halting knock.

Mrs. Cobb did not hear it. "This is just the kind of day when my last words might come in handy. There's that damp chill in the air that gets down into your lungs."

Another knock. Louder.

"You may as well start on something happy to get the chill out. Just in case I survive the afternoon."

Knocking. Downright rude.

"What is that?"

"Someone at the back door."

"Go and see who it is, then."

And so he did, and there stood Lizzie, her hands on her hips again, about as soaked as if she had been thrown into the ocean, wrung out, and thrown in once more. Water dripped down her face.

Turner held the door open.

"You getting hard of hearing?"

"What was that you said?"

"You must think I like standing in the wet, and stop answering a question with another question."

Turner looked around and found a dish towel. It was the best he could do. She took it, still glaring, wiped her face and arms, dried off her legs as best she could, then folded it and handed it back. "Thank you," she said.

She followed Turner into the main house, her feet squeaking on the dark, polished wood of the floor. She held her arms around herself, and when Turner looked back at her, her eyes were large as she looked into the rooms off the hallway.

"Just one person lives here," she said, and shook her head at the thought. "Golly Moses, wouldn't Granddaddy think this was fine?"

"Who is that?" called out Mrs. Cobb, turning in her chair as they came into the room.

"Mrs. Cobb, this is—"

"Oh my sweet Jesus," said Mrs. Cobb. "A Negro girl standing in my house."

CHAPTER

7

THE rain came on gray and cold, pattering with hard, metallic fingers at the panes of Mrs. Cobb's parlor. Drips spilled from Lizzie to the floor—the only other sound in the room.

Turner looked back and forth between Mrs. Cobb and Lizzie, both of whom seemed about as surprised at each other as a new hope drying a last tear. Mrs. Cobb breathed heavily, and her hands throttled the chair arms. Turner wondered if this would be the moment he would hear Mrs. Cobb's last words.

"This is Lizzie Griffin, Mrs. Cobb."

"I know who she is. I know who her daddy was. And his daddy before him."

"You do?"

"Of course I do, and don't be rude, you with all your questions."

Lizzie smirked at Turner.

"This is Mrs. Cobb," he said.

Lizzie said nothing at all as the metallic fingers of the rain pattered about as hard as they could without breaking the glass.

Turner figured that if there ever was a time for a hymn, this was it. So he sat down at the organ and wheezed the air into it. He thought for a moment of "The Battle Hymn of the Republic" but decided it wasn't a good idea to invoke the military. And so he set into "Shall We Gather at the River?" as the most peaceful hymn he knew, even if it was about the afterlife. But Mrs. Cobb seemed not to be interested in the river that flows by the throne of God. "A Negro girl in my very house," she said again after the first refrain.

Turner played through all four verses, with the refrain every time, and when he came to the last verse, he sang the words out loud—"Soon our happy hearts will quiver with the melody of peace"—and finished with a harmonized "Amen."

He lifted his fingers and let the last wafting air carry the notes out into the room. When he turned around, Lizzie was sitting on the floor, her legs tucked up beneath her. Mrs. Cobb was still throttling the arms of her chair, but she was leaning back now and not breathing so heavily.

"Turner," Mrs. Cobb said, "don't ruin the music by singing."

Lizzie's eyes fairly danced. Turner figured she would have said the same thing had she thought of it first.

"I thought you might not know all the words, it being the fourth verse."

"Since I was singing that hymn before your father was born, it's likely I would. Try something snappier."

So Turner pumped again and set into the "Battle Hymn," and then into a couple of missionary hymns written to hold the attention of lost drunkards—they were pretty catchy—and a temperance hymn with a kind of rollick to it. Then he settled down into hymns that liked a trembling vibrato. All the while he did not look behind him but felt Mrs. Cobb and Lizzie holding their breath.

When he finished with "I Have Some Friends Before Me Gone," he turned around and saw that Mrs. Cobb's hands had finally relaxed. She had folded them together and settled them high up on her lap. Her head was tilted back on the chair, and though her eyes were not closed, she certainly wasn't looking at anything in the room. And Lizzie—Lizzie Bright was smiling the kind of smile that showed that happiness had settled in somewhere deep and was glad to be there.

"You always play that last hymn so loud," said Mrs. Cobb.

Turner shrugged. He figured maybe this was just the kind of moment when God wouldn't mind his stretching. "It sounds like a hymn that needs to be played loud."

"It's a morbid hymn, for funerals. No one plays a funeral hymn loud unless they want to wake the dead."

"I suppose I wouldn't want to do that."

"No, I suppose you wouldn't." She looked at Lizzie. "It never does, to wake the dead." She leaned forward. "Come tomorrow at high tide again."

"Yes, ma'am. How did you know it was high tide?"

"You think an old lady doesn't know anything? I've followed the tide since before your father was just a glint in God's eye. Today it came in at two-forty. Tomorrow it will be half past the hour. Come then, and tell your friend here that she can come, too, if she wants. And that I never did think to ... Well, tell her she can come. Now, the both of you scat and leave an old lady some peace."

So they scatted out the back, Lizzie still dripping now and again. And when they came out from the kitchen and stood for a moment in the first sunlight of the day, Lizzie looked at Turner while he smiled back and waited for her to tell him how wonderful he had been, how fine his music was.

And God's truth, that's what she almost told him.

But she caught herself just in time.

"It got a whole lot better once you stopped singing," she said, and skipped out the yard and was gone.

And Turner, Turner skipped across the front yard and through the picket gate. He waved to Mrs. Hurd, who grinned and waved back from her window, and then skipped down Parker Head as thunder came from far, far away. His feet threw up mud with each step, and he hardly cared that by the time he was back at the parsonage, he would be wetter and muddier than the parishioners of First Congregational felt their minister's son should be.

That's how it was for the rest of the week. Day after day the skies quilted over and the houses of Phippsburg shivered and croodled together and the rain spilled down onto leaves that hung brown and heavy with the wet. High tide came too late now, so each afternoon, Turner waited for the bells of First Congregational to ring three times. Then he left the parsonage and sprinted to Mrs. Cobb's house, where Lizzie would be waiting and dripping inside the kitchen—Mrs. Cobb had started to leave the back door open for her. They would take their spots in the parlor, Turner at the organ and Lizzie sitting with her legs bent beneath her on the floor and Mrs. Cobb in her armchair, and Turner would wheeze the organ into life.

He did not try to sing again.

But Lizzie did.

When Turner slipped into "Didn't My Lord Deliver Daniel," Lizzie began to tap her knee. By the end of the first verse she was nodding, by the end of the second she was humming, and by the end of the third she was singing along. "I set my foot on the Gospel ship, and the ship it began to sail. It landed me over on Canaan's shore, and I'll never come back anymore." Turner—who hadn't known the words to the last verse—fretted that Mrs. Cobb might want to grab ahold of Canaan's shore, but when he looked at her, she wasn't holding a hand to her heart or even clenching the arms of her chair. Her head was laid back and her eyes turned to Lizzie, and she was listening to her sweet high voice as if it were the first spring day.

After that, Lizzie always sang the hymns she knew, and Turner cut down on the high churchy tunes to accommodate her. She never spoke to Mrs. Cobb, though, and Mrs. Cobb never spoke to her. But Turner figured Mrs. Cobb's leaving the back door open was enough.

So the two weeks of Turner's sentence ended and he was free—or at least as free as any minister's boy could be. Malaga Island was still *forbidden*, but he began to explore the paths into the woods above Phippsburg and to hike along the peninsula's Kennebec shore and climb down to its barnacled rocks. Sometimes he found himself at Thayer's haymeadow, and he would stand at home plate and see the ball coming in hard and fast the way it was meant to, see it so clearly that he could make out the spinning of its seams and know which way it was about to curve.

He never saw Willis Hurd except at church, and then only because he had to. But there were times, especially down at the haymeadow, when he was so lonely he figured he might as well climb on the Gospel ship and head to Canaan's shore—if he couldn't reach the Territories—because he sure didn't want to come back anymore.

Phippsburg cooled into autumn, and Turner spent an hour or so every morning moving wood into the shed closer to the house and splitting kindling—until he figured he had enough kindling to start a conflagration across the whole state of Maine. The maples shivered into their new finery. The oak leaves wrinkled at the edges, though they had no notion of going anywhere for quite a long while.

Turner felt a kind of unhappy kinship with them.

Still, every day at the ringing of the three Congregational bells, Turner left his kindling and set off to Mrs. Cobb's house, and every afternoon Lizzie would be there. Mrs. Cobb never asked for Mr. Milton and Mr. Addison anymore. Instead, Turner would play and Lizzie would sing, and then she would disappear out the backyard and Turner would wave to Mrs. Hurd, and he'd settle himself for the silent supper—and the still more silent evening. School would begin soon in Phippsburg, and although he would not be attending—Reverend Buckminster believing that a minister's son should learn at home under the tutelage of his ministerial father—he was already beginning to read the theology that would soon be a part of his curriculum: Nathaniel Emmons, *On Some of the First Principles and Doctrines of True Religion*.

Lord, save us all, thought Turner when he hefted the volume.

One day, after the frost had hinted that it might be on its way soon, Turner came out of the woods above Phippsburg where aspens had bleached to a dull yellow-beige and the pines were starting to look haughty in their greenery, and he figured he had better be at Mrs. Cobb's. He sprinted on down, and he might have been there on time if he hadn't been struck by something about as expected as a megalosaurus lumbering up Parker Head.

The door and shutters of Mrs. Hurd's house had been painted green.

He walked across the street and onto her porch. The paint was still glistening. He opened the screen door and rapped with the knocker, but he could tell right away that Mrs. Hurd would not be answering. The house was holding itself tight and lonely,

113

even its curtains pulled together and tied against the day. Turner walked around to the side porch—the shutters had all been painted there, too—and he found a single window whose curtains had not been pulled. When he looked in, he saw sheets laid eerily over all the furniture and even on the carpet, as if an arctic landscape had lifted itself and dropped into a parlor in Phippsburg. Even the wind seemed to be blowing colder, and Turner shivered.

He stood that way for a long while.

Mrs. Cobb was waiting for him with hands on hips. "Three o'clock," she said. "Not two o'clock. Not four o'clock. Three o'clock. Here I've let that child in and she's sitting in my parlor and I don't have a thing to say to her, and Lord knows she hasn't a single thing to say to me."

"I'm sorry, Mrs. Cobb. Mrs. Hurd's house looks closed up."

"All I know is that those awful shutters have been painted a Christian color."

Turner could see that Lizzie was annoyed when he came into the parlor. Her mouth was closed tight, but her eyes said, "Turner Ernest Buckminster, if I had to sit in this parlor alone with her for one more minute, I'd have thrown something through a window, and it would have been your fault."

Turner got right down to his playing.

But the green shutters hung before him, and his fingers seemed to miss half the time, and toward the end of just about every chorus he found that his feet had stopped pumping and that the verses were drifting off into a strangling silence.

"Turner Buckminster, keep your mind on God's songs."

He tried. He did try. But Mrs. Cobb got more and more exasperated. "Are you trying to send me into my last words?" she finally hollered. Lizzie's eyes grew big, and Turner figured he didn't want Mrs. Cobb to die on him. So he picked up the pace with a few Civil War hymns, but even so, she finally waved her hand and told him to stop. There was playing the organ, she said, and there was playing *at* the organ. If she wanted to hear someone playing *at* the organ, all she had to do was listen to that dreadful Lillian Woodward. It was high time for him to go on home and leave an old lady some use of her ears.

Lizzie Bright stood up and walked over to Turner. She took his hand and led him out the back of the house. They stood together on the back porch, as they had done so many times, but now, for the very first time, there was a gentle touch in Lizzie's hand that Turner had never noticed before. He did not let go.

"You know I was about to throw something through the window by the time you got there?"

"I know."

"You know what it's like to sit in there not talking with her? Golly Moses, I kept trying to find a place to put my eyes so she wouldn't think I was planning on stealing something."

"She wouldn't open the door for you every day if she thought that. She just doesn't know what to say to you."

"I know. Just like sometimes I don't know what to say to you."

"Lizzie, you never have any trouble knowing what to say to me."

"Well, Turner Ernest Buckminster, right now I'm trying to figure out how to ask you why a wild turkey could have played that organ better than you today."

"You still trying to figure out a way to ask?"

"Not anymore. I guess it's right out there."

"I don't know. Me leaving Boston. What might happen to you and everyone else on Malaga. And now Mrs. Hurd's house. And then these dinners at home where no one says a single thing. Not one single thing. I guess, I guess I just want one thing to stay the same. Just one thing."

"Well," she said, "if you were still in Boston, you'd never have heard of me."

Turner smiled. "I suppose some changes are as fine as they can be."

"Turner Ernest Buckminster, you best be careful what you say." Lizzie took her hand from his and was gone.

Turner went out to the street, looked at the green shutters of Mrs. Hurd's house, and walked back to the parsonage. The sea breeze, wearing its overcoat, followed him all the way until he closed the door on it. Then it tipped up into the sky and spread out, looking for a maple it could scorch or a beech it could blanch. It found the maple and went about its business, so that if Turner had looked out his front door, he might have seen the maple just past First Congregational shiver some and then coldly begin to burn into reds.

But he didn't look out. He went up to his room and listened to the clicking of the typewriter from his father's study, and he thought about sunlight shutters and strawberry doors and Mrs. Hurd and baseballs hit higher than the dome of the Massachusetts State House and Lizzie Bright, and he suddenly knew that he needed to find a way back to Malaga Island.

And he needed to find out where Mrs. Hurd had gone.

So that night, as dishes were passed around a silent table, and as the clock on the breakfront chimed the quarter hours, Turner decided he would dare the silence and ask.

"Mrs. Hurd's house is all closed up," he said. He was surprised at how loudly his voice crackled around the room, as though it were electric and sparking up the paneled walls. "And her shutters are all painted green."

"Yes, I know," said Reverend Buckminster without looking up. He deliberately cut a square piece of lamb and dipped it into the mint jelly on his plate. He brought it slowly to his mouth and chewed properly.

The clock chimed another quarter hour.

"Do you know where she went?"

Reverend Buckminster slowly chewed. There was a long silence, so long that Turner wondered if the clock might chime again. "Yes," his father said, "I do know. But it's not to be gossiped about at the minister's dinner table."

Turner's mother put down her fork. "Tell him, Buckminster. Tell him where Mrs. Hurd has gone."

"It is a family affair."

More silence, then his mother said softly, "Turner, Mrs. Hurd has been sent to the Home for the Feeble-Minded in Pownal. Do you know what that is?"

Turner shook his head.

"It's an insane asylum, Turner. It's a place where people live in long wards, tied to white iron beds. It's a place where there are strong nurses to tell them exactly what to do."

Turner thought he might throw up. The smell of the mint jelly filled the room, heavy and sickly sweet, awful, wafting around him.

"You don't need to frighten the boy."

"But she wasn't feebleminded or insane," she continued. "I knew her, and she wasn't feebleminded or insane."

"That's for her son to decide. He is a deacon, after all," said Reverend Buckminster.

"For her son to decide," said Turner's mother, looking only at him, "and for two other respectable citizens of Phippsburg to agree to, if she was to be legally committed. One of the respectable citizens was Mr. Stonecrop, who just happens to be looking for capital to build his new hotel. And my, isn't it surprisingly convenient that the good Deacon Hurd now has his mad mother's house to put on the market, all newly painted in colors that everyone expects? And isn't it surprisingly convenient that once it has sold, Deacon Hurd will have a nice sum to invest?"

"Deacon Hurd, Turner, has been fearing for his mother's sanity for some time, and he cannot leave her safely alone. You can hardly expect him to care for an insane woman."

"The other respectable gentleman who signed the committal papers," said Turner's mother, "is best named by your father." And she gathered up her dishes and went out to the kitchen.

Turner did not ask his father who the other respectable gentleman was. As silence descended upon the dining room again, and the ticking of the breakfront clock grew louder, he, too, gathered up his dishes and left his father sitting very still, his hands on the edge of the table.

His mother was gone from the kitchen. Turner stacked his plate atop hers and then went out to the front porch and sat on the steps. The days were darkening earlier now, but down Parker Head he could still make out Mrs. Hurd's house—or what had been Mrs. Hurd's house. "I have some friends before me gone," he sang quietly, but the sound seemed so lonely and lost that he stopped before the chorus. He thought of Mrs. Hurd in some awful gown, confused and afraid, her hair uncombed, in a well-lit ward under sheets white and starched, stretched tight across her chest, and he knew that she was thinking only one thing: if only she could light out for the Territories. If only she could.

So when he stepped into his father's study the next morning to begin the first formal day of tutelage, Turner was about as grim as a dark cloud lowering itself over a Sunday-school picnic. He stood silent, watching his father finish drafting the day's assignment. The collar was tight and perfect around the reverend's neck. His coat fell in folds as precise as those of a marble sculpture. Each sleeve of his starched shirt protruded the same amount from the coat, just enough to show the matched cuff links, gleaming silver. His nails were cut precisely to the pink.

Turner wondered if his father had ever played baseball, had ever hit a fly into air so blue that it hurt his eyes to look at it. He wondered if his father had ever joked around, out-loud lied, gotten into a fight and pushed another kid's nose off to the side, jumped off a cliff about as high as a middle-sized pine into an oncoming froth of wave.

Probably not.

His father looked up. *"Arma virumque cano,"* he said. His first words to his son that morning.

"Arms I sing," said Turner . . . after more than a few moments.

"Of arms I sing, and the man. *Troiae qui primus ab oris Italiam."*

"And the one who first from Italy . . ."

"No."

"From Troy, the coasts of Troy to Italy."

"Fato profugus."

"Fate's . . ."

"Turner, we've done this passage before."

"By fate. Exiled by fate."

"Laviniaque venit litora."

"Come to the shores of Lavinia."

Reverend Buckminster handed Turner an ominously large book. "Do the first hundred lines." He looked at the grandfather clock guarding the study's corner. "An hour and a half should be enough."

So Turner sat at a small desk by the window—a window closed tightly and imperiously against sea breezes exiled by fate—and began the first hundred lines of the *Aeneid*. He tried not to sigh. He tried not to scratch too often. How was he to blame if dang Virgil was so ornery that he wouldn't give up his verbs until the very end of his sentences, as if he thought it would be a fine surprise to snap things around like a cat changing direction?

But there was something here he knew. Someone exiled by fate from a place he loved. A man thrown around greatly—or whatever *multum iactatus* meant—thrown around on the shore and on the sea by something he did not understand.

Turner knew what this was about.

He finished in two hours. He was sweating. His father was not. He was tapping his pen in rhythm with the ticking of the clock. By the time Aeneas's chilled arms were weakening with dread—if *extemplo Aeneae solvuntur frigore membra* meant chilled arms weakening with dread—Turner was wishing that fate would exile the Minister's Son anywhere else.

"You must be done now," said his father.

"Yes, sir."

Reverend Buckminster looked at the clock. A long look. "Read me your translation."

His father quietly tapped his pen through the reading.

"It's not his arms that are chilled," he said when Turner finished. "More like 'chilled dread.'"

I almost touched a whale, thought Turner.

"Write a summary of the passage, one hundred and fifty words." Reverend Buckminster looked at the clock again. "Thirty minutes." And he turned back to his own writing— probably a sermon about hell's torments, one of which was writing a short essay in thirty minutes.

Turner began. And no matter if Aeneas's storms had come to chill his arms or chill his dread or whatever, Turner was determined to finish in thirty minutes. If whole empires rose and fell, continents shifted, and the earth tilted upside down, he would finish in thirty minutes.

He finished as the grandfather clock ticked to twenty-six minutes, and he handed the paper across his father's desk.

His father glanced at it. "Another summary," he said. "From the perspective of Juno."

"Sir?"

"The queen of the gods, Turner. Write it as though she is telling the story. This is Juno here, *regina deum,* line nine. Thirty minutes seems about the right amount of time."

Out in the bay, I almost touched a whale, thought Turner.

He began again, starting with Juno's unforgiving cruelty, sweeping into the cave of winds, and finally breaking into the storm: *ruunt et terras turbine perflant.* He chaffed some at going over a hundred lines for the third time, but he felt Juno's malice as she snatched the daylight from the Trojans' eyes, and as she heaved up the seabed on them. He imagined her as, say, Mrs. Cobb, swooping out from behind her picket fence with eyes aflame, calling down the *turbine perflant* upon a minister's son who threw rocks.

He finished in twenty-four minutes. He thought Mrs. Cobb's swooping gave his summary a kind of flair.

"Now from the perspective of Aeolus," said Reverend Buckminster, and Turner was in the gloomy cavern of the king of the Winds, reining back the storms until he could unleash them at Juno's will. "From the perspective of Aeneas," said Reverend Buckminster next, and Turner despaired with the hero in the groaning and stretching ship—or maybe it was Aeneas who was groaning and stretching. It was hard to tell.

He supposed, in the end, that the morning was about as passable a morning as anyone could pass when he was forging through a Latin exercise.

His father set all four summaries on his desk, side by side, and read each one twice. He tapped his pen on each in turn, underlining now and again, circling a phrase here and there. He tapped some more with his pen, as loudly as the ticking of the grandfather clock, and finally gathered all four together, arranged them neatly, and handed them back to Turner.

"Aside from your multiple spellings of *Aeneas*—which, despite all of your creativity, has, according to Virgil, no *u* in it at all—you have translated and summarized well enough for someone coming back to Latin after a summer's break. You see how important it is to view the story from different perspectives?"

Turner nodded. He waited for his release. He felt the quiet sea breeze stirring outside the house and peeking in at the window.

Reverend Buckminster stood and turned to his shelves. He looked them up and down, one finger at his lip, as Turner's heart stood still, and as the sea breeze paused and quivered.

He pulled out one of the volumes, thumbed through it, put it back, pulled out another. Its leather binding and marbled edges proclaimed to all the world that it was about as dull a book as could ever have been written by any one human being. "Robert Barclay's *An Apology for the True Christian Divinity: Being an Explanation and Vindication of the Principles and Doctrines of the People Called Quakers,*" he said. "Read the first two propositions, and then summarize them after dinner."

Outside the window, the sea breeze dropped and slunk away.

It was a dreary afternoon that followed a dreary and silent

dinner. The *Aeneid* was one thing—at least there were storms and ships being tossed and people being washed overboard. But a proposition on "The True Foundation of Knowledge" was as awful as Mrs. Cobb's seeing him in his underwear in her kitchen. Well, almost as awful.

He wondered if he would be reading propositions by Robert Barclay if he were sitting at a desk in the Phippsburg schoolhouse. Probably not—but Willis Hurd would be there. So he sat in his father's study as the sea breeze frolicked somewhere else, and as Lizzie Bright was probably flying with the Tripps, and read propositions. Long propositions. Long propositions that didn't seem to want to go much of anywhere and that were taking their time not wanting to go there. He sighed, glanced at his father to see if he had heard above the ticking of the clock, and settled in to write about seeking divinity.

It looked to be a long school year.

It was, at least, a mighty long school week. A hundred lines of the *Aeneid* with their summaries for each morning, followed by two propositions by Robert Barclay for the afternoon. Virgil was passable, with the storm breaking up the fleet, and Aeneas finally coming to land, and the gods bothering and fussing at each other. But reading Robert Barclay while the sea breeze waited outside—that was something not even a minister's son should have to do. Aeneas—or Aenaeus, however he spelled his dang name—would never have put up with it.

Maybe even Reverend Buckminster understood that. On Friday, after the Trojans had come upon Queen Dido and all the exciting parts were getting ready to die down, a miracle greater than the parting of the Red Sea descended upon the town of Phippsburg, Maine: Turner's father gave him the afternoon free. Turner supposed something more amazing could happen in his life, but if so, he couldn't imagine what it might be. So he let Robert Barclay drone on by himself and ran outside and jumped off the porch and caught the sea breeze when it raced past him, and he followed it down Parker Head and thought how fine it was to be free, free, free for an afternoon.

He didn't mean, at least at first, to head on down to the shore, since Malaga was still *forbidden*. But the sea breeze did race on ahead of him just that way, and he did think of Aeneaus (or however he spelled his dang name) with his two great spears exploring the coast, and it might be that he would find Lizzie clamming on this side of the New Meadows so that he wouldn't actually be going across to the island. *Forbidden*. So he followed the breeze out of town and through the pines and across the granite ledges to the shore. And when he looked down to see if Lizzie might be clamming, he came upon the second most amazing thing of his day.

Just off the shore of the island, a house was set on a raft, bobbing up and down in the gentleness of the surf. Even Aeneas would have been surprised.

It was about as forlorn a thing as he ever wanted to see. The house perched on its raft as though it were trying not to be sick. Its roof beams sagged in the middle, its shingles clung loosely, and the chimney pipe swayed with each wave, trying to be jaunty but not very good at it. Lashed to its sides were two barrels, a few lobster pots, and an old, battered trunk complaining at being dragged out onto the water.

Faces looked out the windows. Abbie's face. Perlie's face. Tripps' faces.

On the shore stood what looked to be just about everybody who lived on Malaga Island, Lizzie and her granddaddy hand in hand. No one was saying much, just watching as Mr. Tripp circled the raft, tightening a rope, checking the barrel tops, and trying to make it about as shipshape as Aeneas would have made a warship. Then he went back onshore, and there were handshakes and nods, all quiet, until he went back aboard and cast off. A wave kicked up, but he hung on, and soon the house was drifting down the New Meadows, heading out to the coast. Mr. Tripp held on to the door frame with one hand, and the other he held high, his fingers spread out as if he were blessing them all.

In that moment, Lizzie's granddaddy lifted up his voice, quavery but loud, and soon every soul on the shore was singing.

> Yes, we'll gather at the river,
> The beautiful, the beautiful river,
> Gather with the saints at the river
> That flows by the throne of God.

And the raft floated away, the sounds of the singing faded, and the gulls swooped and screeched as if they were announcing a death in the town.

One by one, those on the shore headed back up into the island. By the time Turner had climbed down the ledges and stood just across the New Meadows, only Lizzie and her grand-daddy were standing there, still looking at the raft before it crossed behind the island and so out of sight. "Lizzie," Turner called. "Lizzie Bright."

But she did not answer. Instead, she put her hands to her face and ran up the beach. And her grandfather, after peering at Turner for a moment, followed her.

Turner didn't feel like Aeneas anymore. Suddenly, he felt a whole lot like Mrs. Hurd, alone, with her friends before her gone.

8

IN late September, the sea breeze stole the gold from the maples, the silver from the aspens. The oaks browned; the beeches paled. And in a general disheartening, the leaves let go, twirled and somersaulted, and finally settled down to sleep.

The sea breeze cooled the sun, too, which shone whiter and feebler against aging clouds. Some mornings, it seemed to want to sleep with the leaves.

On such a morning, not long after the day had finished rubbing its eyes and yawning, Turner rubbed his eyes and yawned to a pounding on the parsonage door. He heard his father's slippered feet hurrying down the stairs. Figuring that only a calamity would fetch the minister out this early in the morning and that a minister's son should stand by his father at such a moment, he jumped out of bed, gathered his robe around him, and went downstairs, too. But he could have stayed in bed and still have heard the news Mr. Stonecrop brought, since he was hollering it loudly enough to let folks on the other side of the New Meadows hear it.

"Have you read the Portland newspaper, Buckminster?

Have you read it?" He waved it in front of Reverend Buckminster's face.

The reverend admitted that he hadn't read a single word yet today.

"Then let me read this for you!" Mr. Stonecrop held the paper out with both hands, mumbled a moment until he found the right place, and then began to sputter as though great Lucifer himself had provoked him. "Here, the wretch says that he's been forced off the island that has been his home—as though he had any right to call it his home. Forced to put his house on a raft. And here, that Phippsburg has never given a fig about him, never even tried to help him or his family—as though we'd never built a school or hired a teacher. And here, he claims that now that he's floated all the way down to Portland, he has nowhere left to go. And that's not all, Buckminster. The moving saga of the Tripp family continues: how they had to tie up at Bush Island after being prevented from coming into Phippsburg, how he had to row back and forth three miles to find a doctor to tend his wife, and how all of this is the fault of the good people of Phippsburg." He stopped and took a breath.

"The fault of the people of Phippsburg!" declared Reverend Buckminster.

"The insolence of it all!" declared Mr. Stonecrop.

"The Tripps!" declared Turner.

Silence in the parsonage as Reverend Buckminster and Mr. Stonecrop looked at Turner for a long moment.

"You know these people?" asked Mr. Stonecrop.

"You know these people?" asked Reverend Buckminster.

Turner suddenly wished he hadn't come downstairs. He thought of the house floating down the New Meadows with all the Tripps inside, and Mr. Tripp holding the house together and steady against the waves. Did he know these people?

Hadn't he flown with them around the island? Hadn't he made Perlie laugh?

But he said, "Not much."

"Well," said Mr. Stonecrop, "had he set out to deliberately humiliate the town, he could hardly have done much worse. Good Lord, Reverend, if this town is going to survive, we need not only hotels to house tourists, we need goodwill to bring them in. And this kind of thing does not bring goodwill."

"Perhaps, Mr. Stonecrop, you are depending too much on—"

"Perhaps, Reverend, if you want a town to preach to, you should begin to use some of that influence we understood you had. We need to be done with this business, and done quickly. Write to Governor Plaistead. This very day. Tell him the situation. I know things move slowly up to Augusta, but good Lord, the state declared six years ago that it would adjudicate Malaga Island. Six years! It's time to get things moving. Tell him that."

"I could write to him."

"Today, Reverend."

"Mr. Stonecrop, tourism is at best a chancy business."

"It is the only business left to us. The only business once the shipyards fail—as they will within a year. Write the letter."

Mr. Stonecrop blustered out of the house, and Turner and his father watched him take the street by right of possession. There wasn't a sea breeze anywhere near him, and if there had been one, it would have been trampled into the dust of Parker Head until it wasn't anything but a puff or two.

Reverend Buckminster stood still, watching the striding Mr. Stonecrop, who had paused by Mrs. Hurd's house and was gazing up at it as if to appreciate its value. A long sigh. "Go get your breakfast," he said finally. "I've a letter to write this morning, and you've got a hundred lines of Virgil to translate."

The lines turned out to be a hundred dull ones, as Aeneas—Turner thought he finally had the spelling down—moped about and looked for a place to live. With Robert Barclay in front of him, it promised to be an even duller afternoon. Turner figured he had had enough of Robert Barclay's tormenting propositions, more than enough to satisfy any human being, and he said so.

And as if to prove that miracles can still happen on a dull day, Reverend Buckminster agreed. When they came back to the study after dinner, his father closed the door—something he hardly ever did—and reached for a volume in the glassed case behind his desk. He weighed it in his hand. He looked at his son, as if trying to make up his mind.

Finally he did.

"Turner," he said, "books can be fire, you know."

"Fire?"

"Fire. Books can ignite fires in your mind, because they carry ideas for kindling, and art for matches." He handed the book to Turner.

"The Origin of Species," he read aloud. "Is this fire?"

His father laughed, and Turner suddenly realized that this was the first time he had heard him laugh since they had come to Maine. The very first time. "It is a conflagration," he said.

Turner looked steadily at him. "Should a minister's son be reading this?"

"Who better?" said his father. "Besides, your mother says that maybe First Congregational doesn't need to know everything we're thinking." He laughed again. "Whatever would Deacon Hurd say if he knew you were reading Charles Darwin?"

Turner felt as if the world was suddenly a more mysterious place. He had never before thought that there were things he ought to be doing that might cause, well, fire. When he opened the book and began to read, he was Jim Hawkins at the captain's chest, Sinbad opening his eyes in the Valley of Rubies, Huck himself waking up to a brand-new bend in the Mississippi.

And it wasn't long before he knew that what he was reading was fire, all right.

It was almost like lighting out for the Territories.

He read with fire in his brain through the afternoon; the next day, he rushed through Virgil so that he could read again. Day after day through the week he read, the fire heating him, while outside the sea breeze grew colder and colder, and soon there wasn't a single maple it hadn't nipped or a single oak whose leaves it hadn't curled to a crispness. When Saturday came around, Turner spent the morning with Darwin. He finished in a breathless run just before the three ringing bells and ran down Parker Head carrying the fire in his hands.

He would not warm anyone at First Congregational with it. He had promised his father.

But he could warm Lizzie.

He was at Mrs. Cobb's by the last toll of the Congregational bells, but Lizzie was not there. Still, the fire burned red in him, and when Turner played for Mrs. Cobb, he marched briskly through the "Battle Hymn," then drove through "Swing Low, Sweet Chariot" until it was swinging mighty low and mighty fast. He kept listening for the knock on the back door. It did not come, and after playing long enough for even Mrs. Cobb to shush him out, he waited on the back porch.

But Lizzie never came.

When she did not come on Sunday afternoon, either, the fire in him weakened to a smolder. He played the organ slowly, so that Mrs. Cobb said she had never heard "Shall We Gather at the River" played so mournfully. "I'm not about to say my last words this afternoon, Turner Buckminster."

"No, ma'am."

"So play something a little cheerier."

He played a blood-and-thunder hymn, and Mrs. Cobb clapped to it. "Yes," she said, "those hymns about eternal lakes of fire are always so jaunty, aren't they? Play another." And he tried to find one equally hearty in its pleasures of damnation, but he was smoldering so low that he could not keep the tempo up.

Turner felt about as low as a raft set loose on the New Meadows River.

"Where's that Negro girl been?" asked Mrs. Cobb suddenly.

"I don't know," said Turner. "I don't know where she's been and I'm not allowed to go down to find out and I don't even know if she's there anymore or if she's gone with everyone else on the island and Lord knows they haven't done a single thing that calls for people being so awful to them and taking away their home and I haven't even said goodbye, if she's gone, that is."

He stopped to breathe. Mrs. Cobb looked at him, startled, with eyes as wide as daybreak.

"You said all that in one breath."

"I suppose."

She nodded and looked down at her hands gripping her knees. "I've gotten to like her, too. Awfully much."

"I didn't say I liked her."

"Turner Buckminster, you don't have to be a minister's son all the time."

You don't have to be a minister's son all the time. *You don't have to be a minister's son all the time.* Turner had never thought he could ever, at any time, be anything else. The thought shivered him—as if he had almost touched a whale.

"I do like her," he said.

"Of course you do. And it doesn't matter a damn—yes, even old ladies cuss—it doesn't matter a damn what anyone else in the town of Phippsburg has to say about it. It doesn't matter what anyone else in the whole state of Maine has to say about it."

Turner nodded.

"And if anyone has anything to say about it, it should be me!"

"You, Mrs. Cobb?"

"Yes, me, Turner Buckminster. You don't think people haven't been talking about me letting this colored girl into my house to hear you play? Next thing they'll be taking me down to Pownal. Yes, I know all about Mrs. Hurd. That son of hers, sending her to Pownal so he can sell her house and invest the money. You think there's any other reason?" She shook her head solemnly.

Turner stood up from the organ.

"That's right. Go find out about her as fast as you please, and faster."

And Turner—Turner ran out of Mrs. Cobb's house and down Parker Head. He did not see the lace curtains parting, or Mrs. Cobb watching him sprinting, or hear her humming "I Have Some Friends Before Me Gone." But he felt the sea breeze rolling beside him, and he heard the rising of the gulls, and he felt the fire in his hands again. He felt as if he were standing on the edge of the sea cliff with the green waves roaring in and their yellow froth churning at the tops—and he was ready to leap.

He half ran, half tumbled down past the scrub trees and over the ledges, almost expecting that Lizzie would be waiting for him—and so he was hardly surprised when he reached the shore and she was there, her arms muddied up to her elbows, a bucket of spitting clams beside her, and her dory pulled up against the shore.

"Hey," he called.

She looked up, then back down.

"Hey," he called again as he came up.

"Hey."

"I haven't seen you for days."

"Nine days," she said. "You haven't seen me for nine days."

"Nine days, then."

She went back to her clamming.

"I could clam with you some."

"There's another rake in the dory, if you want to so badly."

Turner went to fetch the rake. "What have you been doing?"

"Same thing I'm always doing."

They raked together and dug, silently.

They raked together and dug a *long* time, silently.

"Lizzie, you mad about something?"

"Well now, Mister Turner Ernest Buckminster, why should I be mad about anything?"

"I guess if there were people in a town trying to take away my home, I'd be mad."

"I guess you would, but it's not hardly likely."

"And I guess if they were taking it away just for money, I'd be madder still."

"I guess you would. And you'd be even madder if you had a granddaddy so sick he couldn't move, and a deacon from the town come down to tell him he had to move anyway."

Turner stood over the clam hole he had raked. "How sick?"

And Lizzie Bright threw her rake across the flats, sat down in the mud, and began to cry. Turner set down his rake, sat beside her in the mud, and took her hand.

Muddy palm in muddy palm they sat, and the sea breeze was quiet. Not even the gulls called out. And Turner did not care if Willis Hurd called down the whole town of Phippsburg upon them.

"You done holding my hand yet?" asked Lizzie after a season or two.

"Not yet."

"You going to tell me when you're done?"

"I suppose."

She nodded. "After a while, this mud will dry so hard we won't be able to get apart."

"It'd be all right by me."

Lizzie looked at him, and it seemed as if she might start crying again, but this time, she'd be crying and laughing at the same time. "I guess it'd be all right by me, too, Turner Buckminster. But what'll we do when the tide comes back in?"

"Go see your granddaddy."

And that's what they did. When the tide came back in, they rinsed their hands together in the seawater, and together they climbed into the dory and rowed to Malaga, and together they hefted the bucket of clams around the point and up to the house.

Lizzie's granddaddy was not sitting on the doorstep smoking his pipe, and Turner felt the loneliness of the place. For a moment he imagined the Tripps wheeling out of the woods and flying around them. But there were no Tripps anywhere on the island anymore. He stretched the fingers of his hand and was surprised that he could no longer feel Lizzie's hand in his own. Is it possible to forget the feeling so quickly? he wondered.

Inside the house it was darker than he remembered, darker than it should have been. Lizzie's granddaddy was propped up in a bed, perched on his angled elbows so that he could see out the window. "Lizzie Bright." He smiled when they came in, and he spoke her name as if he were reciting a blessing. "And Turner Buckminster. Boy, we've missed you here. No, no, don't go explaining. You don't need to go explaining. We're just glad you're here today."

Lizzie handed Turner a knife. "You know how to open clams?"

"I will in a minute or two."

"You think you'll just figure it all out on your own?"

"No, I think you'll just tell me."

"You think so?"

"Of course I think so. You never can keep from telling me something you know that I don't."

"Then I must be telling you a whole lot all the time, because there's a whole lot I know that you don't know."

Lizzie told him a whole lot, even after Turner got the knack of it and could open the shell with the point of the knife, slit the muscle before the clam objected too much, and drop it into the pot along with its juice. It was enough, Lizzie's granddaddy said, to make even a man sick in bed look up and take notice, seeing those clams slip out of their shells. But Turner saw that Reverend Griffin couldn't do much more than look up and take notice, and that once the chowder was set to cooking, he lay back down on the bed, exhausted from having propped himself up. He coughed once or twice, weakly, as if he didn't have the heart for it, and then lay too still.

Lizzie and Turner sat by the shore while the chowder hottened up. They didn't talk much—didn't have to. The New Meadows was quiet, with the tide slow and careful not to scrape itself against the shore rocks. The gulls rode its back as if for a joke, calling now and again to each other, but mostly just riding the waves up and down, then up and down again. They must have been doing this for more years than anyone could count, thought Turner, and for a moment he saw Darwin standing on the bridge of the *Beagle* and watching the seabirds of the Galápagos, and maybe thinking the same thing.

"How do you think that gull learned to swim like that?" he asked Lizzie.

"His mama and his papa showed him. How else?"

"How did they learn?"

"Because they had mamas and papas, too, Turner. You know about this stuff, right?"

"But how about the first one? The very first one. What made him start to swim?"

"God took him in His two hands and threw him out there and got him all wet and told him he should stay put. And gulls are still squawking about it."

"You read that in the Bible?"

"Somewhere in Genesis. Toward the middle."

"Well," said Turner, standing up, "I guess God doesn't mind if He gets squawked at sometimes."

"I hope not, since I've had reason enough myself lately."

She stood, too, and together they watched the gulls riding the waves. Then they went into the shack, and Turner helped Reverend Griffin sit up in the bed, and Lizzie brought over a bowl of the clam chowder and fed him. All the time he was smiling, telling them how it was just like Lizzie's grandmama used to make it for him. All the time Turner held him up and wondered at how light he was, so light it hardly seemed his body could heft his soul. Whatever would happen if he really did have to leave Malaga? And whatever would happen to Lizzie if he couldn't?

Lizzie rowed Turner back across the New Meadows after

her granddaddy finished the chowder. He jumped out and held the dory for a moment, then let it go, and the tide took her out a bit. She turned the boat with one oar, and with the smooth movements of one who knew how, she began to row slowly back to the island. Turner watched her across to the shore, watched her pull the dory up and give a wave. And then she spread her arms out, smiled broadly, and began to fly across the beach, bobbing and weaving until she turned the corner of Malaga and was gone. Turner climbed the granite ledges back toward home.

And as he climbed, a fire grew in his gut, a fire as hot as Darwin's and maybe hotter. He felt it flaring as he went down Parker Head, and flaring again when he passed Mrs. Hurd's empty house, and flaring when he passed First Congregational and climbed the porch steps to his house. He felt it through supper, so that even Reverend Buckminster stared at him sometimes, and Turner's mother dared to break the silence by asking him how his day had been.

"Fine," he said, and burned.

He was still burning when his father told him to get ready for the season's last baseball game that evening. Because he couldn't think of a single reason why he shouldn't go—that is, he couldn't think of a single reason he could tell his father— he went and burned on the sidelines, trying not to watch the people who were laughing and passing around bottles of dark Moxie and waving straw hats at each other and getting ready to turn Lizzie and her granddaddy off Malaga Island. He wondered that God could let such a thing be.

And then Deacon Hurd called to him. "Turner, you going to try again?" He chuckled, and Willis next to him chuckled, and everyone on the whole dang field chuckled. Turner nodded, let himself get chosen up for sides, and felt the fire burning brightly.

He did not lead off. He was set down in the end of the lineup, so that it wasn't until the end of the second inning, with a couple of outs, that he stepped up to home and swung his bat low and set his front leg. The days were shorter now, and the white sunlight cold as it settled onto the field and thought about dropping frost. Every tree was blessed with a halo, and the sparkling silver beams slanted down to Turner as he thought about streaking a ball right back up alongside them until it disappeared in the silver-haloed glow.

"You still have that front leg out pretty far, son. You want to think about that?" Deacon Hurd chuckled again.

Willis, standing easy on the mound, threw the ball into his glove over and over, watching Turner. The holy beams backlit him, so that Turner could barely make out his face. He was just as glad.

"Batter up!" yelled Deacon Hurd.

"Here it comes," said Willis, and lofted the ball into the air, so that it rose into the silver light and took on its own halo.

To Turner, there was nothing but the ball and the sky and the light and the bat in his hands and the fire in his gut. And Lizzie, lofting a rock to him on the beaches of Malaga and hollering at him to swing low to high, and the gulls crying and the waves cresting and the rock coming down and him feeling the tingling in his hands as he began to swing.

As he swung, he broke his wrists forward and took the ball as if it were as big as a melon and curled it skittering and skating along the beams of silver light, twirling it foul far, far off into the woods beyond third base, higher than any pine trees Phippsburg might set against it, high and far and gone forever.

"Strike one!" Deacon Hurd called.

No one chuckled.

Someone from behind the backstop threw a new ball out

to Willis. He took off his glove and roughed the ball up, then put the glove back on and stared in at Turner, not chuckling, but his face dark as the sun spun down and the beams slanted up. The next ball he threw was higher than the first, with a wicked spin he put on with his fingertips just before he released it. Turner sidled his front leg a little to the right and watched the ball come, hearing again the crying gulls and the cresting waves. This time he held his wrists back and sent the ball curling foul past the first-base line, curling away and over the haloed maples and skipping over a gravelly road until it disappeared into a ditch about a county away.

"Strike two!" called Deacon Hurd.

And no one chuckled.

Another new ball from behind the backstop and Willis roughing it up again. A third pitch, as high or higher than the first, without a single bottle of Moxie being passed around, without a single straw hat waving, and Turner waiting, waiting for the ball, and the fire burning in his gut. He broke his wrists again just as the ball came in and threw a roundhouse swing that skied the ball and then curved it foul into the third-base trees.

Whistles from the people of Phippsburg, and shouts of wonder that the minister's boy, the minister's skinny boy should be able to hit a ball that far three times in a row.

But it wasn't three times in a row. It was twelve times in a row. Twelve balls hit as high as pride. Twelve balls hit as far as hope. Twelve balls curling away as though they were lighting off for the Territories. And after every one, whistles and shouts and even clapping for baseballs as foul as baseballs could ever be.

Until when another ball was thrown out from behind the backstop, Deacon Hurd called back, "How many more you got in there?"

"That's the last one."

"You lost twelve balls on us," said the not-chuckling Deacon Hurd.

"I won't lose this one," answered Turner, and he swung his bat, and put his leg out, and waited for the pitch from Willis, still and quiet.

Willis roughed up the ball again. He stepped off the mound for a moment, turned and motioned his center fielder to go out some more, and waved his left and right fielders out against the lines. By now the whole field was in a dusky shadow and the sunbeams were level and tree-high above them. When Willis began his windup, Turner couldn't see his face at all. But the ball, the ball was as big as the moon, floating up into the light, then back down into the shadow, spinning in a way that didn't matter, and ready to cozy up to his bat and then streak on out.

And so the ball came down, down, spinning, spinning, and Turner gripped his bat, brought his front leg in . . . and then stepped back from the plate just as the ball dropped, smacked the granite, leaped up, and then rolled to his feet.

"Strike three!" hollered Deacon Hurd.

For a moment, no one else said anything. Then Turner heard his father call out, and Willis's friends, and probably most every other soul in Phippsburg, telling him that he should have swung, that he should have straightened his swing out and hit the ball, that he should have homered. Straw hats were thrown on the ground, and heads were shaken.

The only one who said nothing was Willis. The only one. When Turner picked up the ball and threw it to him, Willis caught it and turned his face so that the shadow was not so dark—and he saw that Willis was smiling.

Turner did not play the rest of the game, which was just as well, folks figured, since they were down to their last baseball. He went back to the parsonage with his mother, walking a little ahead of her. They didn't talk all the way up to the front steps, where they both paused at the top and turned to looked across at the church—now only the steeple was quickened by the light—and then on down Parker Head. Turner shivered in the shadows, but he wasn't ready to go in yet, not while the light was still on the steeple, so he sat down on the stoop to watch it fade, and his mother stood above him and laid her hand on his head, playing with his hair.

"You know, Turner," she said quietly, "you may have embarrassed your father."

Turner considered that for a moment. "Maybe," he said finally.

"Not that I'm so against it—embarrassing your father, I mean. It's good for ministers to be embarrassed now and again. Helps them to remember who they are."

"I'm not sure the Reverend Buckminster would agree," said Turner.

"Of course he wouldn't. That's when he needs it most."

The light on the steeple began to pink. Malaga, Turner thought, would already be in deep shadow, lying low in the water as it did. He had never been there in the dark, but he imagined it now, him standing on the shore and making out the waves only when they broke. Up above, the sky would be spangled, and he could sit side by side with Lizzie and watch the stars fall out of their places in sudden shrieks of light. The gulls would be quiet. The light from Lizzie's house would throw a yellow column onto the sand. And they would move closer together when the sea breeze got into mischief.

That's how it would be at night on Malaga Island.

The light began to disappear by the far end of Parker Head. The houses were still mostly dark, everyone being down to Thayer's haymeadow playing with their last baseball. Soon they would come home in groups, talking quietly beneath the naked maples, the striped blankets they had used to sit on now wrapped around their shoulders. The lights would come on and throw their columns across from one house to another, and the coal stoves would be stoked against the coming cold of the fall night as the town settled into evening.

That's how it would be at night on Parker Head, where folks knew that, come winter, their houses would still be on Parker Head, not floating down the New Meadows.

Turner wondered what it would be like to float down the New Meadows with his house on a raft, floating to where he did not know. Suddenly, he wasn't so sure about lighting out for the Territories. Suddenly, he wondered if having a house wrapped around him wasn't something he wanted a whole lot more.

It was sure enough what Lizzie Bright wanted.

Turner heard the first group coming back from the game. His mother took her hand from his head and backed up a bit into the darkness of the porch. "Don't stay out too much longer," she said. "It gets cold so quickly here." Turner nodded, listening to her as she closed the door on the town and disappeared into the house. The group passed, did not wave to him as it went on down Parker Head, hushed.

Turner wondered what Darwin might have said about the evolutionary advantages of being silent. He figured they might be considerable. He figured he might give it a try the next time he met Willis Hurd.

Four more groups came by, one after another, laughing as they passed by the parsonage. The last group held Reverend Buckminster, who separated from them and came up the stairs, then went by Turner silently into the house. The purple darkness had rolled farther and farther up Parker Head, rolling in front of it thin, wispy lines of silken fog that hovered chest high over the ground, like ribbons waiting for racers to part them.

When Parker Head quieted and it seemed that there would be no more laughing groups up from the haymeadow, Turner jumped off the stoop and strode with giant strides down to the street, breaking one ribbon after another, leaving them swirling and re-forming behind him, leaving his house deeper and deeper in the purple night, and coming finally to the darkened, empty house of Mrs. Hurd—and seeing someone standing on her porch. He stepped closer, and closer still, until he was close enough to see who it was who stood there.

It was Willis. He was painting the shutters yellow.

Turner walked up the porch steps. "Willis, it's dark as all get out. What are you doing?"

Willis spun around at the sound of Turner's voice, but then he turned back to the painting. "What does it look like I'm doing?"

"Painting shutters."

"Gee, you know how to hit a baseball and you're smart, too."

"You're painting in the dark."

"I'm painting in the dark."

"Because you don't want your father to know."

"I told you you were smart."

"It's for your grandmother."

Willis did not answer. He went on with his painting, covering the green shutters with sunlight yellow.

"You have another brush?" asked Turner.

Willis stopped painting. "Why didn't you hit that last pitch? You could have hit any one of those twice as far as the center fielder, but you didn't. Not even the last one. So why didn't you hit it?"

"Because everyone expects green shutters."

Willis stared at him. He stared at him for a long time. "There's another brush in the pail in that corner. There by the strawberry red. Are you fast?"

"Not especially."

"That's all right," said Willis. "You can hit a baseball so high that God can catch it without stooping. You don't have to be fast at painting shutters."

Turner took the brush and dipped it in the paint can. He moved beside Willis, painting in the dark. Heaven only knew what the shutters would look like come morning. But they would be yellow again. Just as Mrs. Hurd had kept them.

He began to paint, while behind him the stars glittered for all they were worth—which was considerable—and every single one of them held its place in this night's sky without falling. Every single one.

CHAPTER

9

A round and golden moon rolled low along the horizon for the next few days, too huge and weighty to rise up any higher into the sky. When it finally began to shed its weight and loft higher, it lost its golden hue, and the light became grayer. The air began to frost every night, and the stars to glitter more coldly, and so October came upon Phippsburg and Malaga Island. The cold snapped the tethers of the last leaves, and they fell straight down onto Phippsburg's roads and over the gravesites of Malaga. Even the pine trees down to Thayer's haymeadow put on their darker green and hunched their branches closer as the mornings came in colder and colder. It would not have surprised anyone to see the first flakes of snow.

Turner ran to the shore every day now, the *forbidden* having been silently lifted—or at least not imposed. From the granite ledges he could count twenty, sometimes more, plumes of white woodsmoke rising from the houses on the island, but each time he went, there seemed to be fewer, though the days grew colder. Slowly, little by little, souls were drifting away from the island, their own tethers snapped. And the houses, left soulless, died—windows glassless, doors hanging on single hinges, some of the clapboard already pruned.

Usually, Lizzie would be watching for him. He would wave from the top of the ledges with both his hands over his head, and she would run down to the dory, push off, and be across by the time he had climbed down. Once over on Malaga, they would go up to her house to see her granddaddy—he was always propped up on his elbows and waiting for Turner—and then they would go down to the shore until the sea breeze turned too cold for them to sit by the waves. They'd walk across the island, through the quiet green cemetery, past the foundation of the Tripp house, and then around the whole island, hardly talking, hardly needing to. Everything was as quiet as quiet could be.

If Lizzie wasn't there waiting for him by the shore, Turner would figure her granddaddy needed her, and he would wait, hoping she might come around the turn. If she didn't, he would walk home with his coat wrapped about him, a tang of salt in his mouth.

Back at First Congregational, folks were quiet around Turner, though Deacon Hurd had stopped him outside church the Sunday after the game. "Still can't get a hit off my Willis's pitching, can you, Turner?" He had laughed, then stopped suddenly and stared at Turner. "What's that on the tip of your ear, boy?"

"On the tip of my ear?"

"Looks like yellow paint. Have you been painting anything yellow the last few days?"

"Nothing around my house needs painting," Turner said, which was not a lie at all—sort of.

"Then what's that on your ear?"

"It's an old family disease that keeps coming back, no matter what I do."

"Old family disease?"

"My grandfather got it from missionary work. Somewhere in the Galápagos Islands."

That was as out loud as an out-loud lie could be, but it was such a good one that Turner couldn't feel too bad about using it. Especially with Deacon Hurd.

"In the Galápagos, my grandfather shouted, 'Unclean, unclean,' whenever someone came near him."

Deacon Hurd backed away when Turner held out his hand to shake.

"An old family disease?" said Turner's father after the evening service. "You told Deacon Hurd that your grandfather gave you an old family disease?"

"Well, that he might have gotten sick once while doing missionary work."

"Your grandfather did missionary work in Iceland. I don't think people in Iceland call out, 'Unclean, unclean!' And how did you get yellow paint on the tip of your ear? No. I don't want to know."

Turner obliged him.

The next Sunday after services, Willis Hurd nodded to Turner as he filed out with the rest of the congregation to shake Reverend Buckminster's hand. (No one was shaking Turner's hand.) "Next time keep your ears out of the paint," said Willis, and went on to the minister. Turner decided he probably didn't hate Willis so much anymore.

Turner was still playing the organ for Mrs. Cobb on Saturday and Sunday afternoons, and hoping that Lizzie would come. He and Mrs. Cobb waited together by the back door for her. Usually, she wasn't there, but every now and again she'd run across the backyard and up the stairs, and Mrs. Cobb would sniff and say something about being kept waiting for the only pleasure she had left to her. Then they'd process down the hall and into the parlor, and Mrs. Cobb would sit in her chair, Turner at the stool, and Lizzie on the floor against the horse-hair chair, and Turner would begin.

Mrs. Cobb had taken to "Swell the Anthem, Raise the Song," and since it had nothing in it about dying, Turner played it almost every time. All six verses. And Mrs. Cobb would sing along. All six verses. Her silvery voice, dry with gray age, warbled a bit and missed more high notes than it hit. But Turner simply played more loudly to help her out.

She never failed to remind Turner that he was to listen for her last words, and that the paper and pen were atop the organ. She was ready to go whenever the good Lord called her, she said, and so Turner—and Lizzie, too, if she was there—had best be prepared for the worst. Any day. Any hour. Any moment.

Turner tried to look resolute whenever she said this. Lizzie mostly looked panicked—which pleased Mrs. Cobb no end. She would cough through the playing to remind them of the potential of the moment, and shake her head at the frailty of human flesh.

As October turned whiter and colder, Mrs. Cobb turned whiter and colder, too. Walking from the back door to the parlor was more a shuffle and less a spurt, and her singing grew more and more patchy—a line here and a line there, but never a full verse anymore. Her hands lay on top of the armrests as if they needed a place to sit after a lifetime of clenching, and in fact, she seemed to be settling into stillness, quietly and crankily.

The last Sunday in October, she waited in the parlor for Lizzie, too shaky to stand in the cold. She said nothing when Lizzie and Turner came in. She did not pick up the afghan that had fallen from her knees. Turner wondered if she might even fall asleep—so he played soft and low.

"Are hymns always so slow?" she asked after the third one. Turner looked back. "Not always."

"And so soft? Good Lord, if you're going to play the hymn, Turner Buckminster, play the hymn!"

So he played more quickly, and more loudly, Lizzie grinning the whole time, until Mrs. Cobb told him that he was playing too quickly and too loudly. "You'd think a minister's son would know how to play a hymn with reverence. Wouldn't you think so, girl?"

"Yes, ma'am, I surely would," Lizzie said, and then put her hand to her mouth, startled. Turner wheeled about on the organ stool.

"She does talk!" said Mrs. Cobb.

Lizzie stared at her.

"All these days, and never a word."

"I guess I never did have one to say," said Lizzie.

And Mrs. Cobb, cranky Mrs. Cobb, leaned forward and laid her hands against Lizzie's cheeks and held them there, slightly trembling. "Oh my land," she said quietly, "I had too many, but never the right ones for you. Oh, oh," and suddenly, quickly, she lay back against the chair.

Turner stood, and Lizzie pulled the afghan up around Mrs. Cobb's knees. She looked at Turner, then at Lizzie. She took a deep and rattling breath. Her eyes opened, closed, opened again, pale and opaque.

"Get your father," said Lizzie. "Hurry."

"Turner," Mrs. Cobb said.

"We're here, Mrs. Cobb."

Another deep and rattling breath. "'Safely to the mountains lead me. Safely to my heavenly home. Safely to Your mansions guide me. Never, oh never, to walk alone.'" Then she leaned back and closed her eyes.

"Mrs. Cobb?"

Her eyes stayed shut.

"Mrs. Cobb?"

She breathed twice more, gave a little cough, breathed once again.

"Mrs. Cobb?"

"She's gone," said Lizzie.

"No, she's not. She's still breathing."

Lizzie looked at her. "She's not breathing."

Turner put his ear to her mouth. "Yes, she is. She's still breathing."

Lizzie put her ear to her mouth. "I guess so," she said.

Together they watched Mrs. Cobb head to the mountains, and Turner took Lizzie's hand in his without even knowing it. They held their breaths, waiting for Mrs. Cobb's last. They hardly dared blink.

"You need to write the words down," whispered Lizzie.

Turner took the paper from the organ. He dipped the pen and wrote quickly.

"You got them?"

"I got them."

"Let me read it." She took the paper. "It was *walk* alone, not *be* alone."

"It was *be* alone."

"It was *walk* alone."

"Can't you even get that right? It was *walk* alone," said Mrs. Cobb. Her eyes were open and she was staring at them. "*Walk* alone." She sat up straight and let the horsehair gallop up beneath her. "It doesn't matter now anyway. I'll have to come up with a whole new set of last words. Something easier to catch, I guess." She glared at Turner.

"Mrs. Cobb, we thought you were . . ."

"I did, too, or I wouldn't have said my last words. And they were such nice last words."

"They were," said Lizzie.

"Oh hell," said Mrs. Cobb, "it's warm here. Get me a ginger ale."

Turner and Lizzie went to the icebox to get a ginger ale. "I told you she wasn't dead," said Turner.

"Well, let's just get you a black bag and call you doctor."

"She was breathing."

"Yes, doctor."

Lizzie grabbed a ginger ale and pried the cap off, and together they went back into the parlor.

"She was breathing the whole time. You just couldn't tell," whispered Turner.

"Here, Mrs. Cobb," said Lizzie, and held out the bottle.

Mrs. Cobb did not take it.

"Mrs. Cobb," said Lizzie again.

Mrs. Cobb did not open her eyes.

"I don't think she's breathing," said Turner.

Lizzie glared at him, then turned back. "Mrs. Cobb?"

But there were no more words to speak.

Turner had never seen death before. He had been to funerals, but never to anyone's he knew more than by name. But there the bodies were closed up, and it was almost hard to believe that a person lay inside the box, covered with linen and flowers and candlesticks.

But here was death with its dart, having spurted into the house as bold as you please and snapped its chilly fingers. Mrs. Cobb was no longer clenching the arms of her chair, and she was no longer fussing at the organ music, and she was no longer humming to the refrain. She was just no longer.

Lizzie took Mrs. Cobb's hands, laid them in her lap, and

covered them with the afghan. She straightened her dress and brushed the hair off her forehead. Then she bent down and kissed her on the forehead.

"I'm not sure you're supposed to kiss a dead person," said Turner.

"You going to write down her last words?"

"'Oh hell, it's warm here. Get me a ginger ale'?"

"You going to write them down?"

"I'm not going to write down 'Oh, hell, it's warm here. Get me a ginger ale.'"

"You going to lie about her last words?"

"Yes."

"You can't lie about somebody's last words, Turner."

"I better go get my father," he said, and sprinted from Mrs. Cobb's house to the parsonage, from the parsonage to the Hurd house, and from the Hurd house to get Dr. Pelham, who came walking about as fast as he could with the black leather case he would not need to open. Lizzie was gone when Turner came into the parlor with the doctor, but Reverend Buckminster was there, and Deacon Hurd, and no end of folks came in while he examined her—though, Turner thought, anyone with half an eye could tell she had before them gone.

Turner was pushed farther and farther back, wondering why they didn't see that Mrs. Cobb would have hated all the fuss, that they were shoving furniture from where it was supposed to be, that they had bunched up the throw rugs in the front hall. Maybe this was what death was—when no one cared about one dang thing you had cared about.

And then Mr. Stonecrop was there, his large self parting the crowd like Moses holding out his staff over the Red Sea. Murmurs stilled and silence settled. Even Dr. Pelham stood. Mr. Stonecrop leaned over the body and put his ear to Mrs. Cobb's mouth. He stayed there a long time, and when he straightened up, he had taken possession of the situation. "She has gone to the heavenly reward she so richly deserved," he pronounced. "Before Reverend Buckminster leads us in prayer, we must know: Mrs. Cobb was waiting all her life, it seems, to say her last words. Was anyone here to hear them? Was anyone here to tell us what they were?"

"Turner?" asked his father.

Every eye came upon him. "Yes, sir."

"You were here."

"Yes, sir."

"Did you hear her last words?"

Turner nodded.

"Can you tell us what they were?"

"No, no, Reverend," said Mr. Stonecrop. "Not here. Not like this. Let young Buckminster write down her last words. Then let them be read aloud when we come to pay our final respects."

Murmurs of approval.

"Just as you say, Mr. Stonecrop," agreed Deacon Hurd.

"I'm not sure . . . ," Turner began.

"Perhaps you might lead us in prayer now, Reverend," suggested Mr. Stonecrop.

While they all closed their eyes and bowed their heads, Turner went out to the porch. The first snow of the year was just beginning, the flakes so light that they hardly fell. They crystallized in the bright air and hovered, twirled a bit to catch the light on their angles, and then waited for a breeze to waft them away. As people came and went, he sat there looking across the street at Mrs. Hurd's house—the shutters and door painted green again—thinking how soon it had been after he had met them that Mrs. Hurd and Mrs. Cobb had both lighted out for their own Territories.

He thought through Mrs. Cobb's last words again. He closed his jacket, hunched his hands into his pockets, and set off to the spot on the shore where he hadn't jumped on that very day he had met Mrs. Cobb.

And when he got there, he found Lizzie sitting on the edge of the leap, holding a curl of yellow birch bark.

"You know this place?"

"I've lived here all my life. You've lived here a few months. You think there's a whole lot of places you know about that I don't?"

He sat down beside her. "Lizzie, I never saw anyone die before."

"I did. My mother."

"Is it always like that? One second she was here, and the next second she was gone. I mean, really gone."

"That's what it's like."

Together they watched as the green sea lolled about, the waves hardly peaked enough to break against the rocks. The snowflakes were bigger now, and they fell more heavily past Lizzie and Turner, their sharp angles slicing into the bulky sea. They disappeared in less than a moment, and the sea hardly noticed them at all.

"You tell anyone what her last words were?"

"Not yet."

"You going to?"

"I suppose you're right and I have to."

"When?"

"Mr. Stonecrop wants my father to read them at her funeral."

"Well," said Lizzie, "it'll be something folks talk about."

They watched the waves come in, so bulbous and full, as though they had all the time in the world—and more.

"They never stop," said Turner.

"My granddaddy is going to die," said Lizzie.

Turner watched the snowflakes fall even faster. Then he reached over and took her cold hand in his.

❧

The funeral for Mrs. Cobb was three days later. Turner wrote out Mrs. Cobb's last words and gave them to his father, who put them in his front coat pocket, still folded. The whole congregation watched the paper in his pocket during the prayer for peace. They watched it while Lillian Woodward droned the hymns. They watched it while Reverend Buckminster delivered the eulogy. And they watched it when he removed it from his pocket and held it out to them.

"Such has been the beauty of this saintlike life. Such has been the glory of her passing. And at the moment of death, there can be no greater testimony to the Christian life than the final words of the dearly departed."

Turner was sweating enough to wilt even his starched shirt.

Reverend Buckminster unfolded the paper. It was upside down, and he turned it over slowly. Slight laughter from the congregation.

Turner sweated in places he didn't think he could sweat.

Reverend Buckminster was silent and still.

"Read it aloud, Reverend," called Mr. Stonecrop.

Reverend Buckminster cleared his throat. He cleared it again. "It's quite . . . it's quite short," he said.

Murmurs in the congregation. Turner felt sweat dripping into in his eyes.

Reverend Buckminster cleared his throat again. "'The Lord is my shepherd. I shall not want,'" he said.

"Oh," from the congregation, disappointed.

"'Yea, though I walk through the valley of the shadow of death, I will fear no evil.'"

"Well, who's going to bother remembering that?" Turner heard behind him.

"Let us turn to hymn one hundred eighteen," announced Reverend Buckminster. He looked pointedly down at Turner. "Amazing Grace."

And when the sweet sounds of that hymn were finished, the pallbearers carried Mrs. Cobb's casket down the center aisle, followed by the minister and his wife—Turner a good deal behind them—and then the rest of the congregation. She was buried with her people in the cemetery behind First Congregational, straight in front of the headstone that marked the family plot, not far from her grandfather of the perfect picket fence. It was snowing again, and the air was so sharp and cold that most of the congregation, having already shown proper respect by coming to the funeral service, and having been disappointed by the resolution of the mystery of her last words, went home before the burial. But Turner stood by the graveside, along with his mother and father.

"Perhaps," said Deacon Hurd as he finished the final prayer, "you might say her last words once more, Reverend."

Another clearing of the minister's throat. "I think a holy silence might best become her," he said, and bowed his head.

When the committal was over, Turner told his parents he would stay to help the grave digger.

"No need for that," said his mother.

"I think she might like me to be here," said Turner, looking at his father.

"No need for that," said old Mr. Thayer, who had dug more graves for more years than he cared to count.

"I think she might like me to be here," said Turner, still looking at his father.

He stayed, and when old Mr. Thayer began to fill in the

grave, Turner took the shovel from him and filled in most of it himself. He was almost done when Lizzie appeared from out of the woods. "I think she might like me to be here," she said, and Turner handed her the shovel.

"That does beat all," said old Mr. Thayer, and he watched Lizzie fill in the grave and pat the cold earth tight over Mrs. Cobb. Turner and Lizzie stood by the grave as he gathered his tools and left, shaking his head. Together they sang "I Have Some Friends Before Me Gone."

"Your daddy read the last words?"

"He read them."

"He say them out loud?"

"No. He said something else."

"You're not supposed to lie about someone's last words."

"She won't mind."

Lizzie reached down and smoothed the bulge of the grave. "Plant some violets here in the spring," she said.

"We'll plant them together."

But she shook her head. "Turner, look at things straight on, the way they're going to be." She stood up suddenly, then ran, twisting through the stones, leaving Turner alone beside the grave.

Before he walked home, he went past Mrs. Cobb's house and leaned against her grandfather's fence. He could almost hear his own organ music coming out, and he gripped the pickets so hard that he could feel them real and solid, things that had lasted a good long time and would probably last a good deal longer. Even when he could no longer hear the music, he could feel the pickets in his hand, the wood covered with layer after layer of whitewash, standing guard around the house for who knew how many winters. Past the fence, the house stood straight and ruled as it had for two centuries—maybe more. It seemed as solid as the granite on which it was built, and Turner marveled that it could still be so after Mrs. Cobb had gone.

Turner didn't know if he should be comforted because the house still stood, or afraid because it didn't care. Or both.

Three days later, he had another reason to think of Mrs. Cobb's house.

Turner knew that most of the business of any church happened right after the Sunday morning service, when everyone was breathing easy because the week's sermon had been successfully endured, the wheezing organ playing politely excused, and the tithing accepted as one of life's necessary hardships. While the congregation filed past the minister, exchanges were made, bargains agreed upon, transactions completed, and announcements announced.

And it was an announcement that Mr. Stonecrop made as he gripped his minister's hand and stood close to him.

"Mrs. Cobb's will was read last night," he said too loudly.

There is nothing for quieting a crowd like announcing that a will has been read.

"Did she have family?" asked Reverend Buckminster.

"Not a single living soul she would lay claim to. And even if she did, she didn't have a fortune to leave."

"She had the house."

"Yes, Reverend Buckminster, she had the house, sitting on the prettiest piece of property on Parker Head. Probably worth more than she could have ever imagined to some city folks from New York looking for a summerhouse in a town gearing up for the tourist trade."

"I suppose so, Mr. Stonecrop."

The congregation was edging in closer now, considering what Mrs. Cobb should have done to remember some kindness they had gone out of their way to show her.

"Reverend Buckminster, you sent your boy over to read to her, didn't you?"

Reverend Buckminster looked at Turner for a moment. "Yes, I did, Mr. Stonecrop. Most every afternoon this summer."

"And on Sundays, too?"

"And some Saturdays."

Mr. Stonecrop slapped Reverend Buckminster on the shoulder. "Reverend, you're more conniving than I thought." He looked around at the congregation as if to include them in his joke.

"Conniving?"

"The situation might lead some of us here to think for a moment—just for a moment, of course—that you had foreseen this very possibility, and so sent young Buckminster here to Mrs. Cobb to create this—we'll call it a situation."

Turner could see that his father was feeling his own situation moving away from him. He adjusted his robes, then his glasses. "Mr. Stonecrop," he said, "you have me at a loss. What situation do you mean?"

"I shall speak it plainly and bluntly, Reverend. This house, which might have been left to the town to fund a coming prosperity, was left instead"—and here he focused accusing eyes on Turner—"to your son."

A general murmur of disappointment and dismay. A general sense that the parishioners of First Congregational had been cheated out of something that was due them.

"Mrs. Cobb has left her house to Turner?"

"Yes."

"My son, Turner?"

"Now you have a grasp of the situation. What do you intend to do about this?"

The Reverend Buckminster looked at Turner, and Turner suddenly had the impression that his father was seeing him for the first time as someone more than his son. It almost frightened him.

Reverend Buckminster looked back to Mr. Stonecrop. "I suppose we'll have to see about the legalities," he said.

"Legalities!" Mr. Stonecrop almost shouted. "It is a mighty poor parson who hides behind legalities, sir. Your son made his way into Mrs. Cobb's household and so ingratiated himself that he has inherited a great deal of money that ought properly to belong to the people of this town."

Turner saw his father draw up. "Your implication, Mr. Stonecrop, that I have done this purposefully—" But Mr. Stonecrop shook him off.

"Implications mean nothing. Legalities mean nothing. The only thing that means anything is what you do with the house. And I suspect that your congregation—indeed, every soul in Phippsburg—will be watching what you do with it."

Reverend Buckminster looked down at Turner again, and Turner wondered if he was expected to speak. The silence was sharp enough that it seemed almost to wedge its point against his throat.

But silent or not, Turner did know what he would do with the house. He had known from the moment Mr. Stonecrop had announced that he had inherited it.

Still, the disapproval of First Congregational stifled him like the silence a fog brings upon the ocean. And when his father spoke again, he sounded like an invisible buoy. "We will do what is good and honorable in the Lord's eyes."

"Don't neglect," suggested Mr. Stonecrop, "to do what is good and honorable in the town's eyes as well. I think you may find, Reverend, that they are the very same thing." Mr.

Stonecrop moved off into the foggy silence, and the rest of the congregation passed quietly, most hands extended, some not. Only when they were finally all gone, and the fog with them, did Turner feel the old familiar sea breeze coming in at the doors and pulling him outside.

It had snowed during the service and was snowing still—a crisp and cold snow that didn't melt as soon as it struck. Already Parker Head was covered, and the ground was frozen enough that where the congregation had walked and driven carriages, the road showed through but the snow hadn't changed to slush. Turner felt the cold air deep down when he breathed it in, and the snow that fell on his lashes and into his hair stayed there, gleefully stubborn.

The snow fell on the maples, on the aspens all along Parker Head. It gathered on the oak leaves and drooped even those sturdy branches down. It clotted the cedars. All three Buckminsters stood on the steps of the First Congregational and watched it come down, clean, tasting of the salt air, whirling about in a joyous jig—swinging partners and do-si-doing and promenading as if it were a whitened barn dance.

"'A gust, shrieking from the north, strides full on his sail and lifts the waves to heaven,'" said Turner, trying to smile.

"Not a bad translation," said his father. "But *Franguntur remi,* 'The oars snap.'" He crossed Parker Head and slowly climbed the steps of the parsonage.

Turner's mother wiped off the snow collecting on Turner's hair. "The house is yours," she said. "Don't listen to what anyone says. She gave it to you because she wanted you to have it."

Turner nodded. "And I know what she wanted me to do with it."

"Then you had better do that."

"And if Mr. Stonecrop doesn't like what I want to do with it?"

"Then," said Mrs. Buckminster, standing tall and straight, and the blood reddening her cheeks, "then the profound Mr. Stonecrop will be profoundly disappointed." She shook her head, and together they laughed out loud in the falling snow of Parker Head on the steps of First Congregational, risking the disapproval of any parishioners who might have seen them just then.

"Go on," she finally told Turner. "Go on and disappoint him." And Turner went to do just that.

So it was not very long until Turner, having slid and sprinted, sprinted and slid, stood at the granite ledges and began climbing down, kicking the snow off the footholds, and finally jumping onto the dark gray mudflats that wouldn't abide a single snowflake to freeze on them, no matter now much cold the sea breeze brought in. The snow wasn't so thick that Turner couldn't see across to Malaga, but it was thick enough that probably no one would be out on the water. He looked above the tip of the island, hoping he might at least see the smoke rising from Lizzie's house, but he couldn't make it out at all. Probably because of the snow.

It seemed to him that he might do best to just go on home and wait for a better day when there might be a dory or two out. He would have to be a dang fool to stand on a mudflat that was doing its best not to freeze, in a snowstorm, waiting for a friendly boat to take him across. But then again, maybe it wasn't such a terrible thing to be a dang fool sometimes. Maybe, he thought, it was just what you were supposed to be. So he wrapped his arms around himself and stood back against the ledges, waiting.

He waited for a long time, walking up and down the beach, stamping his feet to keep the blood moving, until it got so cold that the mud really did start to freeze, and he thought that maybe being a frozen dang fool might not be a good idea. He might have left then and there if he hadn't seen the Easons' dory butting its prow against the waves as it came down the New Meadows, trying to find its place somewhere between the white water and the white air. Turner ran to the edge of the tide and waved his arms, hollering as loudly as he could, though his voice seemed to be drawn up in the snowy wind.

Whether he was heard or seen, the dory turned to him and began taking some of the waves just a bit broadside until it came square to Turner, then let itself be swept to the shore.

"It's one awful day to be digging clams," called Mr. Eason.

"I'm hoping that you could take me across."

Mr. Eason looked at him a long time. "You know, boy, sometimes it's best to leave things be."

"This isn't something to be left, Mr. Eason. I've got some news for Lizzie. The best news."

Another long stare. "Well," he said, "it's not my place." He motioned for Turner to step in, then used an oar to shove the dory back into the New Meadows, flat against the waves but steady enough.

Turner felt that he was hovering in some unearthly place. With the snow and the spray from the waves wafting against the boat, they seemed to be in neither air nor water, or maybe in both, and the queasy, uneasy feeling came upon him that he didn't know where he belonged—and wasn't sure he could find his way.

Mr. Eason, rowing hard against the waves, said nothing, not even when the waves turned and he began following them in to Malaga. Turner stepped out first and dragged the boat up on shore, and Mr. Eason jumped out to haul beside him. Once the boat was past the high-tide mark, he pointed down across the shore. "You'll find her at my house," he said, and turned back to the boat.

Then Turner knew why he hadn't been able to make out the smoke. And he didn't want to know why.

He walked slowly, brushing the snow off and shaking it from his shoes now and again. Although he was cold, the tips of his fingers hurting and his eyes watering some, he didn't hurry. Maybe there wasn't even a need to hurry. He smelled woodsmoke and passed a stack of old lobster traps, blown over and the staves broken in, then a heap of firewood guarded pitifully by some old barrels, also broken. The woodsmoke grew stronger, and he passed a stand of thick pines and was there. He stood and stared at the house as if wondering how it was holding itself together, layered as it was with patches and odd boards. He kicked the snow off his shoes once more, brushed it from his hair, and thought he probably looked like a dang fool standing there in the snow.

The door opened, and there was Lizzie, just wrapping a red shawl around herself—a shawl that needed about as many patches as the house had. She walked to him and stood by him. "Do you want to see?" she asked, quietly, so quietly in the snow.

Turner nodded. She took him by the elbow, and together they walked back across the island to the graveyard, where there was one new mound, piled higher than the others but still covered by scudding snow like the rest of them. And they stood in the quiet of the snow as it settled all around them.

"We'll plant violets here in the spring," said Turner, but Lizzie did not answer.

Afterward, they walked together, silent, around to the tip of the island and into the deserted house that had been Lizzie's home. Already it seemed as if no one had lived there for a very long time. None of the furniture remained. The house had been emptied and even swept out neatly; the only thing on the floor now was the snow, in soft piles that had drifted in through the cracks. It was as cold as cold can be, the cold almost like a presence.

"No one lives here anymore," said Lizzie simply.

They went outside and stood by the door, facing the gray and white sea that was so very silent, rolling into the shallows, its spume blown off into the wind.

"He died while he was asleep," said Lizzie. "Mr. Eason came by and called in the morning, and I told him not to call too loud since Granddaddy might be just asleep, after all. But then he came in, and I knew Granddaddy wasn't just asleep. So Mr. Eason, he brought me up to his home, and came back here and took care of him. And then he went up and dug the . . . dug the hole and carried Granddaddy to the coffin he'd already built, and we stood there, me and the Easons, and not one of us knew what to say, because Granddaddy had always done the words."

Turner stood next to her as her words broke the snow, and he felt again as he had in the boat, somewhere between two worlds and drowning because he couldn't find his way in either one. And just when he thought he might be lost entirely, the snow stopped, Lizzie said, "Oh," and the waves began to sound again with their frothy roars. The sea breeze bent the pines behind them, blew across their backs, and sped out over the water, tearing the whitecaps back even as they came to shore. With a ripping groan, one of the snow-laden pines wrenched itself free from the rocks and toppled, slowly at first, then faster and faster, until it swept onto the ledges beneath it, its branches thrusting a boiling cloud of snow into the air.

Together they stood.

"Nothing stays the same, does it?" said Lizzie. And Turner, who found himself breathing hard, nodded.

10

ON top of the fallen pine—both of them still quivering from the crash of the thing—they walked where no one had ever walked before, shaking the wet snow from the branches, balancing against the trunk, which gave beneath their feet, until they came close to the very point. "We can't go any further," Lizzie called back to him.

"Lizzie," said Turner, "I've got a house."

"Of course you've got a house."

"No, no. Mrs. Cobb left me her house. In her will. It's mine."

"She gave you her house? Why did she give you her house?"

"Because she figured you might need one."

Lizzie played with the branches that spread up between them, pulling at the needles. "Thank you, Turner Ernest Buckminster," she said quietly.

"We'll be neighbors," he said. "The house is big enough for the Easons, too. Then they can build a hundred hotels and it won't matter."

"Turner," said Lizzie, tightening the red shawl around her. "Turner, it *will* matter. The Easons won't be able to live in that house. Not me, either." She jumped down, and the tree bobbed up against Turner's weight.

"What do you mean, you won't be able to live in that house?"

"They won't let me."

Turner stepped off the trunk. "It's my house. It's my house to do what I want with."

"Turner . . ."

"No, Lizzie. You listen for once. They're already taking away your house. They're taking away the entire island. But they can't take away Mrs. Cobb's house, too, because it isn't theirs to take. It's mine."

"Turner, you never can look at things straight. Look at me. No, look at me. Look at my skin. It's black, Turner. No one in Phippsburg is going to let someone with skin as black as mine live with them. They're not."

"It won't make a bit of difference," he said.

"It won't make a bit of difference," he said, waving to her on the shore.

"It won't make a bit of difference," he said to Mr. Eason, rowing across in the dory.

It won't make a bit of difference, he said to himself on the road back to Phippsburg.

But each time he said it, he believed it less.

By the time he reached Parker Head, the sun had come out dully and shone on the brassy undersides of the high clouds. They looked heavy enough to fall into the sea, maybe to fall on top of Phippsburg itself, crushing the steeple of First Congregational and all the fine houses on Quality Ridge.

It won't make a bit of difference, he said to himself as he climbed the porch steps. Not one bit, he said as he opened the door.

But now he hardly believed it at all.

"Turner, is that you?" called his father.

Turner took off his boots and left them outside. Then he went to his father's study, where Mr. Stonecrop was filling the room. Turner's mother sat in a chair by the window, her hands discreetly clasped in her lap; Reverend Buckminster sat behind his desk, his sermon notes discreetly covering Darwin.

Turner wondered what Darwin would think of being covered by sermon notes.

He began to burn again.

Reverend Buckminster glanced at the grandfather clock. "Mr. Stonecrop and I were discussing what might be done with Mrs. Cobb's house. He has brought the keys over."

Turner saw that they were still in his hand.

"I believe we have come up with a fine, equitable solution to the situation," said Mr. Stonecrop. "The house will be sold for the benefit of the town. And since Mrs. Cobb obviously intended you to benefit from such a sale, young Buckminster, we shall put aside a percentage of the proceeds to be held in trust for your ministerial education." Mr. Stonecrop pocketed one of the keys.

"My ministerial education?" Turner looked at his mother.

"So that you might follow your father, as he followed his," said Mr. Stonecrop.

"To be a minister?"

"That is what a ministerial education would be for, certainly."

Turner felt the Territories moving farther west. He looked at the pile of sermon notes and felt the bulk of a ministerial education covering him. He took a breath.

He had almost touched a whale.

"Well, Reverend Buckminster," said Mr. Stonecrop, "I think everything is most satisfactorily concluded."

"No, sir," said Turner.

Mr. Stonecrop looked hard at him.

"No, sir," said Turner again.

Mr. Stonecrop looked harder still. "It is not the place of a young boy to question," he said slowly.

"I wonder," said Turner's mother, "if Turner hasn't already made plans for the house."

"Plans for the house?" Mr. Stonecrop now looked more than irritated. "What plans could you have made so quickly?"

"I've decided to give the house to Lizzie Griffin and the Easons."

"Jake Eason?" Mr. Stonecrop stood.

"Yes, sir."

"Jake Eason from Malaga Island?"

"Yes, sir."

"And Lizzie Griffin, that Jonah's daughter?"

"Yes, sir."

Mr. Stonecrop leaned over the desk. "You realize, Buckminster, that she is as black as the ace of spades!"

Reverend Buckminster sat silent.

Mr. Stonecrop took two steps across the room, two steps back. He glared at Reverend Buckminster and then at Mrs. Buckminster. He glared especially long at Turner, who saw the word *homicide* spring into his mind. Turner wondered if the tendency toward homicide might be one of the multiform individual differences or slight variations that were introduced into a species by moments just such as this.

"By God, Buckminster, this is the result of your lackadaisical handling of your son—this after all the warnings we have given. Do you see how those people have brought him to this? But I won't have it. I won't have a Negro living in Phippsburg. What do you think we've been about these past months? Do you imagine there would be a single soul come up from Boston to summer in a town populated by them? A single soul? We brought you—all three of you—here to be a part of the new Phippsburg, but I can see now that you have no such interest."

"Mr. Stonecrop," said Reverend Buckminster, "nothing is decided yet."

"Lizzie doesn't have a house," said Turner. "And the Easons might not have one soon. What are they supposed to do? Float down the New Meadows and hope to tie up somewhere?"

"Let them head wherever they see fit to go. It's none of my affair, and nor, by the way, is it yours."

"I'm giving the house to Lizzie," said Turner.

He looked at Reverend Buckminster, expecting the disappointment he knew his father must feel. But his father's eyes were upon him, and they were not disappointed.

"Buckminster, this is your son. Have you nothing to say as the minister of this town, if not as his father?"

Then Turner saw his father stand like Aeneas with his two spears, pausing beside burning Troy and putting it all behind him, his face to an open world.

"What would you have me say, Mr. Stonecrop? That my own boy shouldn't find shelter for someone in need? That my own boy shouldn't care for the outcast?" Now he leaned across the desk. "By God, that my own boy shouldn't stand up—as his father should have stood up—against the money of the town when it set about to destroy a community that never harmed it, merely for the sake of tourists from Boston? Is that what you'd have me say to him?"

Mr. Stonecrop went to the door of the study. "Ethics are a fine thing to have, Reverend. You can take them out and wave them around like a flag whenever you feel a qualm of conscience. And all that flag-waving will make you feel just like you're up there in heaven with God Himself. But God has seen fit to set me to live in the here and now, Reverend. And I do what it takes to live in the here and now."

Turner's father reached over his desk and pulled away the sermon notes. "Have you read this book, Mr. Stonecrop? *The Descent of Man,* by Charles Darwin. Turner and I have been reading in it quite a bit together. We've already finished *The Origin of Species.* I suspect you might not recognize it."

"Are you, a minister of the gospel, taunting me with god-lessness, even while teaching it to your son?"

"Darwin writes that man is liable to slight variations, which are induced by general and complex laws."

"The deacons will hear of this."

"I have no doubt they will. But consider this, Mr. Stonecrop, my slight variation, induced by general and complex laws: I will not stand with you at the destruction of Malaga Island. I will instead stand with my son."

Mr. Stonecrop narrowed his eyes. Turner had never seen anyone do it in quite this way before, and he thought once again of homicide. "There will never be a Negro living in the town of Phippsburg," Mr. Stonecrop said quietly. "I will see to it myself." He flung the keys onto the floor.

That night, in the quiet of his dark room, while a deep and clear cold frosted the starlight over the town, those words came back to Turner: "I will see to it myself." He sat up in his bed and looked out the window. He stayed that way for a long time, as if to guard the world.

He guarded the world most nights through that next week. When he was more angry than afraid, he recited Virgil: "Of arms and the man I sing!"

He was more than halfway through the *Aeneid* now, and

getting faster at his hundred lines. After lunch and a chapter of Darwin—he did not mind the summaries—his father told him he was free to find Lizzie Bright. She waited for him by the pines above the granite ledges—it was too cold to wait down by the shore—and together they explored the New Meadows coast, watching everything hunker down for the winter: the chipmunks and the squirrels with their last cheekfuls of larder, the deer toward dusk with their heavier coats, the rabbits whitening except for the tips of their ears.

Every day Turner asked Lizzie to come live in Mrs. Cobb's house.

Lizzie would smile at him and shake her head. "Turner, they'll never let us," she said.

"It won't make a bit of difference," he said.

And she would smile again and tell him he didn't look at things straight on, and then she would find some mouse tracks in the snow and they would follow them until they disappeared beneath a small bank.

Mr. Stonecrop wasn't at church the next Sunday. At least, not at First Congregational. There were, in fact, quite a few souls of the Phippsburg faithful who did not come on that Lord's Day. Even Lillian Woodward failed to show for her prelude, and Turner found himself taking her place at the organ bench and looking over a mighty small congregation. The Newtons were there, with all the little Newtons. Deacon Hurd was there, and Willis, but none of the other Hurds. Reverend Buckminster waited for a few minutes past the hour to give the opening prayer, but the congregational singing that followed was thin, and Turner had to tone the volume down about as low as it could go if he was to hear any voices at all.

From the organ bench, Turner listened to his father preach as though he were addressing a house packed full of the saints, but he could also see his mother fidgeting in the front pew, opening and closing her Bible, taking out her handkerchief and twisting it in her hands until she realized what she was doing and put it away. Then she'd take it out a minute or two later and start all over again.

Turner imagined the houses up on Quality Ridge falling to the trumpets of the Hebrew host.

It didn't take too long to shake hands with folks after the service. Most of the congregation didn't meet the eyes of their tight-lipped minister. When Deacon Hurd went past, he nodded curtly. "There's a deacons' meeting this Wednesday night," he said.

"I'll be there."

"No, Reverend. For meetings of this sort, the bylaws tell me I have to inform the minister, not invite him."

Turner wondered if his mother might swing out her right arm and go for Deacon Hurd's nose, then his eye. That would be worth seeing. And he was sorely disappointed when Mrs. Buckminster simply shook the deacon's hand as he went on past.

But all thoughts of a bloodied deacon disappeared a few seconds later when Willis whispered to him, "Tonight. It's tonight," and then went on by, holding Turner's eyes with his own for as long as he could. Turner felt himself go cold in the center, a cold so deep it made him nauseated. He felt as though he were standing on a cliff over the sea.

Tonight, something would happen to Mrs. Cobb's house.

He did not tell his parents what Willis had said. They sat in silence through dinner, but it was not the same as the silence that had been there before. His parents' eyes often met, and sometimes they reached out to touch each other's hands. They ate quietly, glad to be together.

So Turner let them be glad together.

It turned out to be the coldest night Turner had spent in

Maine so far, the kind of night that let him know that fall was pretty much wrung out, and that deep winter was on its way to freeze the salt water out into the New Meadows. Turner lay in his room, shivering even though he was still dressed, listening to the familiar sounds of his parents moving around in the room below him, coming up the stairs, closing the door. Their quiet talk. He listened to the mantel clock chime the quarter hours and to the house tightening itself against the cold.

He figured he would leave the house just at midnight, but he got so fidgety that he couldn't wait that long, and around eleven-thirty he crept downstairs. Across the hall. Into his father's study for the keys to Mrs. Cobb's house. Back to the front hall. Slowly turned the doorknob and opened the door. The air was so cold it rasped in his throat, as cold as a hardened heart. He sat on the top porch step, put his shoes on, shivered, and then set off down Parker Head for Mrs. Cobb's house. *"Arma virumque cano,"* he said to himself, and wished he had Aeneas's arms.

He let himself in through Mrs. Cobb's back door—the door Lizzie had always used. Inside, only a faint starlight shone through the windows. He groped his way through the kitchen, down the hall, and to the front door, afraid to light a lamp, afraid to make a sound. Around him the house seemed huge, with rooms above and beneath him that he had never entered. Who knew what could be there? Who knew if Mrs. Cobb herself could be there, still trying somehow to get her last words right?

Turner shivered, and not only with the cold—though the Lord knew it was cold enough to shiver. His breath frosted the window in the door, and he stepped back, wondering if someone outside might be able to see him—or his breath. But outside, Parker Head was as quiet as the hall inside Mrs. Cobb's house.

Turner went into all the rooms on the first floor, his hands held out in front of him to feel anything he couldn't see. And when he got to each of the windows, he held his breath and peered out, looking for whatever it was Willis had meant was coming—though he wasn't sure what he would do when it came. He figured if someone snuck up to the house and looked in on him, he could pretty well startle whoever it was into a faint. But what would happen when he woke up and found it was only Turner inside?

He fumbled his way back to the parlor and reached around for the organ stool. He sat down on it, careful to keep his feet from the pedals. He let his fingers slowly stroke the silent keys, tapping out "I Have Some Friends Before Me Gone." He didn't need any light to find the notes, and the feeling of something so familiar on his fingertips kept him from thinking about a ghostly Mrs. Cobb.

He was in the middle of the third verse when he heard something upstairs creak four times—four separate times—and he knew that while he had been sitting alone in the dark, someone had come in.

Maybe someone who knew he was there.

Maybe even more than one someone who knew he was there.

In the cold, dead, dark air of Mrs. Cobb's house, Turner began to sweat.

He lifted his fingers from the keyboard and sat perfectly still. He felt his hearing sharpen and sharpen until it seemed like another sense entirely, reaching out and around him. He listened for a step. He listened for another creak. He listened for breathing.

Nothing.

He swiveled the organ stool around, slowly, slowly, slowly, stopping the moment a sound came from it. He opened his eyes as wide as he could.

Nothing.

He stood, put his hands out in front of him, and groped his way across the parlor. He stuck his head out into the hall and looked back toward the kitchen. But it was too dark to see anything. He turned the other way, then stopped. Suppose there was someone standing there, a pale face at the window? Or suppose there was someone standing in the very hall?

He turned quickly, afraid that the fear suddenly welling up in him might overtake him. There was no one in the hall. There was no one at the door.

Two more sharp creaks from overhead, like someone walking across a floor and trying not to be heard.

He would have to go upstairs.

He groped back up the front hall and around to the staircase, not swallowing. He set one foot on the first stair, and then the thought that maybe it was Lizzie Bright upstairs warmed him. She knew it was to be her house. Maybe it was so cold on Malaga that she had come in. Maybe she'd meet him at the top of the stairs with her hands on her hips, her head to one side, laughing at him.

For less than a second, the thought filled him with relief. For less than a second.

Because Lizzie had no key.

He began to climb the stairs. Freezing at every creak he made. Freezing at the silences. Listening with quick ears for any sound. Watching with sharpened eyes for someone to appear suddenly at the head of the stairs.

When he reached the top, he crouched down and looked around the hallway. There was more starlight up here, and he could see clearly. Three open doors, and a fourth, closed. He stayed still, watching, until his crouching legs began to hurt. Then he stood up and moved as silently as a murderer to the first open doorway and peered inside. A bedroom that hadn't been slept in for a hundred years.

To the second doorway. A sewing room. He could make out the trestle of the sewing machine, and the straight-backed chair behind it.

To the third doorway. But before he reached it, he heard the creak again. From behind the closed door.

He did not move for an eternity or two. Then he figured he could either run down the stairs and out of the house and let whatever was going to happen, happen, or he could pull open the door.

Another loud creak decided it: his eyes open wide; he bolted across the hallway, pulled the door open, shouted, "I see . . . ," and smashed into a flight of steep stairs, striking shins, knees, a hip, elbows, and his nose, which began bleeding. But he couldn't stop to staunch it now. He clambered up the stairs with his hands and feet, missing a step and stumbling, picking himself up, all the time crying, "I see you!" even though he couldn't see anything, and then, suddenly, he was at the top of the stairs and crouching again on a floor as cold as a ledge of granite and it seemed to him that he was suspended in the night sky over Phippsburg.

There was glass all around him—even above him. When he stood, his arms held out for balance, the whole town was laid before him, the houses black against the snow that reflected the silver starlight. The spire of First Congregational rose until it was itself a part of the night sky. He could make out Parker Head heading down to Thayer's haymeadow and the coast; its snowy backside showed between the bare trunks.

And above him, straight above him, the stars followed their own tides. He could almost see them move. His knees bent; he could feel the sea breeze wrapping itself around the cupola and leaning into it some, setting the frame to creaking cheerily at the familiar nudge. Turner set his hands against the freezing glass. Wouldn't Lizzie think this was fine, he thought. And with the thought, he stood on his tiptoes and looked out to where Malaga Island lay in the dark of the New Meadows.

But the island wasn't dark.

This high above town, Turner could see lanterns moving up and down and across Malaga—some in a line down by the coast, some clustered more toward the island's far side, blinking on and off and on again as they passed stands of trees. There must have been fifteen, twenty of them. Then the lanterns on the far side seemed to come together and grow suddenly brighter, until Turner realized that it wasn't lanterns he was seeing—it was a full fire shining a weird orange on the island's snow.

Then the door at the bottom of the stairs slammed shut so hard that the glass rattled around him.

He abandoned the starlight and scrambled down the dark steepness, shouting like the enraged Aeneas until he fell against the door, which did not yield. He stood and pounded, then sat back against the stairs and kicked at it with both feet.

"Strike three," he heard a voice say on the other side of the door. "You're out." Then footsteps down the stairs.

Turner pounded again, but the door had been bolted.

Breathless, Turner ran back up into the light of the cupola. Out on Malaga Island, the orange light flared higher, and a line of lanterns headed toward shore, disappearing from Turner's sight as they neared the granite ledges. Desperate, he looked down at the darkness of the town, but there was no one to call to. Pressed against the glass, his hand began to burn on the icy pane.

The glass.

Turner sat down on the floor of the cupola, held his legs

up, hoped that Mrs. Cobb wouldn't mind too much that he was about to do a whole lot more to her cupola than he had ever done to her grandfather's picket fence, and kicked against the glass.

It shattered around him. He kicked again and again, knocking shards out of the pane until he could crawl out onto the roof. It was, he knew as soon as he put his hand on it, a very icy roof, and it slanted more than he wished it did, and the elm branches that lay upon it looked more brittle in the dark cold than they did in the dark green of early fall.

"'Safely to Your mansions guide me. Never, oh never, to walk alone,'" said Turner, and let himself slide off the sill and down into the branches—which did not break, but which gathered him up like the pocket of a baseball glove catching a falling ball. Holding on to the elm, he drew himself across the roof, then crawled down the trunk and onto Parker Head Road.

He ran panting, grimacing with the cold air that struck deep into his lungs, hoping, praying that Malaga was not lost.

When the road gave way to the woods, he ran on, using the light on the snow to guide him, holding his arms out across his face to ward off the branches that swiped at him, hoping, praying.

And when he reached the granite ledges and looked across to Malaga, he could almost believe in hope and prayer.

Because there was nothing to show that the lanterns had been there. Not a sign. He could hear the waves quarrel as they made their way up the New Meadows, but no other sound. Turner lifted his face to the sea breeze and sniffed. Not even the scent of smoke. He thought about climbing down the ledges, but in the dark he wasn't sure he could find the holds. Some of them might even be iced over.

The moon came up, jumping right over a sea cliff to hang

above the horizon. And it laid its veil over the island, so that Malaga shone with a luminous silver—every stone, every pine—as if an artist had engraved it and set it on the water. For a moment, even the waves stopped, and the island held its breath, and Turner thought, This is how I'll always remember it. This is how it will always be.

Then, in the quiet of that whitening night, standing in new snow with the pine boughs coated above him, Turner felt the hand that he had feared all night long grab him by the shoulder.

Felt it spin him around.

Felt the roar of a shotgun blast flash into the night, a white explosion almost in his face that startled the sleeping gulls up into the air.

Turner screamed as he fell backward into the snow. He scuttled to the edge of the ledges, felt his hand miss, pulled himself back, and tried to get his legs under him. He could hardly see for the explosion, and he held one hand out to ward off whoever had shot at him.

"You're all right, boy. Nobody's going to hurt you."

Turner wasn't sure he was making out every word, what with the ringing in his ears and the clanging in his brain.

"It's the sheriff. Sheriff Elwell. Stand up. Nobody's going to hurt you."

Turner crawled away from the ledges and stood up unsteadily, as if the blast had loosened the granite beneath him and it was swaying with the quarrelsome waves.

"You all right?"

Turner tried to stop the swaying beneath him. He bent his knees, then decided he would do better back on the ground. The bright white spot that was his whole vision began to darken at the edges.

"A shotgun blast right up close to you sure is enough to

knock you down, isn't it, boy? There's lots of ways to knock a man down, and that's one of them. I took this shotgun away from a friend of yours just a little while ago, a Mr. Jake Eason. He had it pressed up against my chest at the time, and he was ready to pull the trigger."

Turner kept blinking, trying to darken the bright white. He could just make out the sheriff off to one side, standing tall and dark, the shotgun held up over his shoulder.

"I wanted you to know what it felt like, boy. Wanted you to know what one of your friends was about to do."

Turner wasn't sure if his clanging brain could make sense of the sheriff's words. He shook his head.

"You stick to your own kind. Better for you and your folks. Go on home."

Turner stood again, trying to straighten his knees. His brain was still clanging, but the ground was steadying. He could see more of the sheriff's outline now. He could see his face.

And Turner was filled with a stony, granite rage.

"Boy, you watch yourself." The sheriff backed up a step and leveled the shotgun from his shoulder. Turner could almost see him against the moonlight thrown up off the snow. He could see sudden fear. He could smell it.

"Lizzie was in Mr. Eason's house," Turner said.

"Maybe so, but she isn't there now. You're not understanding, boy. They're all crazy over there. They're not even right in the head most of the time."

"Lizzie was in that house," Turner repeated. "Did you blow a shotgun off above her, too?"

"As a matter of fact, I didn't need to. She just got up and went along quiet, like she was supposed to."

"Went where?"

"Where all the crazies go. Down to Pownal."

Turner leaped at him, screaming something out of his still-clanging brain. The sheriff backed away, tripped, and went down, and when the butt of the shotgun hit the ground, the other barrel exploded, its white roar glazing the snow around them. But Turner did not even pause. Not for a second. He was on top of the sheriff, pounding at anything he could pound at, leaping back when the sheriff brushed him off, battling like Aeneas, knowing that the battle he fought was a hopeless one, and crying, crying, crying at the hopelessness.

He wasn't ready to stop when his father first shined his lantern on him and pulled him away from the sputtering sheriff.

But he did.

Because he saw his father grab the sheriff by his coat, heft him to his feet, shake him, and toss him back on the ground. Then he reached down and picked up the still-smoking shotgun, turned toward the sea, and flung it spinning over the water, the circle of it shining in the moonlight as it flew over the ledges; over the New Meadows; Lord, maybe over Malaga Island itself; and on and on until the moon set and the night sky darkened once more.

Turner went to stand beside his father, his father of the flinging arm, his father of the heaving chest. "They've taken her away," he said.

"They've taken who away?"

"Lizzie. And the Easons with her."

His father looked at the sheriff.

"Phippsburg has to look after its own," the sheriff said, standing up. "Everyone around here has known for years that Jake Eason is crazy as a loon—him and his whole lot. Sooner or later they would all have gone to Pownal anyway. We did tonight what we should have done long ago."

"What you did tonight you didn't do for the sake of the town. You did it for yourselves."

"We are the town. Everyone around here seems to understand that except for you. You come here and act like you're still in Boston. But you're not. You're here. And in this town, we don't need someone from outside to tell us which way is up."

"Which way is up? By God, Sheriff, you're getting way ahead of yourself. A man who would send a little girl off to an insane asylum just so he could grab her land, he doesn't even know which way is down."

"This way," said the sheriff, and he grabbed Turner by the coat as Turner's father had grabbed him, half lifted him, and threw him back behind him, not even watching to see where he fell.

By the time Turner had spun around and looked up, his father—his father!—and the sheriff were gripping each other's arms and pushing back and forth, sliding and stumbling and tripping over rocks. By the time Turner had gotten to his knees, they had shoved each other close to the edge of the granite. And by the time Turner stood, the sheriff had suddenly let go and backed away as his father's arms windmilled in the moonlit air, and he was over the ledge.

The last thing Turner saw was his father's moonlit eyes.

CHAPTER

11

THE deacons' meeting on Wednesday night was as awkward as a deacons' meeting could get. Deacon Hurd had it all arranged: a typed-up agenda, a written-out prayer—and the formal deacon's letter to the congregation recommending that First Congregational dismiss Reverend Turner Buckminster from its pulpit. But with Reverend Turner Buckminster lying in the parish house with more ribs broken than not, with a leg smashed and his scalp laid open, and still unconscious after three days, Deacon Hurd wasn't eager to begin the meeting. And when Turner walked in just at the stroke of seven o'clock, it was even more deucedly awkward.

"Turner," said Deacon Hurd, "we're more grieved than we can say about your father. But this is a closed meeting of the church."

"Sir," said Turner, "the bylaws say that the minister may appoint a representative to act in his place if he is unable to attend any meeting of which he is a voting member. My mother looked it up this afternoon. She'd be here herself, but . . ."

"I'm not going to allow it," said Deacon Hurd.

Mr. Newton crossed the room and took down a copy of the bylaws from a shelf.

"Page fifteen," said Turner helpfully.

Mr. Newton turned to page fifteen. He looked up, smiling. "Unless you want to go against the bylaws, Deacon, I don't see that you have much of a choice."

"Then read the minutes and let's begin," said Deacon Hurd angrily. "He can stay if he wants."

"Don't you begin with prayer?" asked Turner, as sweetly and innocently as if he were a minister's son right out of a Sunday school book.

Deacon Hurd looked at him hard. "Let us pray," he said slowly, but Turner thought that the prayer he prayed wasn't rising much above First Congregational's steeple.

"Amen," said Deacon Hurd.

"Amen," said the rest of the deacons' board.

"You didn't pray for my father," said Turner.

Deacon Hurd prayed for Reverend Buckminster. Turner figured the prayer didn't rise much off the table this time.

They dispatched the Old Business quickly. They voted the money to repair the supports under the front three pews. And they voted to replace the bell rope, seeing how it was so frayed it would certainly come down by springtime.

Turner was very quiet through the Old Business but sat forward when they came to the only item on the agenda under the New Business: "The status of Reverend Turner Buckminster." Given present circumstances, Deacon Hurd began, this was a difficult matter, but he felt it was the sworn biblical duty of this board to bring a recommendation to the congregation.

"What would that recommendation be?" asked Mr. Newton.

Deacon Hurd did not look at Turner. He cleared his throat,

then cleared it again. "I suppose," he said, "that that is what we are deciding right now."

"I'm not sure that's quite so, Deacon," said Mr. Newton. "You wouldn't be asking us to recommend that Reverend Buckminster be asked to stay. We already decided that last fall. So it must be that he be asked to leave."

Deacon Hurd straightened some. It looked to Turner as if he was about to deliver a speech. Which he was.

"I speak," said Deacon Hurd, "as one who has the confidence of the congregation. When we invited Reverend Buckminster to our pulpit—and I must speak plainly, even if it brings pain to you, Turner, but it's you who insists on being here—when we invited him, we expected a minister who would bring God's message to the town, who would support us through his strong connections in our coming trials and tribulations, who would pastor a flock. Instead, we found a man who has shown no interest in preserving the prosperity of the town. He has thwarted us at all turns, even to the point of threatening to bring Negroes to live right in the town center. I tell you, it would destroy the town—and there's not a soul in this room who doesn't see the truth of that."

"I'm not so sure that—" began Old Mr. Thayer.

"And when the town is engaged in the philanthropic task of bringing the less fortunate to a place where they will be cared for, this minister follows his duties by attacking our sheriff. I'm sorry he got hurt, but if he hadn't been interfering where he shouldn't have been interfering, he might be sitting here right now."

Silence, as Deacon Hurd dared the board to challenge what he knew to be true. Most of the deacons sat grim-faced, their mouths set. Some stared at the table in front of them; others fiddled with pencils. Turner sat with his hands clenched, seeing his father's eyes as he had gone over the ledge.

"Deacon Hurd," Mr. Newton began slowly, "a minister surely does need to support the town. But I'm not sure that means the same thing to me as it does to you. Seems to me you're saying that a minister should go along with whatever the town decides is fit. But I'm wondering if what we need is a minister who makes us ask what is fit."

"What is fit is what is good for the town."

"I know you think so, Deacon. I know Mr. Stonecrop thinks so, too. And maybe the rest of the congregation, I don't know. But I do know this: what we did down at Malaga wasn't philanthropy, and we're only lying to ourselves if we say it was. They all could have lived there another hundred and twenty-five years without bothering a single soul, but we wanted them gone. And that's the truth." He pointed down the table to Turner. "And that boy there saw someone who had no roof over her head, and he set doing something about it, and I'm ashamed because I didn't stand with him. I'm ashamed that not a single deacon on this board stood with him."

"Saints are hard to live with, Mr. Newton. Usually they end up getting burned."

Something of a stunned pause before Mr. Newton spoke again.

"Whether I'm—"

"You've made the point, Mr. Newton. Are there any other comments about drafting a recommendation to the congregation that Reverend Buckminster be dismissed from our pulpit?"

The stunned pause hadn't finished playing itself out yet. It laid its huge hands on the shoulders of each of the deacons—except Deacon Hurd. He got up to toss another log into the woodstove. He stared a moment at the open fire before he threw one in.

Then he came back to sit down.

"Hearing none," he said, "we'll proceed to the vote. Those nonvoting members of the deacons' board are dismissed. That's you, boy. That's in the bylaws, too."

Turner stood. "My mother did ask me to tell you that we'll be leaving the parsonage just as soon as my father's well enough. We'll be moving over to Mrs. Cobb's house. My mother says to tell you that she would rather not have anyone think we were beholden to you in any way."

He walked to the door and paused, his back to them. "And she says for me to tell you this: 'Take whatever dang vote you please.'"

"Turner," said Deacon Hurd, "if you hadn't come up with the idea of handing over one of the finest houses in Phippsburg to a pack like the Easons, none of this would have happened. Don't blame us for where your own ideas take you."

Suddenly, Turner was back in his father's study. His father had just lit his pipe, and the sweet tobacco scent of it was curling around the room and mixing with the smell of leather and polished wood. He had come to the last heady page of *The Origin of Species,* had felt a thrill crawling up his back and into his gut with the closing sentence of praise and wonder: "From so simple a beginning endless forms most beautiful and most wonderful have been, and are being evolved."

His father had looked up as he closed the book, and he had smiled. "Who knows where these ideas will take us," he had said. "But won't it be exciting to find out." They had nodded together, not only father and son, but two people with an open world in front of them.

"The 'dang' is from me," Turner said, and left the deacons' meeting room.

He stood outside the door and felt everything in him start to drain away until he stood there shaking, hoping he wouldn't cry, trying to breathe slowly so that he wouldn't.

He thought of Lizzie.

"What do you think you're doing?" she would have said to him right then.

"Well, trying to help my father, for one."

"No, that's not what you're doing. You never could see things straight."

"You think you know so much."

"I've learned a lot in the last couple of days. You learn a lot in a god-awful place like this."

"When are you going to get out of there?"

He couldn't hear her answer.

"Lizzie, what am I going to do? I've messed up everything. If I'd never met you . . ."

"If you'd never met me, I'd still be in Pownal. What I wouldn't have . . . well, you know what I wouldn't have. I don't have to say it."

Turner went home to a house mostly dark. The light was turned low in his parents' bedroom, where, when Turner looked in, his father lay still and white, his scalp covered with linen bandages, the blankets pulled tightly around him right on up to his chin. His mother, wrapped in a blanket and sitting in a rocker, was asleep, too, and Turner didn't wake her.

Turner went to his room and stood by the window. The clouds were low, but the half moon was lower still and shone a gray, feeble light on their quilted undersides. The spires of the high pines seemed about to poke up into them, and Turner imagined them ripping open the quilts and the feathery snow drifting down upon the town, making everything warm and cozy and weighted with sleep.

"Forms most beautiful and most wonderful." It was the last

thing he thought of before the warm and cozy weight of his own quilt took him.

The decisions of the Board of Deacons of the First Congregational Church were understood to be secret until they were announced for the consideration of the full congregation. But it would have been more likely for a whale to blunder its way down Parker Head unnoticed than for this decision to be held secret until Sunday. The tides didn't have the time to change before the recommendation was general information around Phippsburg. When folks came by to wish the minister well, they looked at Mrs. Buckminster with embarrassed eyes, and she, too, knew—though she had known all along, Turner supposed.

In the hours while Turner read to his father—he was full along in *The Descent of Man*—his mother loudly packed. When they had left Boston, packing had taken weeks, with trunks and crates and loads of straw to cushion whatever might break. Now there was none of that. Turner would push a wheelbarrow up to the front steps, go into the house, and grab whatever she had piled at the foot of the stairs. He carried it out huggermugger—books, dishes, the downstairs rocker, all in a great mix—and carted it right down the middle of Parker Head.

Turner was glad all the mud had frozen and there was just a patina of frost.

Whenever his mother was in Mrs. Cobb's house, Turner would wait by his father's bedside. He'd listen to the slow breathing, try to figure how he might get down to Pownal, and imagine how his father would awake and come with him to rescue Lizzie Bright, storming the gates like Aeneas himself. Then he'd listen again to the slow breathing.

When Turner wasn't watching his father, he translated the *Aeneid*—he figured his father would want him to be keeping that up—or he walked along the far coast, away from Malaga Island. One late afternoon he met Willis standing alone above the Kennebec, and together they climbed down to the water, cracked sheets of ice from the rocks, threw stones from the beach through the wave troughs to skip them before the white water buried them.

Turner soon took to going down there most afternoons, and more often than not, Willis was there, too.

They always began the same way.

"Hey."

"Hey."

"Minister about the same?"

"About."

Willis would nod, and then they would head to the shore, even when the wind scudded up and drove the salt spray at them, even when a new snow covered the beach so that they couldn't find any stones, even when it was so cold they had to wrap their scarves around their faces.

It was Willis who told Turner about the graves over on Malaga Island. How Mr. Stonecrop had hired men from the shipyards to dig up the markers, then hack through the frozen ground to the coffins—or what was left of them. How the workers jumbled everything they found into five caskets and carted them off the island.

"I never saw anyone working up at the church cemetery," said Turner.

But Willis shook his head. "Down to Pownal," he said. "The town wouldn't let Negroes in the church cemetery."

Turner couldn't help thinking of Lizzie's grandfather, dug up and tossed around, not allowed to stay on the island where he had seen the sun rise and set ten thousand times.

Two days later, Turner didn't need Willis to tell him what

was happening on the island. Mr. Stonecrop's workers were not yet finished. The Eason home had already been burned to the ground, but now fire was set to the Griffin home, and one by one to every house, shack, privy, pier, barrel, stack of lobster traps—everything that could burn on the island. White smoke covered Malaga, and then, the sea breeze being what it was, the smoke blew inland, crossing the New Meadows and drawing up the granite ledges. Still roiling and billowing, it pushed through the woods and came out in torn clouds from the trees and gathered down Parker Head. It passed Mr. Newton's grocery, passed Mrs. Cobb's house and Mrs. Hurd's house, passed the parsonage, and then circled around First Congregational until it rose up to the top of the steeple. It went on even to Mr. Stonecrop's fine house, passing through the wrought-iron fence and coming up onto the fine front porch.

And everywhere the cloud touched, it left ashes. On the street, on the houses, on the church steeple, even on Mr. Stonecrop's fine porch. Ashes fell on the pine boughs, on the bare limbs of the maples and aspens, on the dried brown leaves of the oaks, on the snow. Folks who had to go out held handkerchiefs to their faces and walked quickly. Most stayed in.

Turner, between carrying books from his father's study, watched it all from the cold cupola of Mrs. Cobb's house. The smoke came in, he thought, as if it knew what it wanted to do. He wondered what Lizzie might think about that. He figured she would smack him on the shoulder and tell him to see things straight. But maybe he already did.

The ashes fell against the books Turner carried down Parker Head that afternoon. With each load, Turner felt he was leaving something behind, and though he could not say why, he felt lighter. It no longer mattered to him how the people of First Congregational voted; he imagined that his father would hardly care, either. Maybe they would leave Phippsburg. Once his father was conscious again, they could go down to Pownal, pluck Lizzie Bright from the asylum, and leave forever.

Maybe they would head out for the Territories, after all.

But the next new snow covered the ashes on the trees, covered the ashes on the houses, covered the ashes on the steeple of First Congregational, and covered the ashes Turner had strewn over the newly dug grave of his father.

❧

The funeral service was strained. Turner's mother declared that Deacon Hurd was not to have a thing to do with it, and so the deacons sent over to Bath for the First Congregational minister there. He came in late, brushing the wet snow from his coat and blustering about the roads, and he said all the right things at all the right moments. But it was clear that he had never met Turner's father and so could only speak of the Lord's Anointed as if the Reverend Buckminster had just stepped out of the Epistle to the Galatians. They sang the hymns Turner's mother had picked out, and sang the hymn that Turner had picked out: "I Have Some Friends Before Me Gone." They prayed about God's calling Reverend Buckminster home to do His work in heaven.

Then the Bath minister asked if the bereaved would like to come forward and speak some words to the assembled congregation about this good man, comforting others through an account of this holy man's homegoing.

This part had not been planned. Turner heard his mother draw in her breath. He heard, more nearly felt, the congregation draw in its breath. He knew that the congregation would rather not have the bereaved say a single thing. And he knew that his mother was afraid that if she stood up, she might say what was truly in her heart.

So he stood up instead. The Bath minister held his hand out to invite him to the pulpit and moved aside, smiling as Turner went up.

Behind his father's pulpit, Turner was surprised that he was tall enough to see over it easily.

"My father," he began quietly.

"Speak up, son," said the Bath minister. "Gladden the hearts of this grieving congregation."

But Turner had no intention of gladdening the hearts of this grieving congregation. "My father is with God, just as the minister here says. But God didn't call him there because God had work for him to do. My father died because he was doing God's work here. He wanted the people of Malaga Island to live in a place that was their own."

The Bath minister's smile was gone.

"The best way to honor my father would be to rebuild the homes on the island and invite everyone back. It would be to go down to Pownal for the Easons and"—he stopped, his face tight—"and for Lizzie Griffin. But I don't think any of you will do that."

The Bath minister was probably wishing that the service had ended with the last prayer.

"So everyone on Malaga is gone. And my father is gone, maybe to do God's work in heaven. I don't know. All I know is that they're all gone." When he finished, Turner could feel again his father falling away from him. He was empty.

And then, about halfway back in the sanctuary, Mr. Newton stood, his big hands set on the pew in front of him, leaning over so far that he looked like he might topple. Then Mrs. Newton stood beside him, and all the little Newtons, one by one.

On the other side of the aisle, close to the front, Willis Hurd stood. He looked at Turner and didn't need to say a thing. When Deacon Hurd grabbed at his arm, he ignored him.

One by one, a few—not many—of the people of First Congregational stood. No one said anything. It was as quiet as if the roof had been lifted off and the new snow falling outside had blanketed them all in soft down.

To Turner's mind there came again the image of his father that had been with him of late every night when he fell asleep and every morning when he woke: his father's eyes as he fell over the ledge of the granite cliff. What was in those eyes? What was he saying?

Turner sat back down by his mother. She took his hand in hers.

The Bath minister stepped behind the pulpit again, wheezed some to gain time, and then figured that they would conclude the service with "Bringing in the Sheaves."

It was an unfortunate choice. If he had been hoping for a sprightly rhythm, he didn't get it. Lillian Woodward played the hymn like a dirge, and there is nothing like playing a march like a dirge to irritate a congregation. Not that they needed much more to irritate them. As Lillian Woodward droned on, most of them whispered—loudly—to each other instead of singing, and their words came to Turner even over the bass.

"That he would stand there and lecture us!"

"The apple doesn't fall far."

If Mrs. Buckminster heard, she gave no sign of it. When the hymn ended, she held Turner's hand and walked behind her husband's casket as the deacons carried it out of the church. They crossed the vestibule and went down the stairs and on to Parker Head. The snow had mostly stopped, and Turner smelled the salty sea breeze taking up its place behind him—not playful but solemn and steady.

And so they came to the First Congregational graveyard and committed Turner's father to the earth and to the Lord. The deacons lowered the casket into the ground and dropped the ropes in afterward. Turner took a shovel, and Mr. Newton took a shovel, and Old Mr. Thayer took a shovel, and together they laid the Reverend Turner Buckminster II to rest. Then Turner took a vial of ashes from their own hearth and sprinkled them across the mounded grave. And the snow covered them.

That night, the snow came thick and thicker, heavy and wet and piling up so quickly that Turner could watch it mound itself up from his bedroom window. It was the first real snowstorm of the winter, and he imagined the snow lying hip deep across Phippsburg, down Parker Head, across the granite ledges, and on to smoldering piles of the houses on Malaga Island. He imagined it sweeping all the way down to Pownal, and he thought of Lizzie looking out a window, her head in her hands, missing the sounds of the New Meadows tides, missing her granddaddy, missing Malaga. Missing him.

And he knew that he would have to get down to Pownal to free her himself.

But the snow never let up through the night. The snow never let up through the next day. And when the clouds finally shredded themselves and the silvered moon looked down upon Phippsburg again, it looked down upon a town strangely changed, its sheds turned into hills, its woodpiles into igloos. Parker Head had become a curved slope lolling easily and lazily up against houses and over fences, leaving a bare patch now and again to show just how high the snow had reached.

It had sloped up so high onto Mr. Newton's house that when Turner got there the next morning, Mr. Newton had crawled out the second-story window and was shoveling off the roof of his porch. Turner—who had been up not long after first light and had shoveled off his own porch and steps and walkway, then had gone on down to shovel the porch and steps and walkway of Mrs. Cobb's house—hollered up to ask if Mr. Newton had another shovel. Soon he was clearing the porch and watching the sheets of cascading snow Mr. Newton pushed down from the roof above him.

Together they cleared the steps and the short walk out to the road. By the time they were finished, the walls of snow rose above Turner's shoulders, and he had to pitch the snow so high that his arms were starting to ache. Afterward, they went into the store and Mr. Newton stoked the woodstove—"Don't know why. Won't be anyone out on such a day," he observed. He went in the back to the brewed coffee and brought it out in two mugs. Turner cupped his hands around his, and they sat silently together for a time, feeling the warmth of the woodstove and of the coffee thawing their frozen selves.

"You haven't asked me yet," said Mr. Newton.

"Sir?"

"What you came to ask. You haven't asked me to take you down to Pownal."

"Will you take me down?"

"That why you came to shovel me out?"

"Maybe so."

Mr. Newton laughed, a laugh that probably would have been loud had any sound come out. But he laughed with no sound at all, his mouth open, his eyes watering some, his ample belly moving up and down, until finally he drew in his breath, gathered himself together, and took another gulp of his coffee.

"I suppose it's good to be honest if you're a minister's son."

"I'm not a minister's son anymore."

Mr. Newton reached over and laid his hand on Turner's knee. "You'll always be a minister's son. You'll be a minister's son until you take your last breath in God's sweet world. Now, there's a load down to the textile mill in Brunswick that's been waiting for me to pick up this last week. And after that, there's a fellow down to Yarmouth who still has some of last year's syrup to sell, and I'm all out. I figure if you come along and help me load, we'll be able to make it down to Pownal, too."

"I'll help load," said Turner. "Whenever you're ready to go, I'll be ready."

"Well, you talk to your mother about it. And we'll need to wait until I roll the roads. And until we have a clear day."

"I'll tell my mother."

"And Turner, you might . . . what I mean to say is, I don't want you to be too disappointed about what you might find there."

"I'll be ready when you are, Mr. Newton," he said, and he finished his coffee.

Now that the trip down to Pownal was real, Turner could hardly think of much else. The snow had stopped him from wheeling their household over to Mrs. Cobb's, and so mostly Mrs. Buckminster spent her days sorting and looking things over. In the study, she would stand and hold a book for a long time without even opening it. In the parlor, she would finger a vase as if it were some sort of talisman. She never cried in front of Turner, but Turner could hear her sometimes, late at night. And he felt his heart beat like a bird's.

It snowed all that week, ending a white November and beginning a whiter December. Turner shoveled most of the time, stopping to watch Mr. Newton's great Frisians pulling the rollers to pack the snow, their breath steaming out of their nostrils and their heads turning with ease and power. Their flanks were so massive that it would not be hard to imagine them pulling Malaga Island right up to the mainland, if they could only find the right place to tie on to.

Turner shoveled out the parsonage again, and Mrs. Cobb's, and Mr. Newton's. He even shoveled out First Congregational in time for Sunday services, which Deacon Hurd now led and which Turner and his mother did not attend.

Finally, when the sun decided it was time to rise clear and white, Mr. Newton was at Turner's door, the bells jingling on the Frisians' harnesses, the buffalo robes draped in the sled, and the hot soapstones on the seats and the foot warmers almost glowing with coals at their feet.

They stayed warm all the way to the textile mill in Brunswick, with the wind at their backs and the heat under the robes. They brought the soapstones in to hotten by the mill's coal stove and loaded up the sled with bolts of cloth wrapped in brown paper. Then Turner fetched the soapstones and they headed to Yarmouth, the wind on their beam now and colder, so that Turner hunched the buffalo robe up around him and wished that the embers in the foot warmers weren't dying so quickly. At Yarmouth they were disappointed: the man had already sold more than half of the promised syrup, and he had doubled the price on what remained, a price that no righteous anger or bargaining could bring down. "Lots of buyers to take it if you won't," was all the man kept repeating. Since this was probably true and since old Mr. Thayer had told him he would "have his scalp" if he didn't find some syrup to stock, Mr. Newton paid the price, and they loaded the syrup onto the floor of the sled, in front of the bundles of cloth.

And then they headed down to Pownal.

By now it was late morning, and the sun was about as high as it was going to get. Even so, the light was weak and paltry in the cold air. The Yarmouth man had given them new embers for the foot warmers, but the air grew even colder as they got farther from the sea, and the road more desolate, and the houses a little more desperate, as though they were already losing the battle against winter. Woodsmoke hung heavily over them, lowering across the housefronts and onto the spruce branches patterned around the foundations.

Turner grew less and less hopeful the farther they went, and he wondered what he would say when they got to the asylum. How would he get Lizzie out? And what would Phippsburg say when he brought her home?

Well, he would bring her home anyway.

But when they finally reached the Pownal Home for the Feeble-Minded, Turner almost thought they should just turn around. An iron fence surrounded it, topped with sharp spikes, sharp as needles. Beyond them, a frozen expanse of gray, dirty ice, the snow whisking across it in wispy curls and then disappearing. Beyond that, a few bare elms, arching high and graceful, though in that bare landscape looking like the skeletons of trees. And beyond them, a brick square of a building with small windows—barred on the first two levels, bricked over on the third. No smoke came out of the center chimney. It all looked as deserted as if the Flood had newly receded and left this one cold building in its wake.

A cold and annoyed guard left the gatehouse to let them onto the grounds.

Another cold and annoyed guard opened the front door to their repeated knocks.

And a cold and annoyed matron led them to her office and sat them down on one side of her desk, while she ascended to the lofty chair behind it. She listened to Turner say that they had come to fetch Lizzie Griffin. She pointed out that one could not simply waltz into the asylum and remove those committed to it. Turner asked if they might at least see Lizzie. Without answering, the matron went to her files. She returned with a card and informed them that that would be impossible.

Mr. Newton asked why.

"Because," said the matron, "Elizabeth Bright Griffin died ten days after coming to this institution."

Turner felt the cold of the place come into him. He could not move. It was as though the bricks surrounded him and him alone. He felt that he would never escape them, never see anyone he loved again, never see the ocean waves again. That he would always be cold, and the cold would be in him more than around him.

The matron stood. "Those people hardly ever last long when they come here," she said. "Will there be anything else?"

C H A P T E R

12

THE storm that had thrown such snow at Phippsburg was the first of many that winter. Sometimes the storms came so fast and so close that one had hardly finished tapering off before the next came, with winds Turner could hear before he could feel. Sometimes they were separated by a few days, and those days were the clearest and bluest Turner had ever seen. He figured if Darwin had written about snow, he would have said it was one of the things in the world most beautiful and most wonderful.

In February, Mr. Newton called on Turner and his mother. They were missed at First Congregational, he said. He wondered if the time wasn't right for them to come back.

They waited two more weeks.

When Turner and his mother did appear at church, silence followed in a spreading wake as they walked up the center aisle. They passed into an empty pew about halfway up the sanctuary, feeling the wake of the silence pass over their heads and carry forward, so that folks in front looked back and then turned away quickly. Turner picked up a hymnbook and thought he might fling it at the next set of peering eyes. He imagined it circling end over end, its pages fluttering like wings, until it struck, oh, say, Deacon Hurd, just on the side of his nose.

The church filled silently. The ushers tried not to look their way. No one sat in their pew. The prelude began, Lillian Woodward playing too slowly. The candles were lit. The ushers brought up the latecomers and searched for a place to insert them.

But no one sat in their pew.

"I think we should go," whispered Turner to his mother.

"So do I," she said.

They might have gone then and there if Mr. Newton and Mrs. Newton and all the little Newtons had not suddenly stood up from a pew toward the front and flocked down to Turner and his mother. "Oh, Mrs. Buckminster," said Mrs. Newton, "would you mind terribly if we came to sit with you?"

So they did, all the little Newtons bustling past them, the two boys putting up their fists as they passed Turner and grinning like loons when he put his fists up, too; the four prim and pink girls putting their fists up and hitting him full in the belly as they passed, one by one. Mr. Newton tousled his hair, and Mrs. Newton sat next to his mother and took her hand.

Turner put the hymnbook back.

Each of the little Newtons took a turn sitting on his lap to get through the sermon. And Turner couldn't help tickling each of them in the stomach—especially Ben and Meg Newton, who laughed like Abbie and Perlie.

When he didn't have a Newton on his lap, he looked out the window to watch the snow falling.

❧

With all the snow, Turner could hardly keep the walks clear in front of the church, the parsonage, and Mrs. Cobb's house, where they were living now. There were still boxes and one trunk to cart over, but the books from his father's study had already been set on the shelves in front of Mrs. Cobb's books until they could be sorted out. Turner had cleared away the round study table in the library and left only his father's Bible, the *Aeneid,* and *The Origin of Species* on it, along with the lamp.

When his mother saw the table, she put her hands to her cheeks and nodded, her eyes brimming.

Willis helped Turner move the heaviest things, and it took them most of a week. Afterward, Willis had supper with them, and he told stories about teachers in the Phippsburg school, and for the first time in a long time there was laughter over a meal—so that even the apple crisp Turner's mother forgot to take out, which baked to a hardness no spoon could ever breach, meant only more laughter.

On a gray, low day at the end of February, they closed the door to the parsonage for the last time. Mrs. Cobb hadn't believed in electric lighting, so Turner settled into the tasks of trimming wicks and cleaning lamp chimneys, of banking fires at night and starting them come morning, of doing the hundred things that must be done each day to keep a house older than the country tight and warm. In between, he was in the library, surrounded by his father's and Mrs. Cobb's books, sitting at the study table in the morning to translate the *Georgics*—which he thought had nothing on the *Aeneid*. The afternoon was all Wordsworth, Longfellow, and Coleridge—Turner figured Coleridge would do—and last of all, Mr. Darwin's *Journal of Researches into the Natural History and Geology of the Countries Visited During the Voyage of H.M.S. Beagle.* Just knowing that the *Beagle* was ahead made it easier to plow through the *Georgics,* and he figured he'd best read it now, since in the fall he'd be going to school in Phippsburg, and Darwin was probably not in the curriculum.

He did not read Mr. Barclay.

Turner did not go back to the granite ledges. And he did not go back to Malaga Island. Even when March came in on an unexpectedly warm sea breeze and the snow began to melt and it was no longer so very hard to keep the rooms in Mrs. Cobb's house warm, he did not go back. When the seas softened and were more blue than green, when he and Willis rowed up and down the coast in the Hurds' tender until Turner felt the muscles in his arms toughen into cords, even then Turner kept the New Meadows at his back.

It was after a Sunday-afternoon row down to Cox's Head and back—Willis had had to sneak off with the tender, Deacon Hurd being a strict Sabbatarian—that Turner came back to find Mr. Stonecrop standing on the porch of the house, his mother holding the door open to speak to him.

"Here he is now," he heard her say. "You'll have to discuss it with him."

"Mrs. Buckminster, really, the two of us . . ."

"Circumstances being what they are, you'll have to discuss it with him. Turner," she said, "Mr. Stonecrop has something to propose. Won't you come in, Mr. Stonecrop? Perhaps the library will do."

Turner followed them into the library, Mr. Stonecrop seeming too large for the house. She motioned him to a chair—which he did not take—and then, without saying anything more, left the room.

Turner felt an assault about to begin.

"So," said Mr. Stonecrop, "you are the man of the house."

Turner didn't think Mr. Stonecrop expected a reply, so he didn't give him any. Mr. Stonecrop walked around the study table, picked up the *Aeneid,* and put it down after he flipped through some pages. "I don't know what good this will do you," he said. "I built a whole shipyard, and I don't know a word of Latin past *e pluribus unum*. No employer will hire you merely because you know Latin, young Buckminster."

Turner almost said that the whole state of Maine would have to pull up its skirts and dance a reel before he would hire on with Mr. Stonecrop. But he didn't think that needed saying aloud, either.

"And you're still reading this tripe," observed Mr. Stonecrop, holding up *The Voyage of H.M.S. Beagle.* "You won't learn much from a fellow who thinks we came from monkeys." He looked at a couple of pages, closed the book, and tossed it onto the chair. Then he rounded his hands into fists, set them on the table, and leaned down, his arms pillars supporting his top half. "Son, I came here this afternoon to discuss a business proposal with your mother. She tells me I need to discuss it with you—I suppose since Mrs. Cobb left you the house."

"I'm not your son, Mr. Stonecrop," Turner said simply.

"No, you're not. If you were, you'd be in the boatyards, learning a trade, instead of translating a language not a single soul speaks anymore, and then this monkey foolishness to boot. It's a practical world out there. And people who aren't practical get—"

"I know what happens to people who aren't practical, Mr. Stonecrop. I've seen what happens to people who aren't practical."

"Blunt. You're blunt, aren't you? That's good. Men of business should be blunt. They don't have to like each other to do business, but they do have to be blunt."

Yet another comment that Turner didn't think needed a reply.

"So here is your business proposal, Mr. Buckminster. I propose to purchase Mrs. Cobb's house from you outright. I'm prepared to offer you better than the market price."

"Why, Mr. Stonecrop?"

"This is a business matter."

"If this were a business matter, Mr. Stonecrop, would you be giving us an offer above the market price?"

Mr. Stonecrop smiled. "Well, young Mr. Turner Buckminster, all grown up. Handles his business affairs better than his father might have, and him only thirteen—no, probably fourteen years old now. Maybe there's more to Latin than I thought. Maybe I should be hiring you down to the shipyard after all."

"Did you know that Lizzie Griffin is dead?"

"Malaga Island is in the past. What matters is the future. I'll put it simply: you're not wanted here. Neither you nor your mother. A boy as sharp as you, a boy who reads Darwin, should be able to tell that. I'm giving you the opportunity to go back to Boston. This is a business proposal you can't turn down."

"You see things only one way, Mr. Stonecrop. We're not selling the house."

"Today is your best offer, young Buckminster."

Turner nodded.

"Boy, are you stubborn just to be stubborn? Or is there something else to it? You think some other Negro will come live with you? Will you be sweet on her, too?"

"Mr. Stonecrop, you're a rich man. And you'll be a whole lot richer once you build your hotel. But I don't think Mrs. Cobb would have wanted to help you. And I don't think I want to help you."

"Blunt again. Very good. But you're missing your chance, boy, just as your father missed his. You won't hear me make this offer again."

"I won't expect it."

"You'll regret living in a town where no one wants you."

"I'm getting used to it."

"I was the one who brought you here," shouted Mr. Stonecrop. "I was the one who insisted upon your father. I thought he was an up-and-coming preacher. A man with his wealth, with his connections—I thought he would rise like a star in Maine."

"I was the one who saw him fall over the cliff."

"And what do you imagine he was thinking then? He must have realized what was about to happen. He must have hoped that you would make good decisions and take care of your mother."

What had his father been thinking when he went over the cliff? What had been in his eyes? And it came to Turner, no matter how much he tried to hold it back, no matter how hard he tried to make the night darker so that he couldn't see it: his father tottering, arms reaching forward to nothing, leaning back. And his eyes.

And then he remembered. He had already seen what was in his father's eyes.

He had seen it in the eye of the whale.

Turner hardly noticed when Mr. Stonecrop left, snorting. He let the moment at the cliff's edge come to him again, wincing with the hurt of it but watching his father's face closely. He let it come again and again, until he was absolutely sure he could see his father's face.

What had been in their eyes? What was it that the whale knew? What was it that his father knew?

In May, Mr. Stonecrop's shipyard failed. He abandoned the house on Quality Ridge and lit out for parts unknown, taking with him what remained of the investments of half the town. All of Phippsburg raged. Quality indeed! What hope was there for a hotel on the New Meadows now? Here were all the workers in the shipyard unpaid for the last month. And the Hurds! All their investments were gone! They'd been left penniless!

The sea breeze carried the news up and down Parker Head—"Did you see?" "Did you hear?"—until most souls in town were swearing they had known long ago that Mr. Stonecrop was a scoundrel, and wasn't it too bad about the Hurds?

Most souls in town except Turner and his mother, that is. They had stayed to themselves pretty much through the spring, settling into Mrs. Cobb's house. The rooms upstairs felt as if they hadn't been lived in for a very long time, and so Mrs. Buckminster set about bringing them alive again. She had Turner cleaning and painting, dragging rugs outside and beating them, opening windows for new air, and bringing light to rooms that hadn't seen any since the century began.

They had not gone back to First Congregational since February, but soon after Mr. Stonecrop's absconding, the Ladies' Sewing Circle, led by Mrs. Newton, called on Turner and Mrs. Buckminster to invite them back to services. It was, to be charitable, a little awkward, and Turner kept sensing that Mrs. Newton was about to stick the steel point of her umbrella into any of the ladies who didn't behave. But they all did, and Turner and his mother returned to First Congregational.

Deacon Hurd, beset with financial woe, was no longer preaching. The Bath minister was rushing over after his own service, and he preached well enough, though he was always a little out of breath.

The Hurds had sold their sloop but kept the tender, and one day, late in May, Turner borrowed it to row his mother over to Malaga Island, carrying with them a pot of violets. He walked with her along the shore to the point of the island where Lizzie's house had stood, and there, at what would have been the doorway, they troweled up the earth and planted the violets, turning their hardy blossoms toward the sea. Afterward, Turner rowed all around the island, and his mother was surprised by how sure he was on the water.

"Goodness," she said, "I hope you don't ever go too far."

"I've seen whales," he told her.

"I never realized they came this close to shore."

Turner concentrated on his rowing.

The Hurds, unable to meet the loans upon loans the deacon had taken out to grow wealthy with the town's coming prosperity, sold the tender, too—or more properly, the bank sold it, along with their home, and Willis's grandmother's house, and everything else they owned. Speculators from Philadelphia bought up most everything, but not for what Mr. Hurd or the bank had hoped for.

The Buckminsters bought the tender.

The Sunday after the auction, the Hurds sat in the last pew of First Congregational, stone-faced, haggard, bent over. Since everyone knows that trouble can be contagious, they were alone until Turner and his mother sat down next to them. Turner's mother took Mrs. Hurd's hand.

"I'm so sorry," she whispered.

"How could we ever have known Mr. Stonecrop was such a scoundrel?" Mrs. Hurd replied quietly.

They sat through the service and listened to the Bath minister's breathy sermon from Galatians, and when the last chords of Lillian Woodward's postlude finished, they stood up. Mrs. Hurd fell into Mrs. Buckminster's arms and held back tears as the congregation walked past them, trying not to watch.

"I don't know what we'll do," she said. "I just don't know what we'll do."

"You'll come and live with us," said Turner.

Mrs. Hurd looked at him. Mr. Hurd looked at him.

"Of course," said Mrs. Buckminster. "We've got more rooms than we know what to do with."

Mrs. Hurd looked at Mr. Hurd, who looked down at the floor, his hands rigid on the pew beside them.

"We haven't . . ."

"Just until you're back on your feet," said Mrs. Buckminster.

A long moment passed, almost long enough for another breathy sermon.

"Thank you," said Mr. Hurd, finally. "Just until we're back on our feet."

Willis punched Turner on the arm.

So high summer came to Phippsburg that year, and it promised to be the hottest anyone could remember—just like every other summer. Together Turner and Willis spaded up a new garden in the yard behind Mrs. Cobb's, and they planted pole beans and snow peas and russet potatoes and a couple of rows of corn—which the deer and rabbits and every one of God's creatures living between the New Meadows and the Kennebec thought was just fine. They put new glass in the cupola, painted the fence Mrs. Cobb's grandfather had built, and then painted the porch. When they finished with that, they went down to Mr. Newton's store and bought some sunlight yellow and strawberry red paint to take care of the shutters and door.

Mr. Hurd helped paint until he began to clerk at Mr. Newton's grocery.

Turner and Willis got themselves hired on a lobster boat out of Bath, and even though, as Willis pointed out, Turner was a whole lot scrawnier than he was, Turner did heft his share of the traps and do his share of culling out the shorts. After the first two weeks, Turner was pegging lobster claws as fast as Willis and not getting pinched any more than anyone else.

The days were long, beginning before dawn when the sea was purple black, ending with the sunset when the sea was burning red. Turner was tired and sore most of the time, shivering in the morning and so hot in the afternoon that he and Willis worked sweating. "Probably there's better ways to earn money," said Willis most every morning, but even if there were, Turner wouldn't have taken another way, because hardly a day passed when the lobster boat didn't fool with a pod of whales as playful as kittens in the sun, showing off their dorsal fins, spraying the boat with their spouting, sometimes jumping full out of the water and grinning for all the world to see.

Watching them was when Turner got pinched the most.

Sometimes they would lay traps up the New Meadows, and they would sail past Malaga Island, going so close that Turner could stand by the rail and see the patch of violets planted by Lizzie's doorway. His heart stopped every time.

When Turner and Willis weren't lobstering, they were sleeping—even when they were trying to eat their supper. Mrs. Buckminster and Mrs. Hurd would try to keep them talking through the meal but would finally give up when the boys' yawns got longer than their sentences. They would stagger up the stairs to sleep.

And the eyes of whales would fill Turner's dreams.

One night, when the sea breeze remembered that autumn wasn't far away and so began to blow colder, Turner told Willis he wanted to take the tender out into the bay.

The next dawn, Willis was at the dock with him, loading in a jug, some cheese sandwiches, and some corn muffins, then casting him loose, waving him out into the incoming tide. Turner's arms felt strong against the long, smooth swells, so low they were not breaking, the sea the color of the inside of a mussel shell. He rowed down past Cox's Head, across the mouth of Atkins Bay, around Popham, keeping inshore along the line of tiny islands where the tide was weakest, and finally up and around Small Point Head and Bald Head and into the New Meadows. He let the last of the high tide carry him up the shoreline, the long swells growing ever smoother and lowering with the rising of the sun, until the tide gave its last gasp and settled down for a bit just as the tender tipped its nose onto the south point of Malaga Island, and Turner stepped onto it.

The sea breeze found him and twisted around him like a cat asking for a bowl of milk. It followed him up into the island and didn't stop its play even when Turner went up to the Eason place—the burned ruins already cleansed by the winter and starting to find their way back into woods. At the Tripp place the sea breeze scattered last fall's oak leaves inside the outline of foundation stones. At the graveyard, a few depressions, but otherwise the ground was filled with pine boughs the snow had brought down.

At the Griffin place, nothing. Nothing at all. He could have stood there like Darwin at the Galápagos and known that if he had come a thousand years earlier, everything would have been the same.

He sat down on the rocks and looked out.

When he had sat there long enough to see that the tide was beginning to empty out of the New Meadows, he rose and followed the shore of Malaga Island back to the tender. He got in and cast off, letting the tide take him out and away from the island, using the oars just enough to keep himself square to the swells. The island rocked gently as he moved farther and farther away from it, the chuckling of the water underneath the boat and the wooden creaking of the oarlocks an unrhythmic lullaby.

Rowing now and again so that he could feel the tautness of his muscles, Turner let the lowering tide carry him away from Malaga Island, down the New Meadows, and, some time past noon, out into open water, where the shoreline was a blue blur, the waves higher and longer, and the only company he had in the whole world was the sea breeze that followed him on out.

Mostly he drifted, though once he rowed inshore a ways to a spot where gulls were screeching and diving and trying to lift themselves back up into the air. But before he could reach them, they came out to him; suddenly, he was in the middle of a school of shimmering blue fish, all of them turning to their sides to feed and waving their silver fins up into the strange air. The sea was so smooth it looked sleepy, and the tender, even when Turner rowed as hard as he could, left no wake.

"Who's looking at things straight now?" he called out into the air.

"I suppose you think you are." He could almost hear her, just as if she were sitting in the boat with him on the lonely ocean. "What are you doing out here?"

"Looking for whales."

"That's a good thing to look for," she said. "I've seen some myself."

"I guess."

"I have. They look at you like they know things."

"I know."

"Like they know things older than you could ever imagine."

"I know, Lizzie."

"They look at things straight."

"Are you looking at things straight now, Lizzie?"

Her laugh was in the boat. "Golly Moses," she said. "I always did."

Lizzie Bright.

And that was when Turner saw them: great mounds of water moving between him and the shoreline, following the coast. Above them, seagulls and black terns hovered and circled, screeching and cackling at each other, until suddenly the mounds erupted, and whales—two, four, five, seven, oh good Lord, nine—rose out of the water like easy behemoths. Turner hollered, waving his arms and standing up in the boat until it began to rock with the waves the whales made. He rowed toward them, in his excitement slipping the oars out of the locks, setting them back in, and slipping them out again, desperate to draw up alongside the whales, desperate to know what they knew.

The whales waited for him. Sometimes they went below the surface and came up again, but mostly they waited for him in his puny tender. The gulls circled them like feathered halos, until Turner shipped his oars and let the swells carry him.

He could not tell if the waves were drifting him closer to the whales or if the whales were swimming closer to him. In any case, soon he was so close that when he held out his hand over the water, all he had to do was reach down and he would touch the dark gray rubber of a whale's skin, stretched to a perfect tautness, smelling of the deep sea. He felt more than saw the size of the whales, and the deep knowing within them.

He turned from one to another, their sea-washed eyes open and watching, and then finally he leaned out. And he touched the cool, wet, perfect smoothness of whale.

Then he knew. Then he knew.

The knowledge in his father's eyes and in the whales' eyes.

The world turns and the world spins, the tide runs in and the tide runs out, and there is nothing in the world more beautiful and more wonderful in all its evolved forms than two souls who look at each other straight on. And there is nothing more woeful and soul-saddening than when they are parted. Turner knew that everything in the world rejoices in the touch, and everything in the world laments in the losing.

And he had lost Malaga.

So he wept. With his hand still on the whale and the whale's eye on him, he wept. He wept for old Mrs. Hurd, and he wept for Mrs. Cobb, and he wept for his father, and he wept for Lizzie Bright. In the open sea, with the land blue in his eyes and the sea green in his hand, he wept. And all around him the swells grew still, and the sea breeze quieted, and the perfect sky above him vaulted like a painted dome. Beneath him he felt the currents eddying around the bodies of the whales, felt the tides and shifting water that they created as they passed him, one by one, until the sea closed over the eye of the one he was touching, and they had all lowered into the cool, wet, smooth sea—and they were gone.

And still Turner wept.

He wept until the sea breeze would have no more of it and bucked the swells up, frothed them at the top, and sent some of the spray over the stern. Turner took the oars without thought and kept the tender moving into the waves. Then, again without thought, he began to row slowly, rowing through the watchful ocean until the blue land changed to gray and then brown and green. Then he struck the shore and turned south, keeping outside the breakers and inland of the islands, until he found Popham and rowed up the shining waters of the Kennebec.

He had floated in the ocean with whales.

He had seen them and touched them.

They had seen him and touched him.

It was something to tell somebody, and for a moment he

smiled at what Lizzie would say when she heard. "Of whales and of Malaga I sing," he said. Then he remembered that she would never hear anything in this world again. So he had no one to tell of this thing most beautiful and most wonderful.

The sun had almost decided to set by the time Turner reached the dock. The first stars weren't out yet, but they were close. The sea breeze had come up behind him and the swells had started to tumble over themselves just a bit, pushing the tender's stern along and letting it know that it was time to be safe abed.

Willis was waiting, and he waved and halloed as Turner rowed closer. Turner wondered how long he had been waiting there. A couple of hurricane lanterns stood at the end of the dock, and Turner figured Willis had been about to light them. He rowed hard the last stretch—he didn't want to show how tired he really was—but when Willis threw out the line and Turner could hardly tie the knot, he figured Willis would know. And also he figured that was all right.

Willis's outstretched hand pulled him up onto the dock.

"You still don't know how to tie that hitch. You go far out?"

"I guess."

"Pretty calm. I suppose even someone from Boston could manage."

"You want me to break your nose again?"

"Be still and carry these up with me."

Turner picked up one of the lanterns and looked straight on up toward Phippsburg. A few lights were already glowing, and there was woodsmoke in the air against the chill. He could see the cupola of Mrs. Cobb's house, the glass reflecting the reddening sunset. And there was the first star.

"Willis," said Turner, and he told him about the whales.

AUTHOR'S NOTE

In the spring of 2012, the Maine State Museum in Augusta, Maine, opened the state's first exhibit on the history of Malaga Island; it was titled "Malaga Island, Fragmented Lives." Hundreds of artifacts—pottery shards, cutlery, tools, fishing gear, cabin furnishings, photographs—evoked the life of the island at the end of the nineteenth century and beginning of the twentieth. Those artifacts showed a mostly African American and Irish American community living close together and adapting itself to a forty-acre island surrounded by the New Meadows River—a tidal river. Through hard and constant labor, they created a life of dignity and faith and compassion and cooperation.

Perhaps their sense of community arose out of the knowledge that they represented two of the most despised groups in New England at the turn of the century, and so they would be wise to band together. Perhaps it arose from their common situation: to survive, they would have to wrest a living from the cold waters around them. Or perhaps it arose from the fact that the community had to work together to survive on such a small plot of land in such inhospitable waters. But however the Malaga settlement grew up, the 2012 exhibit showed a people of strength and tenacity—qualities they especially needed a bit more than a century ago. Though in the end, the community would not survive the bias that other, more powerful groups would use against them.

I visited that exhibit accompanied by a group of middle school students who had recently put on a stage version of *Lizzie Bright and the Buckminster Boy.* They came from an island off the Maine coast, so they knew something of island life. Most of these students had never been to Augusta, the state capital; some of them had never been off their island other than on a lobster boat. They were bright and excited, eager to see the city and to attend an exhibit that would show them the story they had been reading about and acting out on stage.

But none of them expected what was waiting for them, a surprise that stunned them into silence.

When we got there, the curator of the exhibit introduced us to three women, representing three generations of the Tripp family: a grandmother, mother, and daughter. Only recently, the younger two generations had discovered that the grandmother had grown up on Malaga Island. She had been a member of one of those families that was forced by the state and town governments to leave their home and to yield their rights to Malaga, under the claim that they had no legal deed to that land. The grandmother of this group was quiet, but she pointed to a blown-up photograph of the islanders that showed her as a very young girl, looking out from the picture with the eyes of a child who knew trouble and grief. Her daughter, the mother in this group of three, said that her mother had never revealed the story to them, so ashamed was she of having lived on the island—because that is what hatred and bias can do: make people believe that they should be ashamed of who they are.

But the shame does not belong to the people of Malaga Island.

Malaga was first settled by the descendants of Benjamin Darling, a freed or possibly escaped slave, who had come to the Maine islands in the 1790s with his white wife, Sarah Proverbs. The Darlings had two sons, and those sons had fourteen children, and by the mid-1800s, they had been joined on Malaga Island by about fifty people—Portuguese, Irish, Scottish, African American, Native American, and others not accepted in nearby towns.

It was a rough life: many of the houses were ramshackle and makeshift, some with dirt floors—in other words, the community was like many poor fishing communities up and down the coast of Maine. The islanders lived by fishing, farming, lobstering, and sometimes doing odd jobs on the mainland. For years, the adjoining towns of Phippsburg and Harpswell insisted that they did *not* own the island, since whoever did would bear financial responsibility for the people who lived on Malaga—and both towns believed that they should not be expected to use their tax money to aid people who did not look like them. By 1905 the squabbling had grown so rancorous that the state, in a very questionable legal maneuver, took over the ownership of the island; a school was built and a teacher hired.

But Governor Frederick Plaisted was not pleased. He saw the island's homes as a blight on Maine, and believed that because many of the people there were a mix of Irish and African descent, they were unfit to live in society. Perhaps even more telling, powerful people like the governor knew that over the previous fifteen years, the Maine coast had become a tourist destination—a place for "rusticators," as they were called. They believed that the island community was an embarrassment to the state and that its presence on the coast would hinder the growth of this new economic opportunity—an opportunity they judged to be very important since shipbuilding, which had for a long time dominated the economy of Maine, was now declining. In 1911, Governor Plaisted crossed the New Meadows River to see the Malaga community for himself, and he did not like what he saw. "I think the best plan," he said, "would be to burn down the shacks with all of their filth. Certainly the conditions there are not credible to our state. We ought not to have such things near our front door."

The plan to remove the community from Malaga Island was launched soon after. In June 1912, the Cumberland County sheriff delivered the governor's ultimatum to the islanders: they would have to leave within thirty days *with their houses* or they would be forcibly removed. Some of the islanders were removed against their will: the Marks family, for example, were confronted by a sheriff and a doctor, declared unfit, and then arrested—some would say abducted—and taken to the Maine School for the Feeble-Minded in Pownal, despite the desperate efforts of the island's teacher to keep them free. At Pownal, the patriarch of the family, Jacob Marks, died within two weeks, and his son followed soon after. Two of his daughters remained confined to the "school" until the 1920s, when they died there. Another of his daughters, Lottie, was eventually released. Three additional islanders were imprisoned without cause at that site.

The rest of the islanders were slandered as "feebleminded" because of their "mixed race," and as they left the island, they struggled to find refuge. The local towns had heard of the community and believed the slander, and they did not want to add paupers to their tax rolls. Most of these refugees, carrying the racist stigma, were lost to history, some because they themselves wanted to keep the story hidden, as if the slander itself were true and would stain their own lives. Today, diligent historians—many of them descendants of the community—are trying to recover those stories.

After all of the community had left the island, any remaining homes were destroyed and the island was wiped clean. The schoolhouse that the state had built was removed and brought farther up the coast to Louds Island, where it was dismantled and used to build a church. Even the graveyard on Malaga Island was destroyed; seventeen or eighteen graves were dug up and violated, and the remains jumbled into five zinc-lined caskets. The caskets were then buried again, north of the School for the Feeble-Minded, near the burial sites of six of the eight islanders who died while at the school. Lottie, the daughter of Jacob Marks, lived until she was 103 years old; at her death in 1997, she was buried in Brunswick, not many miles north of where she had been imprisoned when she was just a child.

Since then, the state of Maine has tried to atone for this shameful attack on the community of Malaga Island. In April 2010, a "Joint Resolution Recognizing the Tragic Expulsion of the Residents of Malaga Island" was passed by the state legislature—though descendants of those residents were not notified of the action. In September of that same year, Governor John Baldacci visited the island—the first governor to step foot on it since Governor Plaisted—and he apologized for the actions of the former governor. In May 2012, Governor Paul LePage, at the opening of the Maine State Museum exhibit, echoed Governor Baldacci while speaking to descendants whose families had carried a slanderous stigma for generations: "We apologize for the hardship we have caused you." He pledged to create a scholarship fund available to all descendants of the Malaga Island community, and this was established in 2014 and is now administered by the Maine Community Foundation in Ellsworth. Then in 2017, a large memorial plaque, listing the names of the islanders whose graves had been violated and those who died at the "school," was erected on the grounds of what is now called Pineland Farms—the renamed Maine School for the Feeble-Minded.

Today, Malaga Island is completely uninhabited. It is owned by the Maine Coast Heritage Trust, which acquired the land in 2001 and turned it into a preserve open to the public. It is accessible only by boat, but should you get to the island, you can walk a marked trail through the forty acres and see it as it has been for the last ten thousand years, marked only by the trail, a sign, and some piled-up lobster traps. There is also some evidence of the archeological work that contributed to the development of the Maine State Museum exhibit.

Lizzie Bright and the Buckminster Boy is a novel, not a history. To that end, the characters are fictional. Turner is the character who is the witness: he comes to the island unaware of many of its conflicts and learns about them as the reader does. Mr. Stonecrop similarly is fictional, though he stands for the greed and callousness that led to the destruction of the island community—the hotels he envisioned were a real dream of some who lived in Maine, but they were never built. Some of the characters' names are borrowed from real islanders, and Lizzie's name is a combination of two of those. She herself is based on a photograph of a young islander, taken presumably by a white photographer to highlight the poverty of her community. In terms of the timeline, I have shifted the date of the forced exile of the island's inhabitants for the purposes of narrative, and conflated the destruction of the houses with that exile. And in terms of geography, I have thinned out the peninsula to make the characters' travels a bit easier, and invented the cliffs upon which Turner stands—though not those upon which the frock coats stand. Most of the geography is as described. If you were to drive toward the now-popular beach at Popham that Turner rowed past, you might well see the First Congregational steeple as you pass through Phippsburg Center.

After my visit to the exhibit, I was sent a small piece of pottery from the archeological work on the island; it is on the desk beside me as I type these words. It is small, maybe an inch squared, its white surface decorated by a line of faded green flowers. It is probably from a bowl, or maybe a mug. I find myself in New England antique stores now and then, looking for dishes with that pattern—but it is not the kind of fine china that antique stores tend to carry. It is more a sturdy kind of crockery, everyday stuff, strong enough to have survived being broken and then spending more than a century in the ground, and now unearthed as if to attest to something, as if to bear witness to what was done once, to what has been done over and over, and to what must never be done again.

Another powerful novel by
Gary D. Schmidt

GARY D. SCHMIDT

orbiting jupiter

★ "A powerful story
about second chances."
—*Publishers Weekly*, starred review

o n e

BEFORE you agree to have Joseph come live with you," Mrs. Stroud said, "there are one or two things you ought to understand." She took out a State of Maine * Department of Health and Human Services folder and laid it on the kitchen table.

My mother looked at me for a long time. Then she looked at my father.

He put his hand on my back. "Jack should know

what we're getting into, same as us," he said. He looked down at me. "Maybe you more than anyone."

My mother nodded, and Mrs. Stroud opened the folder.

This is what she told us.

Two months ago, when Joseph was at Adams Lake Juvenile, a kid gave him something bad in the boys' bathroom. He went into a stall and swallowed it.

After a long time, his teacher came looking for him.

When she found him, he screamed.

She said he'd better come out of that stall right now.

He screamed again.

She said he'd better come out of that stall right now unless he wanted more trouble.

So he did.

Then he tried to kill her.

They sent Joseph to Stone Mountain, even though he did what he did because the kid gave him something bad and he swallowed it. But that didn't matter. They sent him to Stone Mountain anyway.

He won't talk about what happened to him there. But since he left Stone Mountain, he won't wear anything orange.

He won't let anyone stand behind him.

He won't let anyone touch him.

He won't go into rooms that are too small.

And he won't eat canned peaches.

"He's not very big on meatloaf either," said Mrs. Stroud, and she closed the State of Maine * Department of Health and Human Services folder.

"He'll eat my mother's canned peaches," I said.

Mrs. Stroud smiled. "We'll see," she said. Then she put her hand on mine. "Jack, your parents know this, and you should too. There's something else about Joseph."

"What?" I said.

"He has a daughter."

I felt my father's hand against my back.

"She's almost three months old, but he's never

seen her. That's one of the biggest heartbreaks in this case." Mrs. Stroud handed the folder to my mother. "Mrs. Hurd, I'll leave this with you. Read it, and then you can decide. Call me in a few days if . . ."

"We've talked this over," said my mother. "We already know."

"Are you sure?"

My mother nodded.

"We're sure," my father said.

Mrs. Stroud looked at me. "How about you, Jack?"

My father's hand still against my back.

"How soon can he come?" I said.

Two days later, on Friday, Mrs. Stroud brought Joseph home. He looked like a regular eighth-grade kid at Eastham Middle School. Black eyes, black hair almost over his eyes, a little less than middle for height, a little less than middle for weight, sort of middle for everything else.

He really could have been any other eighth-grade kid at Eastham Middle School. Except he had a daughter. And he wouldn't look at you when he talked — if he talked.

He didn't say a thing when he got out of Mrs. Stroud's car. He wouldn't let my mother hug him. He wouldn't shake my father's hand. And when I brought him up to our room, he threw his stuff on the top bunk and climbed up and still didn't say anything.

I got in the bunk below him and read some until my father called us for milking.

In the Big Barn, Joseph and I tore up three bales and filled the bins — I told him you have to fill the bin in the Small Barn for Quintus Sertorius first because he's an old horse and doesn't like to wait — and then we went back to the cows in the tie-up to milk. My father said Joseph could watch but after today he'd be helping. Joseph stood with his back against the wall. When the cows turned and looked at him, they didn't say a thing. Not even Dahlia. They kept pulling on the hay and chewing, like they do. That means they thought he was okay.

When my father got to Rosie, he asked Joseph if he'd like to try milking her.

Joseph shook his head.

"She's gentle. She'd let anyone milk her."

Joseph didn't say anything.

Still, after my father was done and he'd taken a couple of full buckets out to the cooler, Joseph went up behind Rosie and reached out and rubbed the end of her back, right above her tail. He didn't know that Rosie loved anyone who rubbed her rump, so when she mooed and swayed her behind, Joseph took a couple of quick steps back.

I said, "She's just telling you she's —"

"I don't care," said Joseph, and he left the barn.

The next morning, though, when the three of us went out to the Big Barn to milk, Joseph went to Rosie first, and he reached out and rubbed her rump again. And Rosie told Joseph she loved him.

That was the first time I saw Joseph smile. Sort of.

Joseph had never touched a cow's rump before. Or her teat even. Really. So he was terrible at milking. And even though I kept rubbing her rump while Joseph was being terrible at milking, Rosie got pretty frustrated, and finally she kicked over the pail because Joseph didn't have his leg out in front of hers. It didn't matter much because there was hardly any milk in it anyway.

Joseph stood up just when my father came in.

My father looked at the pail and the spilled milk.

Then at Joseph.

"I think there's something you need to finish there, Joseph," he said.

"You need milk this bad, there's probably a store where you can get some like normal people," he said.

It was the longest string of words he'd said.

"I don't need the milk," said my father. He pointed at Rosie. "But she needs you to milk her."

"She doesn't need me to —"

"She needs you." My father stacked his two

pails to the side, then righted Joseph's pail underneath Rosie. "Sit down on the stool," he said. It took a few seconds, but Joseph came and sat down, and my father knelt beside him and reached beneath Rosie. "I'll show you again. With your thumb and forefinger, you pinch off the top—like this, and then let your fingers strip the milk down—like this." A squirt of milk against the metal side. Another. Another. Then my father stood.

A few seconds. More than a few.

Then Joseph reached under and tried.

Nothing.

"Thumb and forefinger tight, then run down your other fingers."

Joseph tried again.

My father took over rubbing Rosie's rump.

She mooed once, and then the squirting began. It was slow and not all that steady, but Joseph was milking, and soon the sound in the pail wasn't the sound of milk on metal, but that foamy sound of milk in milk.

My father looked at me and smiled. Then he went around behind Joseph to pick up the pails he'd stacked.

And—*bang!*—Joseph leaped up as if something had exploded beneath him. His pail got knocked over again and the stool and Rosie mooed her afraid moo and Joseph stood with his back against the barn wall with his hands up, and even though he usually didn't look at anyone he was looking at us and breathing fast and hard, like there wasn't enough air in the whole wide world to breathe!

My father looked at him, and I could see something in my father's eyes I'd never seen before. Sadness, I guess. "I'm sorry, Joseph. I'll try to remember," he said. He bent down and picked up his pails. "I'll finish here. You boys better go back to the house and get washed up. Jack, tell Mom I'll be a few minutes."

It was almost dawn when we went outside, Joseph and me. The peaks to the west were lit up and spilling some of the light down their sides and onto our fields, all harvested and turned and ready for the long winter. You could smell the cold air and the wood smoke. The pond had broken panes of ice on the edges, enough to annoy the geese, and from the Small Barn you could hear Quintus Sertorius at his grain, snorting in his bin. Rosie mooed inside the barn. Everywhere in the gray yard, color was filling in — the red barns, the green shutters, the green trim on the house and the yellow trim on the chicken shed, the orange tabby clawing into the fence rail.

Joseph didn't stop to see anything. He missed it all. He went into the house, still breathing hard. The door slapped shut behind him.

Still, that afternoon he was back in the Big Barn. And he rubbed Rosie's rump. And she mooed. And then he milked her. All the way, even though it took a long time.

"Do you think Joseph will fit in?" my mother asked me later.

"Rosie loves him," I said.

I didn't need to say anything more. You can

tell all you need to know about someone from the way cows are around him.

O N MONDAY, JOSEPH and I tried to ride the bus to school, which I'd done a million times and it wasn't exactly a big deal. You wait in the cold and the dark, the bus pulls up, most times Mr. Haskell doesn't talk to you or even look at you because it's cold and it's dark and he didn't spend all his life wanting to be a bus driver, you know, so you better shut up and go sit down. So you shut up and go sit down and the bus bumps over to Eastham Middle.

Like I said, not a big deal.

But that morning I got on and Joseph got on behind me and Mr. Haskell looked past me and said, "You're that kid that has a kid," and Joseph stopped dead on the bus steps. "I couldn't believe it when Mr. Canton told us. Aren't you a little young?"

Joseph turned around and got off the bus.

"Hey, if you want to walk, it's no skin off my

nose. Two miles, that way. And—What do you think you're doing?"

That last part was to me, because I got off the bus too.

"You're nuts," said Mr. Haskell.

I shrugged. Maybe we were.

"You know, I didn't mean anything. Just getting to know you, kid."

Joseph stood still. His black eyes stared at Mr. Haskell.

Mr. Haskell's face got hard. "Suit yourselves," he said. "It's twenty-one degrees out there." He closed the door and shifted into gear. I saw the faces of Ernie Hupfer and John Wall and Danny Nations plugged into his ear buds all looking out the windows, staring at me like I was the biggest jerk in the world, walking to school in twenty-one degrees. And then the bus was nothing but rising exhaust down the road.

I blew my breath out, long and slow. I'm not sure it was even twenty-one degrees.

"Why'd you do that?" said Joseph.

"I don't know," I said.

"You should have stayed on the bus."

"Maybe."

Joseph took off his backpack. It was pretty much empty, since he hadn't gotten any of his books yet. "Give me some of your stuff," he said.

I gave him *Physical Science Today!* and *Language Arts for the New Century,* which was sort of out of date because the new century was a dozen years old already. I pulled out my gym stuff, but he said I could carry my own stinking jock. And he took *Octavian Nothing* and looked at the first page and then looked at me, and I said, "It's supposed to be hard," and he shrugged and stuck it into his backpack.

Then he slung his backpack over his shoulder and nodded down the road and we set off, two miles, and it wasn't any twenty-one degrees.

Joseph walked a little behind me the whole way.

I won't even tell you what my fingers felt like by the time we turned at old First Congregational.

I looked behind me. Joseph's ears were about

as red as ears can get before falling off and shatter-
ing on the road.

"Would you have known you're supposed to
turn here?" I said.

He shrugged.

When we got to school, the late bell had rung
and the halls were empty except for Mr. Canton,
who is the kind of vice principal who really wanted
to be a sergeant in a foreign war zone, but he missed
out so he's patrolling middle school halls instead.

"You miss the bus?" he said.

"Sort of," I said.

"Sort of?" he said.

"We got off," I said.

"Why did you get off?"

"Because the bus driver is a jerk," said Joseph.

Mr. Canton got bigger. Really. He stood taller
and his shoulders spread and his arms widened
away from his body.

"Mr. Brook, right? Maybe one of your prob-
lems is a lack of respect."

Joseph knelt and unzipped his backpack. He handed me my books. Except for *Octavian Nothing*.

"This means a tardy for both of you. You understand?"

"Yes, sir," I said.

Mr. Canton waited, but Joseph just zipped up his backpack and stood.

"Get to class, Jackson," Mr. Canton said. "Joseph, you come with me and I'll go over your schedule. You do have a schedule, you know."

Joseph didn't say anything. He followed Mr. Canton, walking a little behind him.

At supper, I told my parents Joseph and I were walking to school from now on. Joseph kept eating. He didn't even look up.

"That right?" said my father. He looked at Joseph, who still didn't look up, and after a while my father said, "You boys will need some warm gloves and hats. And probably some heavier sweaters. It's already pretty cold out. It looks like we're in for a wicked winter."

My mother had them all ready for us the next morning.

Which was good, since this time it really wasn't even close to twenty-one degrees.

When the bus drove past, catching us a little after the turn by old First Congregational, Ernie Hupfer and John Wall and Danny Nations with the wires to his ear buds flapping hard pulled down their windows and they hollered out to tell us what idiots we were, and didn't we know it was like ten degrees?

When they were gone, Joseph said, "Hey." I looked behind me. He'd dropped his backpack and picked up a stone from the side of the road. He turned and lobbed it toward the bell tower of old First Congregational.

I'd never heard that bell ring before.

I dropped my backpack too. I missed with my first throw. It's hard to throw with your gloves on.

I missed with my second throw too. And my third. And, well . . .

"You're throwing off your front foot. Push off with your back."

So I did, and the second time, I hit the bell pretty square. The second time!

"See?"

I nodded. I might have said something if my whole face hadn't been frozen.

And Joseph?

His second smile. Sort of.

After that, we walked to school together every day. At least, kind of together. He was always a little behind me. We followed the Alliance River—running dark and fast this time of year, and cold as all get-out. We'd stop at old First Congregational to clang the bell. If we'd taken a right turn past it, we'd go onto the bridge that humps over the river—or it used to. Now most of the wooden slats were broken through and a gate with a Bridge Out sign stopped traffic.

We turned left to head to school. And even

though we didn't talk much, I think Joseph might have been glad I was there.

But I'm not sure all the teachers were glad Joseph was at Eastham Middle.

For Social Studies with Mr. Oates and Language Arts with Mrs. Halloway, he sat in the last seat in the second row next to me, since I sat in the last seat in the first row. Even though he was in the eighth grade and I was in sixth. He did go to eighth-grade pre-Algebra with Mr. D'Ulney because he was great at math, but Mr. Collum wouldn't let him into his eighth-grade science class, so we were lab partners in Principles of the Physical World. In PE with Coach Swieteck he lined up with the eighth-grade squad, which is across the gym from the sixth-grade and seventh-grade squads, and once he looked at me from the end of his line and shook his head because he hated being told what to do in PE, but he was trying. Fifth period, we had Office Duty with Mr. Canton together.

At least in the classes he had with me, the

teachers were careful around him. Not like they were afraid of him, exactly—they didn't hear what he said in his sleep at night, how he'd holler, "Let go, you . . ." and then words I didn't even know. Or how he'd start to cry and then he'd only say a name, and he'd say it like it was someone he'd do anything, anything to find. Maybe if the teachers had heard Joseph late at night, they might have been a little afraid of him.

But they were still careful. I guess it was enough that once, Joseph tried to kill his teacher. That would make a teacher wish Joseph wasn't at Eastham Middle.

I'm really sure that's what Mrs. Halloway thought whenever she looked at him.

Joseph had a picture he carried around. Sometimes he took it out from his wallet and looked at it. He held it so no one else could see it. Not even me. During Language Arts on the second day he was at school, Mrs. Halloway told Joseph he wasn't paying attention, and she walked down to the end of the row and held out her hand

and said he should give her whatever he was holding. Joseph didn't. He put the picture in his wallet and he put his wallet in his back pocket and then he stared down at his desk. Mrs. Halloway didn't wait very long before she pulled her hand away. She closed her eyes halfway, walked back up to her desk, wrote something in her notebook, put the notebook in her top drawer, and then started in again on Robert Frost and stone walls and stuff.

She never turned her half-closed eyes toward the end of the second row again.

And there was Mr. Canton.

A week after we got to school late, Mr. Canton found me by my locker. I was trying to open it but my hands were so cold, my fingers weren't exactly doing what they needed to be doing. That's what happens when you take your gloves off so you can hit the bell of old First Congregational.

"Mr. Haskell said you weren't on the bus again today," said Mr. Canton.

"I walked," I said.

"With Joseph Brook?" said Mr. Canton.

Nodded.

"What's the last number?" he said.

"Eight."

Mr. Canton twirled the combination to eight and opened my locker.

"Listen, Jackson," he said. "I respect your parents. I really do. They're trying to make a difference in the world, bringing kids like Joseph Brook into a normal family. But kids like Joseph Brook aren't always normal, see? They act the way they do because their brains work differently. They don't think like you and I think. So they can do things . . ."

"He's not like that," I said.

"He isn't? Jackson, when's the last time you had a talk with a vice principal? When's the last time you got a tardy?"

I didn't say anything.

"Last Monday," said Mr. Canton. "And who were you with?"

I didn't say anything again.

"Exactly," said Mr. Canton.

Mr. Canton wore brown shoes that looked like someone shined them ten minutes ago. There wasn't a scuff on them. Not even at the toes. How would you do that, wear shoes without a mark on them?

"I'm telling you to be careful around Joseph Brook," said Mr. Canton. "You don't know anything about him."

He walked away with his unscuffed shoes.

"He's not like that," I whispered.

That afternoon, I met Joseph at the end of the buses, where he waited for me. Mr. Canton stood near the front doors, watching us. He nodded at me like we were sharing a secret.

Joseph walked home behind me, looking like he didn't want to share a secret with anybody.

So a little after we passed old First Congregational, I stopped and turned. "You okay?" I said.

"What?" he said.

"You okay?"

"Why shouldn't I be?"

"Listen, what's your daughter's name?"

He looked at me. His black eyes. "It's not any of your—"

"I'm just asking."

He waited a long moment. And it sure was cold. Maybe fifteen degrees, maybe fourteen, maybe not even that. The bus drove by and John Wall pounded on the window to let me know what a jerk I was.

"Jupiter," Joseph said.

I guess I looked sort of surprised.

"It was our favorite planet," he said.

"*Our* favorite?"

Joseph nodded up the road.

"You mean, yours and . . ."

He nodded up the road again.

Joseph followed me the rest of the way home. My mother took him to counseling a little while later, and when they drove off, his eyes were closed.